Praise for
Shakedown

"Bodenham, a former private equity fund manager, has hit gold with *Shakedown*, a riveting thriller about the high risks in high finance."

—Jerry Kennealy, author
of the Nick Polo mystery series

"Bodenham's unique insight into the world of high finance has created another authentic financial thriller."

—Howard Leigh, Lord Leigh of Hurley

"On the money. Finance and politics mixed into a thrill-ing, deadly cocktail."

—Derek Thompson, author
of the Spy Chaser thriller series

"Martin Bodenham brings an insider's savvy to this tale of intrigue and deception. Think *Absolute Power* meets *The Firm* and you've got the inside track on this heart-pounding thriller. Relentlessly entertaining!"

—Lawrence Kelter, bestselling author

"*Shakedown* is a crash course in corporate intrigue, government conspiracies, and espionage. The action is swift and the characters are relentless. Don't miss out on this ride."

—J.J. Hensley, author of *Bolt Action Remedy*

SHAKEDOWN

ALSO BY MARTIN BODENHAM

The Geneva Connection (*)
Once a Killer (*)

(*) – coming soon from Down & Out Books

MARTIN BODENHAM

SHAKEDOWN

Down & Out Books
3959 Van Dyke Rd, Ste. 265
Lutz, FL 33558
www.DownAndOutBooks.com

The characters and events in this book are fictitious. Any similarity to real persons, living or dead, is coincidental and not intended by the author.

Edited by Chris Rhatigan
Cover design by Liam Sweeny

ISBN: 1-946502-13-8
ISBN-13: 978-1-946502-13-1

In memory of my dear friend,
Ian Hennigar
1958—2016

CHAPTER 1

I prayed my father was right that I could trust the man I was about to meet.

The law offices of Hennigar and Partners were located on Cambridge Parkway, overlooking the boats moored along Boston's Charles River Basin. I found a spot on the road outside the building, fed the meter with quarters, and walked into reception. Compared to the mega-firms I was used to dealing with at work, the place was austere—no oversized vases of fresh flowers, no Nespresso coffee machine, no expensive artwork on the walls. This was a firm with a handle on its costs. It reminded me of Dad's old practice where a large fee was measured in the low thousands, not millions.

The senior partner was a short man in his late fifties, almost bald on top, except for a wavy two-inch thatch of gray above his forehead. The suit he wore looked expensive, but the pants were far too tight, emphasizing his considerable paunch. The missing lower button on his outstretched shirt didn't help much either. *As long as I can trust him, nothing else matters*, I thought.

"Doug Hennigar," he said, offering me his outstretched hand.

"Damon Traynor," I said, trying to smile. "My father speaks highly of you."

"He's very generous. Did he tell you I learned everything about the law from him?"

"He mentioned you worked together, yes."

"If it wasn't for your father," Hennigar's face filled with

pride, and he circled the air with his finger, "none of this would've been possible. So when he called me yesterday, I said I'd be delighted to help his son out." He pointed to the chair on the other side of his walnut desk. "Please take a seat."

"Thanks for agreeing to see me at short notice." I stared at the space behind him. A preserved blue marlin was screwed into the drywall.

Hennigar must have been watching for my reaction. "Caught that one in Hawaii a couple of years back." His face lit up with the memory. "Sure put up a fight, I can tell you."

"I've never tried it."

"You should. It's a lot of fun. They smoke it over there you know. Sort of enhances the flavor."

"I'll add it to my bucket list."

An open box of cinnamon rolls was sitting on the credenza. He picked it up and held it in my direction. "Hungry?"

"No thanks, I've had breakfast."

Hennigar laughed. "So have I, but these babies, well…" He devoured half of one in a single bite then wiped his fingers on a handkerchief. "Your father tells me you run a private equity firm here in Boston."

"That's right. I set up CCP last year, but that's not why I'm here."

"Then I assume this is a personal matter?" Another bite and the pastry was gone.

"It is."

Hennigar looked at his fingers then licked the sugar off them. "What can I do for you?"

"I need you to keep something for me."

"Sure. What is it?"

"A document. Something really important to me."

"I'm guessing a will or some deeds, maybe?"

"No. Nothing like that. I can't tell you what it is. Is that a problem?"

"Not at all. I was just curious. How long do you want me to keep it?"

"I don't know yet."

Hennigar tilted his head. "Okay."

"I'm hoping one day, I'll be able to come and collect it from you." I leaned forward, reached into my briefcase to retrieve a sealed envelope, and slid it across the desk. The man in front of me had no idea of the risk I was taking. To say I was scared witless would be a massive understatement.

Hennigar pointed to the single word written in capital letters on the outside of the envelope. "What does 'MYLOR' mean?"

"It's better you don't know."

He wrinkled his nose. "You said you *hope* to collect this someday."

"That's right."

"So there's a chance you won't be back for it?"

"It's possible. And if I don't come back, there's something I need you to do for me."

"I don't understand. Why wouldn't you come—?"

"It means I will have been killed."

Hennigar stopped reaching for another pastry and suddenly looked worried. "You have my attention." He paused. "Are you in some sort of trouble, Damon?"

I ignored the question—I had no choice. To answer that one truthfully would take me all day, and he'd never agree to help me if he knew the kind of trouble I was in. "Look, if you hear of my death, I need you to open the envelope."

"And do what exactly?" Hennigar's tone was more cagey than concerned.

"Copy the contents and send them to every news channel and newspaper you can find."

"Whoa." He bolted upright in his chair. "I'd like to know what I'm getting into here."

"It's better that you don't. Believe me."

Seemingly lost for words, Hennigar rubbed his two chins

with his left hand. "I hope this is nothing illegal?"

Another difficult question. What was inside the envelope pointed to a mountain of illegal activity, but none of it was mine. "I wouldn't ask you to do anything like that."

Hennigar looked unconvinced. "You know if it wasn't for your father..."

"I get it and I can't tell you how grateful I am for your help."

He exhaled loudly through his nose. "Forgive me, but how will I know you're dead?"

"I'll ask my father to contact you with the news."

Hennigar put the lid down on the box of doughnuts and pushed it out of reach. "Do you think something will happen to you?"

"I hope not, but if it does, it's really important you do this for me."

Four months earlier
President Brad Halley retired at midnight and rose at four—the same hours he'd kept when he was a five-star general in the U.S. Army. Sleep was a waste of time. Now almost seventy, and still sporting a military crew cut, he looked a good ten years younger—a product of his strict vegetarian diet and daily exercise routine. After an early morning workout in the White House gym, he'd wade through his correspondence and make a few phone calls, both tasks he couldn't stand. For Halley was a man who preferred face to face meetings where he could look the other person in the eye, weigh them up, and study their body language. Such meetings could be called any hour of the day or night, and members of his cabinet were expected to be available at all times. Those who needed more than four hours of sleep or simply couldn't take the pressure didn't last long in the Halley administration.

"Everyone is ready, sir," said one of his personal assistants standing in the northeast door of the Oval Office, poking her head into the lion's den.

President Halley looked up from the mountain of papers spread across the Resolute solid oak desk. "Everyone?"

"Yes, sir. I've double checked."

"Very well."

He stood, took a moment to straighten his tie, and slipped on his jacket. He marched through to the adjoining Cabinet Room and took his seat at the middle of the long mahogany table, his back facing the French doors leading to the Rose Garden. The room, which moments earlier had been filled with a cacophony of voices, fell quiet.

Halley held a bunch of papers in his hand and waved them in the air. "I assume you've all read these?" he asked, working around the table, making eye contact and collecting the nods. "Then I'll hand right over to Secretary Allen, who's going to explain how we found ourselves in this shithole." He glared at Allen, who licked his lips and swallowed. "Then we'll discuss how we're going to get out of it." He jabbed his right index finger across the table toward Allen. "Go."

Treasury Secretary Allen cleared his throat. "Thank you, Mr. President," he said, his fingers revealing a slight tremble when he picked up his notes. A career civil servant in his mid-sixties, Allen was a gaunt, weedy-looking man with the pallor of someone badly in need of some sun. "I'd like to start by drawing your attention to page six." He waited until his colleagues had turned to the relevant page and then cleared his throat again. "When this administration took over three years ago, we inherited a record level of debt. For every ten dollars of federal spending, five dollars had to be borrowed. I refer you to the tables on—"

Halley rolled his eyes before leaning forward onto his forearms. "In other words, our nation was living way beyond its means, and only at the expense of the generations who follow us," he said, then pointed to Allen again.

"Thank you, Mr. President. Succinctly put, as usual."

Halley tapped the ends of his fingers together. "Move on to the main issue, would you?"

"Of course, sir. Borrowing at those levels was unsustainable, which is why we had to raise taxes and slash government spending the moment we came into office. Even today, after all that pain, we still have to borrow three dollars for every ten we spend. That was sustainable while foreign nations were prepared to lend to us—"

"He means the Chinese," Halley said. "There's no one else out there with a big enough checkbook."

At the far end of the table, the attorney general laughed, but soon stopped when Halley's face made it clear he wasn't joking.

"Yes, the Chinese," Allen said before looking down at his notes. "They've bought over ninety percent of all U.S. Treasury bills sold to foreign nations in the last decade." He looked up. "Trouble is, three weeks ago, they stopped buying them. They completely shut off the tap."

"One day they were lending to us." Halley clicked his fingers. "The next, nothing. It's a belligerent, calculated move," he said, chopping the side of his right hand into his left palm with each word.

"They say there's better value in European government debt," Allen said.

"I know what they're saying, but it's complete bullshit. Most of Europe is broke. Look at the state of Greece, Portugal, Italy, Spain. I could go on. You're telling me they'd rather lend to that lot?"

Some cabinet members shook their heads in disbelief, while others held their heads in their hands—anything to demonstrate to their boss they were listening and taking this as seriously as he was.

"If we continue as we are, unable to borrow, this country will default on its obligations within months," Allen said. "All of our budget cuts will have been for nothing."

6

"A few months," said Halley, thumping the table with his right hand, "before this great nation is bankrupt. It's economic warfare. The Chinese see our weakness and are intent on exploiting it. Well, we're not taking it. I want you to understand one thing: this country is not going down on my watch. That will never happen."

"Can we really cut expenditures any further?" the secretary of Defense asked, sitting right across the table from the president. "We've seen some social unrest already, but we've managed to keep a lid on it. Deeper cuts and there'll be riots. It'll make Greece look like a kids' party."

"We'd never see a second term," the attorney general said, safe now that someone else had put his head above the parapet.

Halley banged the table again. "Have you heard anything we've said? This is not a debate. We don't have that luxury."

"All I was trying to say—"

"This morning, I instructed Secretary Allen to take another brutal look at expenditures, but even that's not going to be enough. We have to do more," Halley said. "Much more."

"I can't see how—" said the secretary of defense, before being chopped off at the knees by Halley's icy stare.

"We need cash fast," Halley continued. "I've already ordered Secretary Allen to investigate and action the sale of all government-owned assets. Nothing is sacred. I want that understood." He paused a moment, taking the time to look at every member of the cabinet. "If we can sell it, then it goes on the block. No arguments. No special pleading. No excuses. The Chinese will soon get the message. When they see we're not going over the cliff, they'll come to their senses. In the long run, they need a relationship with this country if they want to keep our market for their goods. They know that as much as we do."

The meeting lasted another hour. When Halley had wire-brushed every member of his cabinet, he brought it to a close. "Ladies and gentlemen, you know what we have to do. Our nation is in crisis, and it will not be solved by exercising our jaws in this room. An ounce of action is worth a ton of talk, so let's get on with this." He rose from the table and marched out.

Immediately afterward, Secretary Allen returned to his own office, closed the door, and picked up the phone. He punched in the number from memory.

"Patterson," the voice at the other end of the line said.

"It's me."

"How'd it go?"

"As expected. The president spelled it out so everyone in the cabinet understood."

"Do you think they really get this country is on the brink of financial disaster?"

"They do now."

Patterson paused. "So, are you ready to do this?"

Allen hesitated, pinching his chin with the fingers of his left hand. "I think so."

"You don't seem certain."

"I am. I can't see another way out."

"How much does Halley know about the plan?"

"Everything. I talked him through it before the meeting."

"Better that way. We don't want any misunderstanding."

"And your man in Bethesda. Is he ready?"

"Mylor's in good shape. He's had a whole team laying the groundwork for weeks, just waiting on you and Halley to give the word."

"He knows how to do this, right?"

"Mylor's the best man I have. He'll do whatever it takes to get it done, but we don't have a lot of time."

"Okay. Then start pressing the buttons—quickly."

Allen replaced the receiver then stared at the reflection of his terror-filled face in the monitor of his PC.

USS Dean Franklin broke all records when it was launched two years earlier: the world's largest naval vessel ever built at one hundred and eighty thousand tons, the fastest aircraft carrier with a maximum speed of fifty knots—propelled by eight nuclear powered steam turbines—and, when it overran its initial budget by thirty percent, the most expensive single piece of military hardware ever commissioned, at a final cost of eleven and a half billion dollars. The press called it a monstrous extravagance when the country was broke—proof positive that politicians should never be trusted with the nation's checkbook. It didn't matter that it had been ordered some twelve years earlier in another era when the U.S. ran a budget surplus.

In one of the officer cabins, Ben Mylor shook his head, scribbled another note in the margin and double underlined it. So far, he'd read fifty-two pages of the document in front of him and he'd written comments on every sheet, none of them positive. Since joining the carrier in Hawaii two days earlier, he'd reviewed six sale memoranda drafted by the team at DH&W, and none of them had made the mark. They'd all have to be rewritten. Why was it that the best investment banking brains in the country were unable to write in plain English? This is meant to be a selling document, not a damn technical manual, he thought, throwing the papers onto his tiny bunk.

Someone knocked on the cabin door, breaking the constant background hum of the engines.

"Come," Mylor said.

A young naval officer, in service dress blue, opened the door, letting in a rush of fresh air. "We're ready for you now, sir."

"At last. Another day on board this thing..." Mylor knocked over his coffee cup as he reached for his jacket hanging on the back of the chair. "How do you live in these cramped conditions?"

"Sir?"

"Forget it. Let's go."

Mylor followed the lieutenant along the officers' cabin deck then up three flights of metal steps before reaching the bridge. There, he walked into a sea of blue uniforms crowded around the main Sperry Marine control panel.

"Mr. Mylor, everything's ready. Just waiting on your order," the captain said, emerging from the huddle, his face glowing with pride.

"Where are we exactly?" Mylor asked, rubbing his eyes as they adjusted to the increased light level on the bridge. He slipped on his sunglasses.

"Thirteen hundred miles northwest of Honolulu," the captain said, handing over a pair of binoculars. He pointed toward the horizon. "I suggest you focus on that buoy."

Mylor removed his sunglasses, focused the left lens first and then the right. "Got it. How far is that?"

"Fifteen hundred yards."

"And the sub is on the other side of the buoy, right?"

"That's right. An LA class operating sixty yards below the surface. Are we clear to continue?"

"Just a moment." Mylor lowered the binoculars and turned to the three-man camera crew at the back of the bridge. Two of them held shoulder-mounted Sony camcorders. "Are you guys set?"

"Ready when you are, sir," the one without a camera said. He was in charge and directing the filming.

"Don't screw this up. We'll only have one take."

All three nodded.

"Go ahead, Captain," Mylor said.

The captain turned to the radio operator. "Launch the birds."

"Flight deck, you are clear to go," the operator said, leaning into his microphone.

Mylor looked down at the steel runway some fifty feet beneath them. For the first time in days, he could hardly hear the background noise of the ship's propulsion units in the co-cooned environment of the bridge. The peace would not last long, though. Soon two Lockheed Martin F-35 fighter jets moved into the middle of the metal runway. The bridge's floor vibrated with the deafening roar of their Pratt & Whitney engines as the aircraft accelerated for takeoff. Moments later, they were in the air, and Mylor raised the binoculars to his eyes to track their progress.

The captain glanced at the control panel in front of him. "Proceed."

"Yes, sir," the radio operator said, turning again toward the microphone. "Predator, this is Falcon. Do you copy, over?"

A crackle came over the bridge speaker system then, "This is Predator. Copy, over."

"Predator, you are clear to proceed, over."

"Copy that, over."

Mylor looked over his shoulder at the camera crew and jabbed his right index finger at the spot near the window where he wanted them to stand. The three men shuffled closer to the glass. "Don't move from there until I tell you," he said.

The captain raised his head toward the digital clock above the control panel before looking at the radio operator. "Thirty seconds. Wait for my further command."

"Sir," said the radio operator, nodding.

Mylor focused on the buoy again. Some two thousand yards away, behind the buoy, a small wave appeared. He adjusted the lenses to bring the wave closer. The tip of a ballistic missile emerged from the water, like a blue whale coming up for air. Mylor smiled as he fine-tuned the focus. The missile glided out of the water and appeared to hover in midair before accelerating. He tracked its flight path climbing above the horizon.

"Target two is now airborne," said the captain, his eyes locked onto the screen in front of him.

Mylor lowered the binoculars to water level. A second missile floated above the surface of the ocean. He took the binoculars away for a moment so he could see the two missiles in flight at the same time.

"Commence procedure," said the captain to the radio operator.

"Eagle, this is Falcon. You are clear to go. Copy, over."

"This is Eagle. Copy that, over."

"Eyes to the sky," the captain said.

Everyone on the bridge raised their heads. The missiles climbed further into the bright sky. Mylor narrowed his eyes then slipped his sunglasses back on. A single bright flash came first, followed by an explosion of reds and whites shooting across the sky like a giant firework then, a few seconds after, a deep booming sound. Moments later, the process repeated and both missiles were gone. White smoke trails doodled across the blue sky before drifting toward the ocean.

The captain stood over the radio controls and leaned toward the microphone. "Great work, everyone. Predator, you are clear to go, over."

"Our pleasure, Falcon. Good working with you, over," the submarine commander said.

Mylor ignored the chatter between the senior naval officers and walked over to the camera crew. "Did you get it all?" he asked.

"Every moment, sir," the film director said. "Incredible how accurate that laser is. Where is that controlled from?"

Mylor ignored the question. "Make sure I receive the edited version by Friday. My people will do the voiceover." He nodded to the captain and returned to his cabin to continue reviewing the documents.

Three days later Mylor was back at his office in Bethesda, Maryland. The first call he made on his secure line was to George Patterson, Director of National Intelligence, who as an ex-military man, had seen active service under, then General, Halley.

"How was it?" Patterson asked.

"Like clockwork," Mylor said. "I've seen the first cut of the video and even I'm impressed."

"Good. Who are you targeting with this one?"

"CCP in Boston."

"The same guys about to win the airports auction?"

"Yeah. The airport deal is the bait."

"That's clever. I like it."

Mylor laughed. "I thought you would."

"You're certain they're good for the money? The laser system is a much larger transaction altogether."

"We've checked them out. They've got plenty in their new fund."

"Where are we on the others?"

"Eight deals already in place, including this one. Five almost there."

"And they're all being fronted by DH&W?"

"As we agreed. Orlando Barrett is heading it up over there."

"Okay, press ahead with the eight and keep me up to speed on the others."

"You got it."

"How quickly can you extend this to the wider list?"

"I already have my people working on them. A lot of the prep's been done." Mylor paused. "Maybe a month before—"

"We don't have that much time."

"Then I'll step it up and report back on timescale."

"Do you need more staff?"

"Not right now. I've just hired two more from Langley and I have a few more coming on board soon."

"Be sure to let me know if you need more bodies. Nothing's more important than this."

"Halley knows this won't be pretty, right?"

"Don't worry. I've spoken to Allen. They all understand the consequences."

"I sure hope so, because there's no free ride on this one."

CHAPTER 2

It had just started to rain when my Town Car pulled up outside Saint Peter's homeless shelter on Camden Street. I put my iPhone into silent mode then stepped out of the back of the vehicle. "I should only be a couple of hours," I said, leaning on the driver's door. "I'll call you when the meeting's over."

"See you around four then, sir," my driver said through his open window before tilting his head toward the building. "Watch yourself."

I glanced over my shoulder. A tall man with long, matted hair stood propped against the railing at the shelter's entrance. He was wearing a filthy trench coat, mumbling something, and shaking his head as though he was in the middle of an argument with himself. I smiled at my driver. "Don't worry about him. I'll be fine."

When the car pulled away, I walked over to the disheveled man and put my arm around his shoulder. "Come on, Jarel," I said, feeling his bony frame protruding through the fabric of his coat. "Let's get you inside, out of this rain."

Jarel flinched then his face lit up. "Mr. Traynor." There was a strong smell of alcohol mixed with stale breath.

We entered the building, where I escorted Jarel down the corridor to the open door of the duty manager's office. The manager looked up from her paperwork and stared over her reading glasses.

"I found Jarel waiting outside," I said, hoping for a friendly response. "Let's see if we can get him something to eat and some place to dry off."

14

The manager frowned. "Jarel, you know the rules now, don't you? No one gets to come in before six."

Jarel rolled his eyes. "I guess I'll wait outside." He paused. "In the rain."

"I think we can break the rules today, Talisha," I said, reading from the plastic nameplate sitting at the front of the manager's desk. "Just this once."

She forced a smile, conceding defeat. "Well, seeing as you're the chairman, Mr. Traynor, I guess we can make an exception today."

"That's right," said the shelter director, approaching the doorway from behind me. "Let's get Jarel something to eat."

I turned, smiled and shook the director's hand. "Good to see you. Are we all set for the board meeting?"

"Everyone's here." The director set off down the corridor. "Let's go join them."

I tapped Jarel on the back. "It was nice to see you again, Jarel. Talisha here will take good care of you." I winked at her and joined the director, who was waiting for me outside the meeting room.

"You look tired, Damon," the director said, opening the door for me.

I wasn't offended. He was right. I'd been working all hours recently and, no doubt, it was beginning to show. "We have a lot going on at the moment. In fact, I'm sorry but there's a chance I'll get called away this afternoon." I pointed to the duty manager's office. "I hope you didn't mind…"

"You realize Jarel will be back again tomorrow afternoon asking to come in early?"

"I know, but there was no way I could walk by and leave him standing out there in the rain. I didn't mean to meddle."

"Hey, you put up most of the money for this place. If you can't break a few rules, then who can?"

I felt a twinge of embarrassment, hoping the director didn't think I thought I could do whatever I wanted just because I'd financed the homeless shelter. While I was their main backer, the last thing I wanted was to interfere in operations. I'd always been uneasy with the amount of money people make in private equity. Just because I was good at numbers seemed a strange reason why the market paid me so much more than people who did more valuable work for society. Being able to use some of my money to help others gave me much more pleasure than spending it on toys and things that didn't really matter. I decided to change the subject. "You know Jarel was a doctor when he was in the army?"

"I do." The director shook his head. "They all have a story."

"I'm sorry." I raised both palms. "Don't say it. I know I get too personally involved. I can't help it."

"There's no need to apologize. Just wish there were a few more like you."

An hour into the shelter's board meeting, I felt my phone vibrate in my jacket pocket. When I took it out, there was a text message from my office: *DH&W have promised a decision at four today.* I made my apologies to the other members of the board for having to leave early, called my driver, and headed back to my office downtown.

I glanced at my watch for the third time in five minutes—seven minutes to four. On the street twenty-two floors below me, I watched a group of tourists step off a bus parked at the edge of National Historical Park and pile into Faneuil Hall Market-place. Others crowded around the flame-eating street perform-ers and clapped. For them, it was just another day in Boston, but not for me. In just over six minutes, I would learn whether my private equity firm had won the auction to buy three government-owned airports. And this wasn't just any deal; it was the most important transaction of my career—one that would put Carada Capital Partners on the map and finally an-nounce my new firm's arrival.

Another quick look at my watch—five minutes. Turning away from the window, I dried my clammy palms on the inside of my pockets. I had to appear cool for my team. My mouth was dry as I walked over to the conference table to join my eleven partners. Many of them had come with me from our old employer on Wall Street when I'd taken the bold—some would say stupid—step of walking away from a glittering investment career to set up my own private equity firm in the middle of a deep recession. Like my new investors, they'd placed a lot of faith in me, and I couldn't stomach the idea of letting them down.

"What time do you make it?" asked Chris Gainham, a lumbering giant of a man, his booming voice filling the boardroom.

"Four minutes to," I said, narrowing my eyes as I pointed at his fire-truck red tie on a blue shirt. "Did you get a volume control for that thing?"

"Sorry. I had no say. Carol and the kids bought it for me."

"I guess they bought all your other ones too?"

"No. I can't blame them for that."

I laughed, knowing he could take the ribbing.

"Grab a seat," Gainham said, making sure I could see him tucking his tie into his jacket. "Your pacing up and down is making me nervous."

Seconds later, I walked to the window on the other side of the room and watched the traffic building up on State Street. "I hate this waiting around to hear."

"It's exactly four o'clock now," said Diane Crawford, another of my partners at the firm. "They must know the winning bidder by now. What are they waiting for?"

"They'll know alright," I said, still staring out of the window. *Maybe eight and a half billion dollars wasn't enough*, I thought. *Maybe my partners were right when they'd urged me to pay a bit more. Had I been wrong to overrule them?* Too late to do anything about it now.

Gainham reached for the speaker phone in the middle of the cherry-wood table. "I know someone senior over at DH&W. We used to play football together. I'll call him and find out what's going on."

I turned and raised my right hand. "No, leave it, please, Chris. We need to play this by their rules. They won't thank us for chasing them. It's hard, but we must wait. Besides, we'll only appear too keen if we call them."

With a sigh, Gainham slid the phone back into the center of the table. "Yeah. You're right."

"It's almost five past now. What are they up to?" asked Crawford, shaking her head. "We need this deal. We can't go a year without anything to report to our investors." She poured another coffee from one of the carafes on the table.

"If we lose it, so be it," I said. "Our investors want us to invest their money, not waste it. I'd rather have to explain to them why we didn't do any deals than justify why we overpaid for assets." As I said those words, I desperately hoped I wouldn't have to have that conversation with our investors.

Crawford made a face. "I need a cigarette."

The speaker phone rang, and a chill ran through me. Everyone looked in my direction. Appearing unconcerned in front of my team was one thing but, more than anybody, I knew we had to win this deal. It would take months to find another one this good, and Crawford was right—our investors' patience was wearing thin. It had to be good news.

I ran to the table, sat down, and pushed the speaker button on the phone, my pulse racing. "This is Damon Traynor."

"Damon, it's Orlando."

The British accent at the other end of the line belonged to Orlando Barrett from DH&W. His tone was somber. Did that mean it was bad news? Had he already called the winning bidder on the hour? Was this the call I'd been dreading for days? Having raised the world's largest first-time private equity fund at seventy-five billion dollars, the whole industry was

18

watching to see what we could do. Many in the financial media had said we'd never be able to deploy such a large amount of capital without overpaying for assets. How many more times was CCP going to come second because of my reluctance to pay too much?

"What's the news?" I asked, making eye contact with Gainham. He looked pale.

A pause at the other end of the line. I closed my eyes, gripped the table leg, and stopped breathing.

"You guys have won the auction. Looks like you'll soon own some airports. Congratulations."

I punched the air and collected the beaming smiles around the table. "That's great news. We were confident our bid was a strong one. I'll have my team contact you to agree the process from here."

"Don't delay. We'd like to have this one wrapped up within a few days."

"Why the hurry?"

"I have another, much larger, opportunity for you to look at once this one is out of the way."

"Sounds interesting." I tried, but failed to hide my excitement at the prospect of another deal so soon. After all the worry about having nothing to show our investors, suddenly we were on a roll.

"Same client, as a matter of fact."

"The federal government?"

"That's correct."

"They must really need the money, given the assets they're selling off." I wasn't complaining—the government's need for cash was the opportunity we'd been looking for to start investing our new fund. The more the merrier as far as I was concerned.

"They're keeping me in business. That's for sure."

"Can you tell us anything about it?"

"Not at liberty to do so yet," Barrett said. "But I will tell you it's defense related."

"We'll be ready when you have the details. Thanks." I terminated the call then exhaled loudly through my teeth before thumping the table. "We've done it. Well done everyone. I'm so proud of you."

"That's awesome," Gainham said. "Maybe now I'll be able to afford some decent ties."

"Don't do that, Chris." I smiled at Gainham. "The office wouldn't be the same."

I scanned the room. A mixture of relief and elation filled my partners' faces. It had been a tough few months for all of us, leaving behind successful careers and risking everything to build a start-up fund management business. While none of my partners had said anything, they must have been as worried as I was. But now things were happening fast. With our first transaction almost in the bag and another one already lined up, things would only get easier from here.

I pushed my chair back from the table and stood. "I'm going to book us a table at Firenze this evening. We have something special to celebrate."

"Sounds like a great idea," Gainham said. "We can carry on afterwards at Arabella's."

After the meeting, I returned to my office and closed the door. Reclined in my leather chair, I closed my heavy eyelids as the adrenaline rush began to fade. Slowly, the weight of everyone's expectations was lifted.

We finally did it.

Arabella's was across the Charles River basin in Cambridge, a magnet for Boston's beautiful people, wealthier students at Harvard, and young professionals. Our cab pulled up in front of the nightclub, and I climbed out with three of my team. With the exception of Gainham, all the married partners had decided to go home after dinner. If I'd not been the senior partner, I would have been happy calling it a night too. I was exhausted, and the wine from the meal earlier made sleep seem like a delicious option.

Although Gainham was married with two young daughters, he'd told me during the cab ride over that nothing was going to stop him celebrating this important milestone for the firm with his best friend. He and I had met at Princeton and had been close friends ever since, and he'd followed me in every career move I'd made. After fifteen years of working together, we were like brothers.

I paid the driver then caught up with the others. The deep bass sound wave penetrated my chest when we walked toward the entrance. "Wow, that's loud," I said.

"Hey, granddad, you're only thirty-six," Gainham said, leading the way. "Wait until you get inside if you think this is noisy."

At my request, the four of us found a booth furthest away from the deafening dance floor, and I sat with my back to the flashing strobe lights. *How can we be expected to hold a conversation in this environment?* I thought.

Gainham stood. "I'll get the drinks. What are you having?"

I cupped my hand behind my left ear and leaned forward. "What?"

"You decide," Crawford said. "I'm nipping out for a cigarette."

"Champagne then," Gainham said. "Keep an eye on Damon. Make sure he doesn't fall asleep. It's only eleven-thirty."

I put my hand over my yawning mouth. "I'm sorry. The day's caught up with me." Then I rose to my feet. "Let me give you a hand with the drinks, Chris."

Fifteen minutes later, Gainham and I returned with two bottles of Champagne and two young women. I'd like to say it was my good looks that attracted them, but the truth is it was Gainham's usual charm.

"Sorry about the delay," Gainham said, placing the bottles on the table. "This is Katie and Emma, by the way. We met at the bar and got talking. We invited them to join us."

Crawford rolled her eyes.

I slid into the booth next to Gainham. Katie sat next to me, revealing long legs under her short skirt.

Gainham spoke into my ear, "She's the spitting image of Pixie Lott."

"Who?"

"The singer."

I shrugged and threw my friend a look as if to say "Is that supposed to mean something?"

Gainham looked disappointed. "You need to get out more."

I poured everyone a glass of Champagne then lifted my glass. "Here's to CCP. Let's hope today marks the start of a great fund."

"CCP," everyone at the table shouted.

Katie leaned toward me, her long, auburn hair tickling the side of my face. "CCP?" she asked.

"That's our company," I said before sipping my drink.

"What do you guys do?"

"It stands for Carada Capital Partners. We're investment fund managers."

Katie opened her eyes wide. "Sounds exciting."

"It has its moments." I thought it was nice of her to be so polite. In my experience, most people outside of my industry think finance and investing make dealing with the IRS seem exciting. "And you?"

"Psychology post-grad." As she spoke, I noticed she had a beautiful smile, full lips, and perfect teeth.

An hour later, Gainham and I were in the men's room. "I guess we won't be sharing a cab back to Beacon Hill tonight," he said.

I nudged my friend in the ribs. "Hey. I'm still single. What do you think?" By now, I was feeling light-headed. I wobbled then steadied myself against the sink before washing my hands.

"You okay?"

"I'm fine." I staggered over to the hand dryer. "I think."

"You never could drink much. Come on." Gainham grabbed me around the shoulders and steered me out of the restroom.

The following six hours were a blur. When I opened my eyes the next morning, I found myself alongside Katie in the bedroom of her Cambridge condo. She was burritoed in her duvet, lying on her side and staring at me. She looked younger than she had the night before, when it was dark and I'd been in an alcoholic haze.

"Last night was fun," I said, trying to remember what I could about it. I rubbed my temples and narrowed my eyes. "Trouble is I'm paying for it now. I need some water and something for my head."

Katie sat upright and leaned, naked, against the back of the bed. "I have a confession to make," she said, her tone serious.

"Please don't tell me you're out of Tylenol?"

"I'm only fifteen."

CHAPTER 3

There are few ways to commit suicide. For an analytical man like Tom Laudel, the options were thinner still. Finding a method with absolute certainty of outcome, but without posing a risk to the lives of others, was a challenge.

Metal grated against rock when Laudel's 911 left the dirt road. Panic gripped him, but he kept the gear lever in reverse and eased off the gas. Traction regained, he continued to back the Porsche toward the forest, scarring the frozen ground with its low chassis. Ignoring the clamor beneath the vehicle and the beeping frenzy coming from its parking sensors, Laudel kept going until it crunched into an oak tree. He killed the engine then stared at his reflection in the rearview mirror. Dark bags hung under his eyes, standing out against his milk-white complexion.

A buckthorn bush blocked the driver door, so Laudel had to ram it open before he could climb out. The pants of his custom-made wool suit snagged on the spiky scrub as he stepped away from the car. Crawling on his knees, he began to search, pulling up clumps of ice-covered undergrowth with his bare hands. He found a stone, inspected it, then threw it away, repeating this two more times before settling on a large one. For two minutes, he scraped at the earth with his fingers until he could prise it out of the soil and carry it to the car. With the heavy rock held above his head, he hesitated before smashing it through the back window.

The shattering glass startled two crows high up in the trees. Laudel waited until their squawking died down and scanned the dense forest. No one was around. He'd picked the right spot. Locals called this remote part of rural Connecticut "Tawny Wood." Once popular with dog walkers, very few people had used it since one of Laudel's investment clients, a corporate landowner, fenced it off with razor wire a year ago. Three miles down the private access track, and at six-fifteen in the morning, Laudel was certain he was the only trespasser.

By treading on the buckthorn, he opened the car door, then leaned in and brushed the broken glass from his leather seat. He sat and examined the scrapes on his hands and the dirt trapped under his manicured fingernails. A sliver of glass had lodged into his right wrist, and the wound began to bleed when he extracted it. Laudel was fascinated as his blood dripped onto the brushed steel surround at the bottom of the gear lever. To stem the bleeding, he sucked on the cut, wincing at the sharp metallic taste.

Laudel's body shivered under his overcoat while the cold wet fabric of his suit pants clung to his knees. Using his good hand, he tugged the door closed as far as it would go, trapping the bush against the frame of the car. The electronic temperature gauge in front of him read twenty-seven degrees Fahrenheit. Next to it the odometer displayed two thousand, three hundred and twenty-two miles. He'd had the car only six weeks, having waited nine months for the latest model to be delivered to his exact specification. There had been a time when things like that were important to him, but that life seemed a million years away now.

When the bleeding stopped, he reached behind his seat and lifted a glass-strewn Mulberry briefcase. His trembling ice-cold fingers fumbled with the combination lock. Inside, tucked behind an elastic strap in the lid, was a photo of his wife, Sally, and their two young daughters. *Happy days*, he thought as his eyes welled up. He slid the photo out and kissed their smiling faces. Maybe one day Sally would be able to forgive him, even if she failed to understand what it was that forced him to this dark place. For the last two sleepless weeks, he'd analyzed his situation to death, and there was nothing else he could do with Mylor's blackmail threat hanging over him. The information Mylor had could come out at any time and it would ruin him and destroy his family. Laudel would never let that happen. A tear dripped onto the photo, and he wiped it away before placing it into the inside pocket of his suit jacket.

Coiled up in the main body of the briefcase was a sixty-yard yellow rope he'd bought from Home Depot the day before. Laudel pulled it loose and gripped the cord with both hands. Twice he tested its strength, then stepped out of the car and carried it to the oak tree. By jumping onto the crumpled rear wing of the Porsche and leaning against the tree for support, he could almost reach the lowest branch. He stretched up, threw one end of the rope around the limb of the tree, and then tied a knot. He pulled on it with his full weight before jumping to the ground and picking up the loose end. It took three laps around the trunk of the tree until he was satisfied he had just the right length, then he tossed the remaining rope into the car through the broken window.

No one could disturb him now; he'd gone too far. He walked back to the dirt road to make one last check. As he looked and listened, a passenger plane flew high overhead, its jet stream leaving two perfect white lines against the clear blue sky. Laudel watched it disappear over the tree canopy before returning to the side of the car, confident the area was clear.

He wiped his forehead with the sleeve of his coat before removing it and throwing it onto the ground. Back in the driver's seat, he took off his tie and loosened his collar, watching white mist clouds form as his heavy breathing mixed with the frigid air. Behind his seat, he grabbed the end of the rope, wound it twice around his neck, and knotted it. The loose length still in the car he estimated at around fifteen feet. Would that be enough?

Automatically, Laudel reached for his seatbelt but stopped

himself. Should he buckle up? What would work best? It made sense to be strapped into the seat; the less scope for movement the better, surely? He used the belt, turned on the engine, and closed his eyes, his heart pummeling the inside of his chest.

The frost.

He opened his eyes, unclipped the belt, and struggled with the knot before unwinding the rope from his neck. Outside of the car, he picked up his overcoat and rammed it against one of the rear tires. Needing something to force against the other wheel he searched the ground in vain. Panic took over, and he tore off his suit jacket and used that.

The photo.

Laudel pulled the jacket free of the tire and retrieved the crumpled photo. He tried, but failed, to smooth out the creases across the faces of his girls before tucking it into his shirt breast pocket. He used the jacket to wipe his brow again then placed it back into position.

A minute later he was back in the driver's seat, buckled up, with the rope tight around his neck. By taking long, steady intakes of air, he managed to control his breathing. There was only one shot at doing this properly. For a moment, he caught his face reflected in the mirror again. His cheeks were drained of all color, his eyes wide open and shiny. Angling the mirror away, he stared at the clear morning sky and listened. The slight breeze subsided, then Laudel could hear nothing. It was the loudest silence he'd ever heard.

A wave of calm washed over him as he turned on the ignition.

Ready.

Staring into oblivion, he eased the gear lever into drive and hammered the accelerator.

CHAPTER 4

Fortress Dunbar, Hawkins, and Weinel occupied a whole block on Barclay Street, between Church and Broadway in lower Manhattan. For the last decade, the firm had topped all of the major league tables: leading M&A advisor on international deals, sponsor of the most initial public offerings by capital raised, and the largest equities trading house in the world. With fifty-five offices around the globe, it was an investment banking powerhouse, advising public companies and governments on all continents. More importantly, for eight years in a row, the bank had notched up the highest profit per partner of all global financial institutions. A successful career with DH&W was a guaranteed road to riches. As a result, the firm attracted the greatest talent and the biggest egos in the business.

Heading up DH&W's mergers and acquisitions division was Orlando Darwin Barrett, a pompous Brit with a fearsome reputation for getting his own way. Public companies involved in contested bids did whatever it took to have Barrett on their side of the deal. Knowing they'd be shredded, no one dared face him across the table on a transaction. His track record of winning, and on the right terms, was unbeatable, and it made his division the highest-grossing department in the whole bank. Among the well-hung giants on Wall Street, Barrett was the biggest swinging dick in town.

"I have Mr. Barrett on the line for you," said one of his personal assistants when I picked up the phone. Fortunately, I knew what this meant—I'd be lucky if he was anywhere near his phone. It was some sort of needless power play to show who was more important. As I waited for the great man, I imagined him rising from one of his two leather couches and taking all the time in the world to stroll across his cavernous corner office to his desk while keeping me on hold.

"Damon, it's Orlando here," he said, as if I didn't already know. I heard a slurping sound, and then, "Oh no, dear. This won't do at all. What time is it?" When I heard a woman's voice somewhere in Barrett's office, I realized he wasn't asking me. "You know I don't drink coffee in the afternoon." There was a pause and then, "I'm sorry, Damon. Temporary staff can be so irritating."

I didn't know what to say to alleviate Barrett's first-world problem, so I changed the subject. "What can I do for you?" I asked.

"Well, now that you've put the airports deal to bed, we can discuss the next one. But first I need to know we're not wasting our time."

"I don't understand."

"Well, this will be a sizeable deal for any private equity firm."

"I assume you know our fund is seventy-five billion? There's not much we can't afford." I couldn't hide the slight frustration in my tone.

"I'm fully aware of your new fund."

Barrett had better not be back-sliding on the next deal already, I thought. "If you think our size counts us out, then why did you mention it to us in the first place?"

"Good question. My advice to our client at the Treasury Department was to restrict the search for potential buyers to trade players only. Personally, I'm not convinced private equity buyers can really afford this one." I heard Barrett take another sip of what I assumed, this time, was a cup of Earl Grey. "However, my client insists we cast the net a little wider. In spite of my advice, they've given me a shortlist of private equity firms they wish to include in the auction process, and CCP is one of them."

"Okay." Barrett was good at this game. I could tell, already, he was talking up the price. "What's the deal?" I asked.

"That would be telling, dear boy."

"I'm sorry?"

"Formalities, formalities." Barrett slurped some more of his drink. "We need you to sign another nondisclosure agreement first. After that, we have a comprehensive information memorandum available."

"If you email over the NDA, we'll take care of it."

"You'll have it tomorrow, but don't dither, old chap. We're running this auction on a very tight timeline."

"We'll let you know whether we're interested once we've read the IM."

"Okay. I have to scoot now. Goodbye, Damon." Barrett terminated the call, and I wondered whether he was serious about showing us the new deal.

The next day, somewhat to my surprise, the NDA showed up. I signed it and immediately returned the scanned document to Barrett. A few hours later, FedEx delivered a large package to my office. I ripped it open and flicked through the contents; all pretty standard stuff: an information memorandum with a project codename on the outside, a set of financial statements and forecasts, a copy of the signed NDA, and a cover letter setting out the sale timetable and bid process. Unusually, inside the package I found a sleeve containing a DVD. I looked at it for a moment then threw it back inside with the documents. I grabbed my calculator, tucked the bundle of information under my arm, and walked over with them to Diane Crawford's office.

"Have you got a moment?" I asked, standing in Crawford's doorway. As usual, there was a strong smell of tobacco smoke.

"Yeah, sure," she said, finishing a text message. "What is it?"

"The new deal's in from DH&W. If it has any legs, I'd like you and I to work on it together given the short timetable. It's probably quite a large deal as well, unless Barrett was just talking up the price. He's such an arrogant—"

"Duh!" Crawford laughed. "He works for DH&W. What's the deal?"

"I haven't looked at it yet. It's only just arrived. Let's go through to the conference room where we can play the DVD on the large screen."

"It came with a DVD? How exciting." Crawford said, sliding her chair back from the desk.

We walked to the conference room, opened the package, and spread the documents across the table.

"Let's see what they're selling," said Crawford, flicking open the information memorandum. "Can't imagine why they'd need a DVD."

"Barrett mentioned it was defense related."

"That's amazing." Crawford looked up from the thick document in front of her.

"What is it?"

"The government is selling SLIDA."

I took a seat. "SLIDA? As in the strategic lid over America?"

"Well, to give it its proper name," Crawford said, reading from the document, "the strategic laser infrastructure for the defense of America."

"Unbelievable. Let's see what's on the DVD."

I walked over to the player in the corner of the room and inserted the disc. The large screen at the end of the conference table came to life, and *USS Dean Franklin* came into view, accompanied by loud music. It was an aerial shot, probably filmed from a helicopter. I closed the conference room door when the music died down and the voiceover began: "The strategic laser infrastructure project has been developed over a twenty-year period. Today, it provides a defense blanket over the U.S. and its allies through a network of sophisticated satellites, equipped with unrivaled laser weapon technology. The demonstration you are about to witness will highlight the futility of any ballistic missile attack against our nation. SLIDA is capable of eliminating enemy missiles before they reenter the atmosphere, making redundant any first-strike technology operated by our adversaries..."

Crawford and I kept our eyes glued to the screen as two ballistic missiles launched, presumably from a submarine, and climbed into the air before exploding moments later when struck by the invisible laser. Ten minutes of detailed statistics followed, most of which related to the laser technology behind the system.

"I can't believe the government is selling SLIDA," I said when the video finished. "I know the country is in a mess, but..."

"As you can imagine, there are a whole bunch of conditions relating to the buyer set out in here," Crawford said, wading through the boilerplate at the back of the memorandum. "No buyers from outside the U.S. will be considered, and there's a load of stuff about the Espionage Act." She looked up at me. "Didn't know we had one."

"My guess is this is something they're selling through gritted teeth. They need the money, sure, but they're going to tie up any buyer real tight."

"Get this," Crawford said, reading from the middle of the document, "they're giving a twenty-year contract with this thing."

I smiled. "Depending on the terms of that contract, this could be a goldmine."

"Won't be cheap, though."

"Isn't that normally my line?"

"I thought I'd get it in before you this time."

"I don't mind paying for quality. Could there ever be a safer investment than this?"

Crawford shrugged. "I guess that depends whether you believe that lot in Washington will finally get a handle on the deficit."

"Okay, making that assumption, once the acquisition price has been agreed, the returns are a certainty." I reached for my calculator. "Hand me the forecasts, would you?"

Crawford slid the numbers across the table then continued reading. "You're right about the tight deadline. It says here they want indicative first bids by the seventeenth. That's only a week away."

I grinned. "Good job we have CCP's best brains working on it then."

"Still tight, though. Even for us."

CHAPTER 5

Frank Marcuri walked with a pronounced limp, the result of shrapnel wounds received when the helicopter he was flying was shot down in Vietnam. As a prisoner of war for over two years, he suffered from near starvation and brutal treatment but, never once, did the Vietcong break his spirit. When he was released during a prisoner exchange in 1972, he insisted on returning to his unit. He wanted to get back in the air, but the leg injury, and the lack of medical treatment he'd received during his incarceration, meant that was impossible. Forced to return home to Connecticut, he joined his father's small, regional insurance business, General Risk.

Marcuri channeled all his frustration into the company, expanding it rapidly and taking it national with a network of two hundred offices. Upon his father's death in 1980, he took over as CEO and really stepped on the gas. When General Risk floated on the New York Stock Exchange ten years later, the stock was massively oversubscribed. Throughout the 1990s and 2000s, Marcuri consummated shrewd acquisitions growing the company to the second-largest general insurer in the country by 2010. With no debt, and a mountain of cash on its balance sheet, the company had seen its stock price grow six-fold since the initial public offering. As far as Marcuri's investors were concerned, he could do no wrong.

General Risk generated billions in surplus cash each year, and Marcuri saw it as a key part of his role to make sure that cash was put to good use, earning a decent return without taking unnecessary risks. Like many insurance companies,

General Risk put a small part of its surplus cash into private equity funds, and by far the largest of these investments was the company's stake in the Carada Capital Partners fund. General Risk became my new firm's cornerstone investor, committing thirty billion to our total seventy-five-billion-dollar pot. In making this commitment, I knew Marcuri was investing in me, having backed me several times before at my previous employer in New York. Although I'd made him good returns over those years, I felt flattered by his confidence in me and hoped I would continue to earn it. He once told me he respected my innate caution and investment judgment and, on the day he made the commitment to our new firm's fund, he said, "You're an intelligent money maker, Damon, and, unlike most of the inflated egos in the private equity market, you always listen to the concerns of your investors." His words stuck with me, and I'm sure that's what made me careful to avoid over-paying for assets in those first few months after we launched.

In exchange for General Risk's sizeable pledge to CCP, Marcuri had been appointed chairman of our investor advisory committee, which met twice a year to discuss the firm's investment performance. In addition, the terms of CCP's investment agreement with its investors required me to consult with the committee on certain material matters. The most important of these was any prospective investment requiring more than twenty percent of the fund. In such a situation, the committee's consent was required before we could make the investment. I had no issue with this so-called "concentration limit" as the industry-standard protection to prevent us from putting all our eggs into one basket. That made sense.

But then we came across the SLIDA deal.

I decided to drive from Boston to Hartford to discuss the deal with Marcuri face to face. The drive gave me uninterrupted time alone to think how best to play the meeting. Marcuri was a man who preferred facts over emotion. I couldn't just sell him on the basis that my team thought SLIDA was a great deal.

Marcuri would want to know why. While I thought we had the bases covered, one thing still troubled me: Not once in my career had I asked investors for permission to exceed the concentration limit. Marcuri would know this too. Crawford and I had spent the last three days working around the clock on the numbers and we couldn't avoid the issue. Whichever way we ran them, it was clear we'd have to pay substantially more than fifteen billion dollars to win the auction, and thus exceed the limit. That meant Marcuri could say no, and the deal would be dead.

How was I going to convince conservative-minded Marcuri that CCP should risk more than twenty percent of the fund on only its second deal? It was a big ask, and I didn't want Marcuri to think I was buckling under the pressure from some of our other investors to deploy the fund more quickly. The truth was the numbers stacked up. Crawford and I thought we'd have to pay around $17.25 billion to win the auction. But even at that price, SLIDA still offered us a decent prospective investment return. By our calculations, we stood to make three times our money on the deal. On this one transaction alone, that meant we could generate almost thirty-five billion dollars in profit for the fund. Surely even Marcuri would find that convincing?

I arrived at General Risk's head office on the northern outskirts of Hartford at two-twenty in the afternoon. My meeting with Marcuri was scheduled for three, so I sat in the car going over how best to present my case. In terms of absolute profit, this was the sweetest deal I'd seen in my career. It combined great returns with solid revenues. Sure, I'd seen higher percentage gains before, but those were on much smaller deals with far riskier earnings. How often in my career would I see an opportunity to make this much profit for my investors in a single transaction? In all probability, there'd never be another one like it.

At five to three, I walked into the white marble reception and announced myself to one of the receptionists. On the wall behind the reception counter, lined up with almost military precision, hung three long rows of framed business awards. No doubt about it. Marcuri had built an insurance giant through his unstinting focus on the customer and by giving him what he wanted: good service at fair prices. The man was a legend in his industry and deserved his nickname—the Warren Buffett of New England.

Five minutes later, I was shown into the great man's office. A smell of cigar smoke, pleasant yet acidic, dominated the room. Marcuri hobbled into the room from his private balcony, stubbed out a fat cigar in the ashtray on his desk, and held out his right hand. I shook it—a firm grip, not bone crushing, but enough to indicate who was in charge of this meeting.

"The dumbest thing they ever did was ban smoking," he said, pointing to the balcony. "I'm reduced to smoking out there. Take a seat, Damon."

Although I'd long supported the smoking ban in offices, I wanted to keep Marcuri on my side. When I was growing up, my father had always told me to pick my fights carefully. In business, it was amazing how many times I'd found that advice useful.

"It must have brought down smoker death rates," I said, taking a seat at the small meeting table. Fresh white flakes of tobacco ash had settled on the dark wood of the table top. Clearly, the balcony wasn't the only place Marcuri enjoyed his cigars. "That has to be good for you guys as life insurers?"

"Fair point. Still can't see what it's got to do with the government." He looked like he wanted to spit. "They'll be telling us what we can eat next."

Again, the smart thing to do was agree. "They're micromanaging everything now. Red tape everywhere you look."

"Exactly my view. Those idiots in Washington don't get it, you know." Marcuri sat down on the other side of the table, partially crossing his hands on the tabletop. His wiry fingers had yellow stains at their tips. "Now, you've come to talk to me about a deal. Must be a big one if you need to speak to me about it."

"It is, but it's also a great deal for our investors."

Marcuri glanced at his watch. "I've only got half an hour. Better tell me something about it."

My shoulders stiffened and my mouth felt dry. Why was I so nervous? Doing this deal really was in the best interest of our investors. If it wasn't then I wouldn't have been there. I was about to tell Marcuri how CCP would make his company a lot more money by doing this deal. This was a good news meeting, but it didn't feel that way. I took a deep breath and dove in.

"You've heard of SLIDA, the defense operation?"

"Of course." Marcuri was already frowning.

"Well, we have a chance to buy it."

Marcuri threw his hands open. "That proves my point." He grimaced as he shifted the weight off his bad leg. "That lot in Washington are going to bankrupt this country. Now they're selling off the family silver. I wouldn't leave them in charge of a nursery school."

"Washington's need for cash means we have a once-in-a-lifetime opportunity. There's no way they'd have sold this if their backs weren't up against the wall."

"That's true. How much do they want for it?"

"It's being auctioned by DH&W."

Marcuri sucked air in through his teeth. "Sounds expensive."

No point dancing around the issue. I had to share the number sooner or later, so I decided I might as well table it now. "We think we may need to go to seventeen and a quarter."

Marcuri's face contorted and he pushed his hands against the table, sliding back his chair. "How much?"

"I know it's a lot, but the government is selling it with the benefit of a long-term contract—"

Marcuri raised his right hand. "Are you sure you want to do this, Damon? This doesn't sound like the cautious Damon Traynor I've known for years."

"We've run the numbers on this every way possible. Even at this price, we can still see us making three times our money, with very little downside."

"That's if those clowns in Washington don't bankrupt the country."

"I guess that's the main investment question on this transaction. Will the government be able to honor the twenty-year contract?"

"And?"

"Our judgment is that they will. Anything else is unthinkable."

"I can't tell you how many times I've heard that when we've had to assess insurance risks for the first time. The unthinkable is just that. Don't mean it won't happen."

"But if we thought the country was about to fail, we'd never do any deals."

"We've never been here before. This nation has never had as much debt bearing down on it as right now. I'm really not sure you should be committing this much of the fund to a single deal. I'd be putting some of it to work in Asia if I were in your shoes."

"We're looking at a couple of deals in China. I can't see why we can't do the SLIDA deal at the same time."

"It's a hell of a lot of money to put into one investment. You'd never make a profit on the fund if this one went down the pan, to say nothing of the damage to your reputation."

I paused. Marcuri was right, and if I wasn't careful I'd soon lose all credibility with our main backer. It was time to stop making my case and cut to the chase. "Are you saying no?"

Marcuri rose to his feet, ambled to his desk, and fired up a cigar. He leaned against the edge of the desk and looked back at me. "Look, I don't like to tell an expert how to do his job. All I'm saying is I'm not comfortable. I'd like to think it over then maybe discuss it with the other advisory committee members."

He puffed on the cigar. "Give me a few days and I'll come back to you."

"I'm afraid we don't have the time. The bids have to be in next week."

"Why the hurry?"

"I guess they need the money that quickly."

Marcuri looked away. "In that case," he said, taking another deep draw on the cigar, "I'm going to have to say no. I'm just not comfortable with it."

CHAPTER 6

The Marcuri estate was ten miles west of Hartford, near the prosperous town of Farmington. With twenty-two bedrooms and twenty-eight bathrooms, the sixty thousand square feet of property nestled in thirty wooded acres of Connecticut's most expensive real estate. Neighbors, not that you could see any of them, were the usual mix of new money—bankers, insurance executives, hedge fund managers, and Russian oligarchs. Frank and Barbara Marcuri built the property to their own design ten years back, with every room situated on one floor to save Frank from straining his injured leg.

With a busy day ahead, Marcuri rose earlier than usual. His schedule was crammed with back to back meetings, culminating in dinner with Damon. The night before, Damon had called him to report there'd been some important changes to the SLIDA transaction since they'd last met—changes best discussed face to face. At first reluctant to spend any more time on a deal he didn't like, eventually Marcuri gave in to the pressure. He suggested dinner in Boston as he was going to be in town for a couple of days on business anyway.

"Pipe down that whistling, would you?" Barbara said. She was sitting at the kitchen table, trying to read her newspaper and grazing on a bowl of Bear Naked granola and low fat yogurt.

Marcuri had finished his breakfast an hour earlier and was collecting his papers together on the kitchen counter before placing them into his briefcase. He stopped whistling. "Sorry. I didn't realize I was doing it."

"You're always chirpy when you're going on a trip. I could get the wrong idea."

"You can still come with me if you like. I did offer."

Barbara lowered the newspaper and peered over her reading glasses. "I'm not going anywhere near that thing. Far too dangerous."

"Ray said I can fly it most of the way," he said, beaming back at her.

"How nice of him. You pay him a fat salary as your pilot and then you end up flying the machine yourself." She shook her head. "Explain that one to me, big shot."

"But this new—"

"I bet you don't even have any real business in Boston. It's all an excuse to try out your new toy."

"If you say so, dear." The doorbell rang. "That'll be Ray now." He quickly stuffed the remaining documents into his case and clipped it shut.

"Off you go, but come back safe," Barbara said, kissing him on the cheek.

Marcuri skipped his way to the front door, whistling all the way.

A few moments later the air was filled with the sound of four Sikorsky rotor blades and the roar of two Pratt & Whitney engines. Marcuri was sitting in the cockpit alongside Ray Mountford, an ex-naval helicopter pilot who'd worked for Marcuri for the seven years since he'd left the service.

Ten minutes after takeoff, and when they were clear of the Hartford area, Marcuri rubbed his hands together. "Okay, Ray. I'm all set."

"Are you sure, sir? I'm happy to continue," Mountford said with a cheeky grin.

"Come on, man. I've been looking forward to this all weekend."

Mountford raised his palms. "She's all yours."

Marcuri disengaged the Thales auto-pilot system and took

control of the state of the art helicopter. He'd owned many of them before, but this one was special. He'd been on the waiting list for three years, handing over a sizeable deposit so that, when it was delivered six weeks ago, he was the first U.S. commercial customer to own one.

"She handles well, doesn't she?" Mountford said.

"A beauty."

Marcuri raised his eyes above the two six-by-eight-inch digital displays in front of him and looked out of the window. The sky was bright blue, punctuated by the odd high-level cloud, floating like cotton candy above them.

"You've picked a great day to try her out, sir."

"Sure beats work, Ray." Marcuri pointed to his briefcase in the gap between them. "Reach inside there for me and fire up a cigar. I want to savor this moment. Have one yourself too."

Mountford lit the cigars, and they sat smiling and puffing in silence for a few minutes as the cabin filled with smoke.

"What do you think the true range is?" Marcuri asked.

"Well, they quote five hundred miles, so my guess is nearer five fifty."

"Quite some machine."

"With that range, we can take this one on many more trips."

Marcuri exhaled a cloud of smoke. "That's the plan, Ray."

They were still discussing the technical features of the helicopter forty minutes later when Mountford took over to prepare for landing at Boston's Logan Airport. They were flying at six thousand feet and beginning their descent when the smile vanished from Mountford's face.

"Did you feel that?" he asked, gripping the cobra-shaped joy-stick in front of him.

"No. What was it?"

"Maybe nothing." Mountford's eyes danced across the electronic array.

"Can you describe—"

"There it is again."

"I felt it that time. A slight judder?"

"Exactly."

The helicopter began to vibrate. Both men looked at each other, fear in their eyes.

"Let's get this thing on the ground, Ray. Make it quick."

"I got it."

The helicopter coughed then, suddenly, dropped fifty feet.

"What the hell was that?" asked Marcuri, pulling his safety belt tight.

"I don't know, but it ain't right. Hold on, sir." Two red lights illuminated on the eye-level panel. Mountford looked confused and shook his head. "That can't be..."

"Are they what I think they are?" Marcuri asked, more than a hint of panic in his voice.

"Fuel warnings. Both of them. It makes no sense." Mountford spoke into the radio. "Logan, this is an emergency—"

The aircraft lurched sideways before plunging two hundred feet.

"We've gotta be losing fuel," shouted Marcuri.

Another judder.

"How is that possible?"

Another drop before the engines slowed.

"This is Logan," said a voice over the radio headphones. "What is the nature of your emergency?"

"We're going down," Mountford said, jabbing at the control buttons.

"Please, no," Marcuri said. "We must be three thousand feet above the ground."

"I'm going to try—"

There was a white flash, and the helicopter exploded over Boston harbor before plunging through the air, strewing debris over a three-mile stretch of water.

CHAPTER 7

I needed to take my mind off work, so I decided to spend the weekend with my parents at their home in Barnstable on the north shore of Cape Cod. Although I couldn't stop thinking about Marcuri's death, the last thing I wanted was to let it ruin the weekend for my mom and dad.

Mom has always been perceptive, and the first thing she said when we sat down for dinner on the Friday evening was, "You're very quiet, Damon."

I forced a smile. "It's nothing." I stared at the full plate in front of me. Mom had made my favorite: smoked salmon with pesto linguine. "This looks great," I said before taking my first bite.

The dining table faced the large picture window, and on the windowsill, in its usual place, was a fading copy of *Forbes* magazine. On the cover was a photo of ten people, including me. The text below the photo read: *The Country's Most Powerful African Americans.* Mom had kept it on show ever since the article had been published some two years earlier.

As I took in the view through the window, I could see the sunset over Sandy Neck peninsula. I remembered how excited Mom and Dad had been when they first discovered the area for their retirement home. But when they realized how much they'd have to spend to buy a house on the waterfront in Barnstable, they were about to reconsider until I offered to help them out. Dad wouldn't have it at first, but I insisted. It would have broken their hearts giving up their dream of retiring next to the ocean.

"Damon," Mom said, disturbing my thoughts. She threw me a look as if to say she knew something was wrong.

"Sorry. There's a lot going on at work," I said, having another go at the pasta, in spite of my lack of appetite. "Just a few things on my mind. That's all."

Mom looked at Dad in search of an ally.

"Anything I can help you with?" he asked.

Dad had spent his entire career as a property lawyer with small law firms in Boston. He'd founded his own firm with two partners thirty years back and, by the time he announced his retirement, it had grown to five partners and two offices. He missed the challenge of the work, and if it hadn't been for his declining health, he'd still be practicing today. When I was setting up CCP, Dad's advice had been invaluable, but his knowledge didn't extend to making investments, so I didn't make a habit of discussing the details of our deals with him. The truth is, too, I would have been embarrassed for him to discover the amount of money we could make on private equity investments. It was an unreal amount by most people's standards.

"Do you mind if we talk about it later, Dad?" I knew he wanted to help, but the shock of Marcuri's helicopter accident and the frantic pressure of work since then had left me exhausted.

On Saturday afternoon, I went for a long run along the beach at Chatham and then down Main Street. Out of season, the roads were quiet so I could wear my Apple earbuds without worrying too much about the traffic. It felt good to get some fresh air in my lungs, and the running distracted me from thinking about work too much. Sunday morning, I went cycling with my father on the disused rail track near Orleans. As we headed north along the peninsula, there were fewer people about, so we could cycle alongside each other.

"You know I mentioned that deal on the phone a few days ago?" I said.

Dad glanced at me. "You sounded quite worried about it."

"I was struggling to convince the chairman of our advisory committee that we ought to do it."

"Did you manage to persuade him?"

"No. It's really sad. He died in a helicopter accident this week."

"I'm sorry to hear that. What happened?"

"No one really knows. It was a new aircraft. For some reason it just exploded over Boston Harbor."

"I read about that in the paper. Is that why you've been so quiet this weekend?"

"It's just that I feel torn in two directions."

"How come?"

"When we spoke to them, it turns out the rest of the committee still want to go ahead with the deal. But I feel uncomfortable going against the chairman's advice."

"I can understand that, but I guess you have to do what you think is right for your investors."

"In the end, that's what persuaded me to continue. In fact, we should hear tomorrow if we've won the auction."

"Good luck with it, Son. I hope it turns out well for you."

"Thanks. It's a massive deal for us, and it'll be in all the newspapers once it completes."

"Fame and fortune. I bet you're glad now you set up your own firm. I know you were worried at one stage that it was taking too long to complete your first deal."

"It's been hard, but I think this one will be the making of our firm. Provided we win it, of course."

"Let's hope so." We slowed down when we approached a road crossing. "Look over there, Damon," Dad said, pointing up the road with a nod of his bike helmet. "Isn't that the same car we saw at the last crossing a few miles back?"

"What, the black one?" I asked, looking at the stationary vehicle at the side of the road about fifty yards away from us. "I don't remember it."

"Yes. The two men look familiar. I remember their suits. Don't see many around here, particularly on a Sunday."

We braked and stood at the curb, watching the black SUV. The two suits in the car appeared uncomfortable and looked away. A moment later, they started the engine, pulled away from the verge, and did a U-turn to avoid driving by us.

"That's weird," I said. "It's as though they knew we were talking about them. What were they up to?"

"I have no idea. Come on. Let's head back. I know I'm ready for some lunch," Dad said, turning his bike around.

The following day, I called all of my partners together in the conference room just before noon, so we could hear the call come in from DH&W.

"So come on then, Damon. How much sleep did you get at the weekend?" asked Gainham.

"Not much," I said, sitting on the corner of the table. "How about you?"

"The same. I took a walk by your place early on Sunday morning. Thought I'd call in for a coffee, but you weren't in."

"I went down to the Cape again. I needed to do something to take my mind off the deal. Sorry I missed you."

"You were lucky. I had the kids with me."

Crawford ran into the room, smelling of tobacco. "Sorry. Have I missed anything?"

"Yeah," Gainham said with a miserable face. "We didn't win."

"Not again," said Crawford. "I need another cigarette."

"He's kidding, Diane. We've not heard yet," I said, looking at my watch. "I make it just after noon, though. I hope they're not going to make us—"

The speakerphone in the middle of the table rang. I looked at Gainham for a split second before answering it.

"Damon, I have Orlando Barrett for you," our receptionist said.

I crossed my fingers. That Barrett himself was calling surely had to be a good sign. If it was bad news, he'd have delegated it to one of his team. I looked around the table at the expectant faces, hoping for it to be good news. "Put him through." There was a click on the line. "Orlando, how are you?"

"Fine, thank you," Barrett said in his clipped British accent. "I have a decision for you."

"We're waiting."

"How do you think you fared?"

What's Barrett up to? "Just tell us the news, Orlando. Are we on or not?"

"Well, dear boy, you had better get the check book out. CCP has won the auction again. Congratulations."

"That's great news."

"We'll be in touch to discuss the diligence process."

After I terminated the call, I stood, held both clenched fists above my head and shouted, "Yes, yes, yes!"

The room erupted in a wave of back slapping and high fives.

"I don't care," Crawford said reaching for her purse. "I'm having another cigarette." She lit one up in the room.

"Just this once," I said.

"We've got a lot of work to do," Gainham said.

"The auction process stipulated one week from here to closing," Crawford said, exhaling a white cloud of smoke.

"I don't care if we have to work day and night to get there," I said. "The prize is worth it."

"I can't believe we went almost a year without a single deal and then we pull off two in less than a month," Gainham said. "Where are we celebrating?"

I paused for a moment. "Dinner at Firenze, unless anyone has a better suggestion."

"And a club afterward?"

"Not this time," I said. "I want us all to have clear heads.

We need to get to work on this deal early tomorrow morning. There'll be plenty of time to celebrate once we've closed it."

I wasn't about to repeat the same stupid mistake I made last time when I'd drunk too much and lost control—behavior completely out of character. Let's just say it wasn't my proudest moment. While I blamed the relief of completing CCP's first deal, there was really no excuse. I'd been a fool, falling for one of the oldest scams in the book. In hindsight, it was obvious the young woman had targeted me and probably many other suckers before me. She had to have been lying about her age to extort money. No way she was as young as she said she was, but it had been easier to pay her off. I didn't like it, but she'd threatened to contact my investors if I didn't cave into her blackmail demands. I couldn't risk the bad publicity even though I knew I was dealing with a con artist. Thankfully, paying her off had worked as I hadn't heard from her again. By now, no doubt, she'd moved on to her next victim.

CHAPTER 8

Ben Mylor avoided the stuffed shirts of Washington, D.C., as much as he could, but when his boss, George Patterson, Director of National Intelligence, demanded a face to face meeting with him at the White House, he knew he had to go. He could count on the fingers of one hand the times such meetings had been called, and each one of them had involved matters of utmost secrecy—things that could only be discussed behind closed doors and without written records.

After passing through security and being kept waiting for twenty minutes, a personal assistant led Mylor into the Oval Office. President Halley was standing, leaning against his desk while Patterson and Treasury Secretary Allen sat on leather sofas opposite each other. Patterson was reclining, but Allen looked nervous perched on the front of his seat cushion. Mylor could tell the mood of the meeting from the deep lines across Patterson's brow.

"Take a seat here, Ben," Patterson said, pointing to one of the two armchairs facing Halley. "We've been bringing the president up to speed on Project Eclipse, and he wanted you to join us, so he could be briefed directly on the details."

Mylor knew exactly what that meant. Halley was a control freak and he'd want to hear the whole story, warts and all, without it being filtered through Allen. As he took his seat, Mylor looked for, and received, the almost imperceptible nod from his boss, indicating he was happy for him to be completely open.

"George has told me what we have in place so far," Halley

said, staring at Mylor, "but I want to know what more we can do to step this thing up. We don't have the luxury of time."

"That depends, Mr. President," Mylor said.

"What does that mean, exactly?"

"On how we handle any resistance." Mylor glanced at Patterson and received another tilt of the head. "You see, we're dealing with some pretty smart people on the other side of these deals. Being astute is how they made their money, so it's no surprise when some of them are quick to discover they've been duped."

"George assures me you can handle them."

"Sure. Most roll over once they know what we have on them. Others have found the pressure too much and have taken the coward's way out."

Allen cleared his throat then asked, "How so?"

Before Mylor could elaborate, Halley said, "How do you think, man?"

"They've killed themselves," Mylor said, his tone matter of fact.

Allen recoiled, but said nothing.

"The resistance I'm referring to, Mr. President," Mylor continued, "comes from a third group: the ones that refuse to accept things and won't stop digging. Not only do they slow us down, but any one of them has the capacity to blow this thing wide open."

Halley looked like he had a sour taste in his mouth. "We cannot allow that to happen." He directed his next words at Patterson. "What do you need, George?"

Patterson slid forward to the edge of his seat. "It's not so much what we need. Ben can deal with all of this. It's more a question—"

"What are you asking me?" Halley's tone was impatient.

"Well, this is more about having the stomach to get the job done."

"That's simple. We must do whatever is necessary," Halley

said, without even stopping to think about the implications.

"That will mean...dealing...with some of these people," Mylor said.

Halley turned to Mylor. "I'm instructing you to do everything possible to make these deals happen and to keep them from blowing up on us. If any of this leaks out..."

"That's very clear, sir," Mylor said. "We will handle them before they become a problem."

"There must be another way," Allen said, his voice almost a whimper. "These are innocent people, U.S. citizens we're talking about."

"Not all of them," Patterson said.

"There is no other way," Halley said. "We have to put the needs of the country first. Sometimes leadership means doing the unthinkable for the greater good."

"The president is right," Patterson said.

Allen gazed at his feet. "I don't want any part of this."

"You're already involved," Patterson said. "Tell him, Ben."

Mylor looked at the president and then Allen. "Getting some of these assets sold in the first place hasn't been easy. Let's just say we've had to use our initiative to eliminate any resistance. How else do you think we've been able to move so fast?"

Allen shook his head no, but said nothing.

"We warned you there'd be some collateral damage," Patterson said. "What did you think that meant?"

Allen avoided eye contact and still gave no response.

Patterson glared at Allen. "You're part of this whether you like it or not."

"Is there anything else you need, gentlemen?" Halley asked.

"Not at this time, Mr. President," Patterson said.

"Then this meeting is over. Keep me informed of developments, George." Halley marched over to Mylor. "Good work," he said, shaking Mylor's hand. "The country is in your debt."

CHAPTER 9

Six days of intense due diligence raced by, swallowed up in a fog of financial and legal investigations in data rooms, Excel spreadsheets, and late night contract negotiations in lawyers' offices, fueled by a diet of pizza, cookies, and too much caffeine. At various stages, every partner took part in the frenetic process of closing the SLIDA deal. Nothing was more important to our firm's success.

The day after the deal closed, CCP appeared on the front pages of both *The Wall Street Journal* and *The Financial Times*, lauded as the "new financial masters of the universe." Journalists talked of CCP pulling off a masterstroke and described in great detail why owning SLIDA was a license to print money. How could the government have found itself in such a mess that it had to sell off key national assets, allowing financial investors to clean up? Private equity journals and specialist online publications focused on what this meant for the industry. Now no company was too big to be acquired by an LBO fund. A new era had dawned.

My partners and I had just pulled off the largest private equity deal in history, more than twice the size of the previous record. As well as countless calls from the media, new investors bombarded us with enquiries. CCP and its partners walked on water as far as return-hungry potential investors were concerned. Keen to get in on the action, they all wanted to know what it would take to obtain access to the firm's next fund. With such a strong appetite from the market, any future fund was bound to be well in excess of one hundred billion dollars, far exceeding any funds managed by our competitors.

The firm's existing backers were ecstatic. They'd all seen the heady stories in the financial press and the speculation that their fund could see profits of at least seventy-five billion on the SLIDA deal alone. Every member of the investor advisory committee called me to congratulate us—even those, like Marcuri, who'd initially been against the deal. And while the winning bid of twenty-five billion for SLIDA had swallowed up a third of the fund, that didn't appear to faze them. As far as our investors were concerned, the money was there to be used.

Two days after the deal was signed, I landed at San Francisco International, where I rented a Ford Edge from Hertz. The twenty-mile or so drive to SLIDA's Sausalito headquarters took me across the Golden Gate Bridge. On the few previous occasions I'd visited the area, the visibility had been poor, and the bay shrouded in sea mist, but not that day. The sun was high in the sky, and the Marin Headlands climbed out of the water on the north side of the bridge like sleeping giants. Life was good. CCP had come a long way in the space of a year, and now I was on my way to the first board meeting of the firm's high-profile investment—a trophy asset and the envy of the buy-out industry.

Besides me, there were seven other members on the SLIDA board of directors, including the CEO, CFO, and chairman, who I'd appointed on the day the deal closed. All of them, with the exception of me and our new chairman, had served on the board for more than ten years. They'd taken the previously government-owned company from its early conceptual beginning, through the prototype stages, and onto its successful development as a strategically important U.S. defense business worth billions.

A seven-foot, razor wire, steel fence surrounded the headquarters building located two miles off the Redwood Highway. The nondescript 1980s-design, six-story office block stood in front of three single-level laboratories which were set back

55

among the trees. I found a parking spot in front of the offices and walked into the reception area.

I was the last person to arrive at the walnut paneled board-room on the top floor. It offered a great view over Richardson Bay toward Angel Island State Park.

"Gentlemen, sorry I'm a few minutes late. Getting through security here is worse than Fort Knox," I said, pulling up a chair in the middle of the boardroom table. "I tried to tell the guard at the gate that I was, in effect, the new owner, but he didn't seem to believe me."

The other directors laughed.

"That's Gary for you. He gives all strangers a hard time," Mike Hansen said, the goateed and balding CEO. "Give him a few months and he'll get used to you."

"Well, it's good to be here, anyway," I said, pouring coffee from the carafe in the middle of the table.

"I think you met everyone during the due diligence process?" Hansen asked.

I looked around the table and made eye contact with everyone. "Yes, we've all met, thanks."

"Good. We have a lot to get through during this first board meeting, so let's get started," George Pellerton said, the wiry, silver-haired chairman. He nodded at Hansen.

The CEO rose to his feet and stood in front of the white screen at one end of the room. "Damon, I hope it's okay to assume the board papers have been read? That's what we normally do."

"Of course," I said. "I'd like to keep these meetings focused on high-level matters. There's no point in them becoming management meetings or just a verbal rehash of the board papers. Otherwise, why bother to have them?"

"That's good to hear," said Hansen. "In that case, I'd like to summarize our financial performance first off."

I smiled before taking my first sip of coffee. It was bitter—

probably a cheap instant variety. *That will have to change*, I thought.

Hansen powered up the screen. "These are our high-level numbers. The main thing to highlight here is that while revenues are right on budget, our profit and cash flow numbers are ten percent ahead of last year."

"It's a great start. What's behind the improved bottom line performance?" I asked, pushing the full mug of coffee away. The sour taste lingered in my mouth.

"In the weeks leading up to the sale by the government, we came under a lot of pressure from the Treasury Department to reduce overheads. Every single line item of cost had to be justified. We were forced to chop some expensive, but highly experienced, people too. The positive impact on our costs was budgeted, but the savings have turned out more than we thought."

"Where were the main cuts?" Pellerton asked.

"Pretty much across the company, but heaviest in technical," said Hansen. "Orders came down from Washington as to where they wanted the ax to fall hardest. We didn't have much say."

"Can we continue to perform this well with the reduced headcount?" I asked.

"I think so," Hansen said.

"Good. What about growing our revenue? I know most of it comes from the government contract, but I'd like to see us moving into third-party consulting pretty quickly. There must be a whole bunch of other ways to expand our revenue base."

Hansen looked confused and glanced at his colleagues. "Well, I guess we could look into that. It's not something we've been asked to do before."

Pellerton leaned forward. "Gentlemen, one of the key differences you will notice between government and private equity as owners is that things will move a lot faster around here, and there'll be a lot more pressure to generate cash to pay down some of the buyout financing."

"Thanks, George," I said, taking in the wide-eyed, pale faces of the executive team. "Don't worry; we don't need to achieve it all next month."

After the meeting, I offered Pellerton a ride to the airport, so we could talk in private.

"I think those guys have a lot of learning to do about working for a private equity firm," I said, pulling away from the security gate.

"Yeah. Moving out of government ownership is going to be quite a culture shock for most of them."

"That's why I brought you in, George. You've been there before. I want you to coach them. I don't want this to be adversarial. It's a great business, and I want to keep them onside if we can. They appear to be motivated to do their best for the company."

"I get it. Don't worry. I know how to handle them."

"Fantastic start, though. I like it when an investment beats its own numbers."

"I hear you."

I pulled onto the Redwood Highway and headed south. "Not sure I appreciated the depth of the staff cuts before it was sold. Did you?"

"It was a surprise when I heard about that too."

"I guess the government was polishing the apple before putting it on the market. I can't blame them for that."

"I spent a bit of time with the guys yesterday, prepping them for this first board meeting. They told me about the headcount reduction. Apparently, the orders came down from on high. They didn't like it at all—thought it was a bit heavy handed."

"Let's keep an eye on morale. If we need to add a few more people here and there, let me know. I want that senior team working with us. We're not the bad guys and we really need this deal to go well. We've got a lot riding on this one."

"Don't worry. I know how important it is to CCP. I have it under control."

* * *

At the airport, Pellerton and I split up to check in for our separate flights. With an hour to kill, once I'd cleared security, I bought a decent coffee and a copy of *The Economist* then found an empty corner in the departure lounge.

Five minutes later, a ponytailed man in his mid-forties, dressed in a baggy suit, sat next to me. He spread the sports section of the *San Francisco Chronicle* across his lap then ripped open a pack of tuna and mayo bagels. Without making it obvious, I leaned away from the man. There was something strange about his demeanor, and I thought it was odd that he'd chosen the seat right next to me as there were plenty of other empty spots in the quiet lounge. He stank of alcohol.

I waited a couple of minutes while downing my coffee. Then I glanced at my watch and packed the magazine into my briefcase. My plan was to find another seat at the opposite end of the lounge, out of sight of the man.

"Please don't go," the man said, resting a half-eaten bagel on his newspaper.

It had already been a long day, and I wasn't in the mood for this. I looked up at the digital display board. "I see they're calling my flight," I said, standing up and grabbing my briefcase.

"I need to talk to you," said the man, panic in his voice.

"I think you're mistaking me for someone else."

"There's no mistake. You're Damon Traynor."

I stepped back. "I don't know you. I'm sorry," I said, turning away.

The man chased after me, tapping my shoulder when he caught up. "I need to discuss something important with you." I carried on walking. "Please."

In the middle of the hall, I stopped and turned to the man. "Look, I don't know how you know my name, but if you don't stop disturbing me, I'll have to report you to security."

"It's about SLIDA."

That caught my attention. "What about it?"

"I know you were there today. I've been waiting here all day to catch you before your return flight. Please, I only need a moment."

Where's this going? I thought. I didn't know the man, but he sure knew something about SLIDA and my attendance at the board meeting earlier in the day. Who was he? "Okay. You have thirty seconds. What is it?"

"We can't talk here. It's confidential."

"You either tell me now or I'm going over to security to have you thrown out."

"I just wanted to make contact at this stage. I'll come and see you in Boston in a couple of days."

I shook my head. "I'm sorry, but I don't want anything to do with you. Please, go away."

The man stepped up to my face. He had a morsel of tuna stuck to his bushy moustache, and his breath smelled of fish and beer. "You'll want to hear what I've got to say, but I can't discuss it here. I said I'll see you in Boston." He backed off and returned to the corner of the lounge where he continued to eat his bagel.

CHAPTER 10

The London arm of the Gulf States' sovereign wealth fund was a giant among investment houses with hundreds of billions invested in assets across the globe. Decades of increasing oil revenues meant its London new deal team, headed up by Paul McCann, was under pressure to find bigger and bigger investment opportunities each year to deploy the fund's surplus capital. McCann's preferred investments were acquisitions of government-owned infrastructure assets, where he could write huge checks and, in return, enjoy a stable and secure yield. He'd enjoyed a good run that year, having acquired two regional ports in the Far East and, a month before, a large oil and gas operation from the U.S. Treasury on the Gulf Coast.

Most days, McCann would still be at his desk at eight in the evening, but that day was a special one, which meant he had to leave early. The equestrian clothing shop on Jermyn Street in London's West End closed at six, and he couldn't risk being late. It was his daughter's eighth birthday and, three weeks earlier, he'd ordered a special pair of waxed leather long boots for her—something she'd wanted for months.

McCann raced out of his office tower on Bishopsgate at five-twenty, cursing himself for leaving it so tight. His last meeting had been scheduled to run until five, but it had run over. He looked west along London Wall and toyed with the idea of jumping in a cab, but the traffic could be hell at that time of the evening, so he walked on—the Central line tube from Liverpool Street to Holborn, then the Piccadilly line to Piccadilly Circus would be far quicker. It would be crowded with commuters heading home, but it was more reliable—twenty-five minutes at most.

He called the shop to say he was on his way before running into Liverpool Street tube station. A swarm of office workers lined up at the barriers, inserting their tickets or swiping their Oyster cards. It reminded him why he never traveled during the rush hour if he could avoid it.

McCann was carried along in the horde toward the westbound platform. When he reached it, people were already standing four or five rows deep. He glanced at his watch—five-twenty-eight. It was tight, but still okay. A train hurtled into the station, and the throng surged forward. Only a few people managed to squeeze into the already full compartments, before the train pulled out. There were still three rows of people in front of him. At this rate, there was a risk he wasn't going to make it. His daughter's disappointed face flashed into his mind. Why had he left it so late? He'd been stupid. It was too late to go back and get a cab now.

"Please stand back well behind the yellow line," announced the invisible staff member from somewhere along the platform. "Another train is only two minutes away."

More people poured in from behind, adding to the crush. McCann looked around. No space anywhere near him. Maybe there would be fewer people at the end of the platform. If he could make it, there was a greater chance of catching the next train.

He tried pushing his way through the heaving mass of bodies, but it was no good; no one gave ground. Another train came and went. Although he missed it, the train's departure momentarily created an opportunity to squeeze his way to the end. He was right; there was a little more space near the tunnel entrance. No doubt he would make it onto the next one. Standing at the platform's edge, he looked up at the electronic display board. The next train was showing as held at Aldgate station. It would be at least another five minutes. The digital clock at the bottom of the board read five-thirty-six. He was going to be late now. He grabbed his phone from his jacket pocket. If he could just get a signal, he could warn the shop he was running behind and was still on his way. Maybe they'd wait for him. The phone's screen indicated no service.

Blast.

Two men pushed up close behind him, forcing him well over the yellow safety line. He turned to the men, threw them a shit-look, and shook his head. What did they think the line was there for?

"Sorry, buddy," said one of the men in an American accent, his half-smile revealing a complete lack of sincerity. "We're getting pushed from behind ourselves."

"No problem," McCann said before looking at his watch again. If the train came now, there was a very slim chance he could still make it.

To avoid the incessant pressure from the Americans, McCann moved two steps to the right, cramming his body against the tunnel's entrance. The shiny steel tracks three feet below him vibrated and a rumble came from somewhere along the dark shaft. The train was on its way.

The crowd surged forward, squeezing the Americans right up against him again. He leaned back as much as he could so as not to be caught in the draught when the train emerged from the tunnel. No matter how tight the squeeze, he had to get on this train; it was his only hope.

The rumbling grew louder, and headlights appeared in the darkness.

"Stand well back from the line," the announcer said.

A pretty blonde woman wearing white earbuds was standing immediately to McCann's left. She turned her head toward him and smiled.

A rush of stale air emerged from the tunnel. It was cold and strangely refreshing on his face. He smiled back at the woman, before leaning further backward to avoid the speeding train.

"Stand well back. The train is approaching," the announcer said.

A sudden and violent lunge struck McCann in his lower back, lifting him off the ground. As he fell forward toward the tracks, he reached out, dropping his briefcase, and grasped at the air in front of him.

The blonde woman screamed.

Time stood still as he floated in midair, the rush of wind from the train enveloping him. The deafening squeal of the brakes and the jarring noise of the metal wheels on the tracks were the last sounds McCann ever heard.

CHAPTER 11

Leveraged buyout transactions rely on a truckload of debt. Too much and the bird won't fly—too little and the equity returns for the private equity firm will be poor or, even worse, the deal will be lost to another buyout house prepared to leverage the target closer to the hilt. The big firms employ whole teams of analysts and Excel jockeys to crunch the numbers, fine-tuning the financial structure of deals before making an offer.

Gainham tapped away at his keyboard and slid the mouse around. He'd been working on the spreadsheet all morning, playing with different sensitivity scenarios and testing whether the debt level on the deal he was working on was right. "I just can't make this thing work," he said, pushing his chair back from the desk. "Take a look at it for me, would you? Tell me what I'm doing wrong."

I stood leaning against the door frame at the entrance to Gainham's office. "Hmm. Can't you give it to one of the analysts for now?" I asked. "I'm hungry. I only came over to see if you wanted to go out for lunch."

"What time is it?" asked Gainham, glancing at his watch.

"Almost noon."

"Already? I've been looking at this thing for hours. My head's going around in circles."

"Come on. When we get back, I'll take a look at it with you if you're too proud to give it to one of the guys downstairs."

Gainham frowned. "I'm not too proud."

"Okay, whatever," I said. "But you always were lousy at numbers."

"I like to keep my mind on higher level issues." Gainham smiled. "Anyone can run the numbers."

"Still amazes me you went into private equity in the first place."

"You told me we'd make a lot of money. Remember?"

I winked. "One day."

Gainham stood up and grabbed his jacket. "Where are we going?"

"You choose. I'm paying."

"Somewhere expensive then."

When we walked through the open plan area on our way to the elevators, our receptionist stopped us. "Glad I caught you, Damon," she said, handing me a piece of folded paper. "A strange looking man left that for you about ten minutes ago. He said you would know all about it."

I unfolded the paper and read the handwritten note. *Meet me at Bertucci's on Merchants Row. I've reserved a table at the back.*

This was confusing. "What did he look like?" I asked, putting the paper into my jacket pocket.

She tilted her head and pursed her lips. "Moustache, late forties, I'd say. Certainly, he looked too old for a ponytail, anyway. He said you know him, but I wasn't convinced. He seemed in a hurry to leave as soon as I started asking questions."

The penny dropped. "I have an idea who he is." I turned to Gainham. "Looks like we're having pizza."

"Not again. Who is this guy?"

"I'll tell you all about him on the way."

Ten minutes later, Gainham and I walked into Bertucci's Pizza, a short walk from the back of CCP's State Street offices. I looked around the room. A ponytailed man was sitting at a table with his back against the far wall, waving a newspaper. As I expected, it was the same man who'd stopped me in the airport departure lounge at San Francisco. Who would have thought he'd actually turn up?

"Leave the talking to me," I said, winding my way through the busy front tables.

"Who's this?" the man asked, looking up and down at Gainham when we arrived at his table.

"He's one of my partners." I didn't sit down and simply rested my hands on the back of one of the empty wooden chairs.

"You were supposed to come alone. I don't like surprises."

It took all my patience to control my temper. Who was this stranger who'd traveled across the country to see us? Why did he think he had the right to start laying down the law? "If you have a problem with him being here then we're out of here."

"I'd prefer to speak to you alone."

"That ain't happening. Now tell me what's going on."

"I guess if he's your partner, I can live with it."

"Nice of you to say so," Gainham said.

I rolled back my sleeve and looked at my watch. "You've got five minutes. We're not staying."

"Please, sit down. This is going to take some time." The man slid a chair out. "I promise, in spite of what you're thinking, I'm not here to waste your time."

Staring at the man, I wondered what to do. There was some-thing about him—something that made me think I should give him a chance to speak. After all, he'd come a long way. What did we have to lose by hearing him out? I nodded to Gainham, and both of us sat.

"Well?" I asked after a few seconds of silence while the man played with his moustache and read the menu. "We haven't got all day."

The man placed the menu on the table, looked around the dining room, and cleared his throat. He leaned into the table and lowered his voice. "First off, I want to apologize for the cloak and dagger stuff." He glanced around the room again.

"My name is Brodie Tillman." He waited, watching my face for a reaction.

I shrugged. "Means nothing to me. Should it?"

"It doesn't matter."

"Whoever you are, why didn't you just pick up the phone?"

"What I have to say couldn't be shared over the phone. I had to make sure you'd meet me, face to face. That's why I tracked you down at the airport. I wanted you to know I was real, so when I made contact you'd take me seriously."

I glanced at Gainham, who looked as confused as I did, then I half-smiled at the man. "Well, it worked. I'm here now. What do you want?"

A waitress came over to take our order. Tillman kept his focus on me. I turned to the waitress. "We're not really—"

"Listen, just bring us three regular pizzas," said Gainham.

"Which ones? You can have—"

"You choose." Gainham handed her the menus.

The waitress dropped the smile and cocked her head to the side. This was off script. "But—"

"Please. Choose anything. I'm sure it's all good."

"What would you like to drink?"

"Just bring some water."

Giving up, she shook her head and left.

"Okay. Why are we here?" I asked.

"I thought my name might be familiar," Tillman said. "Thought it might have been mentioned to you at least once or twice."

"Never heard of you. Who do you think might have mentioned you?"

"Amazing how quickly we're forgotten. Until eight weeks ago, I was head of technical development at SLIDA."

Again, I glanced at Gainham, who was frowning. "Why do you need to speak to us?"

"They let me go." Tillman snapped his fingers. "Just like that. After fifteen years of loyal service. They threw me out like

I was a piece of trash." Tillman's tone became almost belligerent as he talked.

"Look. I don't know much about the layoffs. They all happened before we bought the company. I'm afraid there's nothing we can do about that now. If you've come to ask for your old job back, I can't help you. I'm sorry."

"Hey. I'm not looking for my job back. That's not why I'm here at all."

The conversation was becoming more confusing by the second. "So, why are we here?"

"What exactly did they tell you about SLIDA?"

I sat upright in my chair. "What do you mean?"

"About its performance."

"We can't discuss the company's financial performance. That's confidential."

Tillman leaned forward again. "I'm not talking about the damn financial performance."

"Here we go," the waitress said. The plastic smile was back as she placed the pizzas in front of us. "Three Margheritas. Your water is on its way. Will there be anything else?"

"No. We're fine," Gainham said.

"Are you sure?"

"We're good."

She shook her head again, turned and walked away.

The three of us stared at the pizzas. I wasn't in the least bit hungry any longer. "I'm losing patience here," I said, pushing my plate away. "If there's something you want to say then spit it out."

Tillman took his time to scan the room then stared at me and said, "Did they tell you SLIDA doesn't work?" He picked up a slice of pizza and took a large bite. "It never has."

CHAPTER 12

Tillman chewed with his mouth open as I watched him, wondering what to say. *Why have we wasted almost twenty minutes humoring this man?* I thought. I should have listened to my instincts and ignored him. It was becoming clear why he'd been fired; Tillman wasn't playing with a full deck.

"Listen, I get that you're hurt over losing your job." I tried my best to keep cool. "But I have to tell you if you start spreading malicious rumors about our investment, we'll be left with no choice but to sue you. We can't have that happening."

"Sue me all you want," Tillman said, slapping his lips as he ate. "Still won't change the fact that you guys have been sold a pup. They saw you coming."

Gainham reached across the table and slid the half-eaten pizza away from Tillman. "Did you hear what Damon just said? We'll sue your ass if you continue with this little game of yours."

"If it makes you more comfortable thinking I'm some kind of wacko, then go ahead. But I know what I'm talking about. I ran the development team at SLIDA for years. I know everything there is to know about the system. Sure, there was a time when we hoped the technology would work. It would've made the U.S. invincible. But the truth is it has never worked—not even close. The whole thing's a charade."

"I've seen the system in action myself. I watched it take out two missiles minutes after they were launched," I said, making no attempt to hide my indignation. "Not that we owe you any kind of explanation."

"Then you were deceived."

"You need to be careful."

"I'm telling you it doesn't work. I've seen the demonstration video they showed you. Ever wondered why they scrambled two fighter jets just before the missiles were launched? Think about it. The only reason they did that was so they could take out the missiles. The laser doesn't work."

I shook my head. The man was delusional. "Would you like to explain why the government entered into a contract paying us good money for the use of it if it's no good?" I slapped my hand on the table. "I can't believe we're even having this conversation."

"You guys have been played." Tillman slid the pizza back into reach. "You may not like it, but you've been screwed."

"Come on, Damon," Gainham said, placing his palm on my shoulder. "Let's go. We're wasting our time. I think Mr. Tillman here is running some sort of scam."

"Hey, I'm not here trying to take your money or anything. I'm just trying to do the right thing. You can leave if you want, but there's a lot more you need to know."

Gainham stood. "Come on. Let's go."

I remained seated. "Wait a minute, Chris. We're here now so we might as well hear the whole of his crazy story. You never know. It could be entertaining."

"Laugh at me if it makes you feel better," Tillman said. "SLIDA doesn't work. It's just a stunt to convince the Russians and the Chinese that nuclear proliferation is futile. SLIDA makes that kind of warfare redundant. Well, just as long as everyone believes it works."

"This guy has gone off the deep end," Gainham said, sitting back down. "Do we really have to listen to him?"

"Go on," I said, peering at Tillman.

"It's all about money. This country couldn't afford the heavy investment in the next generation of nuclear weapons. Have you seen the size of the federal deficit?" Tillman waited for a response, and when none came he continued. "That's why they ramped up the SLIDA project. They'd long accepted it was never going to work, but they wanted us to make it look like it did. It saved them billions of dollars."

"Okay," I said. "Let's say I believe you for a moment. If it's all just a pretense, why would the government take the risk of selling it? That doesn't make sense. If what you say is true, they'd sit on it and keep a lid on the whole thing."

"That's because it works," Gainham said, shaking his head.

"You don't get it, do you?" Tillman said. "The government needs the money. By selling SLIDA they received a large chunk of cash. I heard you guys paid twenty-five billion for it. Man, that's a lot of change for an empty box." He smiled at me. "Here's the best part. By selling it for good money, they proved to the world the technology works. After all, why would anyone in their right mind pay that much for something that didn't? It's brilliant, don't you think?"

"That still doesn't address my point. Why take the risk of us finding out about it?"

"Yeah. Answer that one," Gainham said.

Tillman picked up the last slice of pizza and took a large bite. "You weren't supposed to find out. The guys running SLIDA are being paid a bucket-load of money to keep quiet, but they all know what's going on. They knew what answers to give when you were doing your homework. They were well rehearsed. After all, they've been spinning this story for years."

"Why are you telling us this now?" I asked. "What's in it for you?"

"That's a fair question. The honest truth is I was comfortable being part of the deception while I worked there, and while the whole thing was under government ownership. I actually believed we were making our nation a safer place. Whether it worked or not, SLIDA was still an effective deterrent. Then those clowns let me and many others go, so they could sell it off. The more cost they eliminated, the more profitable the company looked. That doesn't sit right with me."

"So you're not looking to get anything out of this?" I asked.

Tillman raised hands. "Nothing."

"Yeah, right," Gainham said. "You're just being a good citizen."

"Why is that so hard for you to believe?" Tillman asked.

"Leave it, Chris. Is there anything else you want to share with us?"

"No. That's it. Now you know what you're dealing with."

"If we need to contact you, how do we do that?"

Gainham shook his head in disbelief.

Tillman scribbled a number on his napkin, folded it and gave it to me. "That's my private cell. Call me if you need to. I'll do everything I can to help."

Fifteen minutes later, Gainham and I were in my office with the door closed.

"I'm telling you, he's crazy," Gainham said. "He's bitter over losing his job and now he's out to cause as much trouble for SLIDA as he can. He's a sad, little man."

I leaned against the window frame and looked along State Street. "Every logical bone in my body tells me you're right. But there's this tiny nagging doubt in the back of my mind. What if he's telling the truth? What if we have been used?"

"Okay. Let me go along with that for a moment. If the technology doesn't work, why would the government have approached trade buyers as well as private equity firms when they auctioned it off? Think about it. Most trade buyers would have their own technical teams pouring over it in the due diligence process. If Tillman was telling the truth, the whole game would have been over the moment the trade started kicking the tires."

I returned to sit at the desk where I rubbed my temples as I rested my head on my fingers. "You're right, but there's something about Tillman…"

"If it was my decision, I'd forget all about it. The man's a loser."

"Maybe."

"You can't be taking him seriously, Damon?"

"I think we owe it to our investors to get to the bottom of this, one way or another. I know there's only a slight chance Tillman is telling the truth, but we have to look into this."

"How do we do that without looking completely stupid ourselves?"

"Not sure yet. I'd like to sleep on it."

"Okay. Let me know what you decide, but remember, I say we drop it right now."

After Gainham left, I closed my office door again, poured myself a coffee, and sat in the armchair in the corner window. A chill ran up my spine. What if Tillman was telling the truth? The consequences would be disastrous. The investment represented a third of our fund and was the most high profile deal ever consummated by the private equity industry. If CCP had bought something that didn't work, we'd never recover the loss. We'd be ruined and our reputation shredded—all in public view. We had no choice but to investigate Tillman's claims, even if there was a strong chance we'd end up looking foolish. But how could we probe Tillman's story without setting alarm bells ringing? I could raise it with the board at SLIDA—just come out with it and see how they react. But if Tillman was right, that would make matters worse. I'd be letting them know I was onto their scheme.

For half an hour, I sipped my coffee, deep in thought. Then the idea came to me. Maybe the best thing to do was go and see Barrett at DH&W first. After all, he was bound to know if there was a problem with the asset. As Gainham said, the trade buyers in the auction would have run a mile the moment they discovered anything wrong with SLIDA.

CHAPTER 13

Her expression would haunt Agent Kerry Ward for the rest of her life. It was there in the little girl's eyes: something innocent, something trusting, something unquestioning. She smiled at Kerry then reached up and held onto her father's hand when they walked down the concrete steps leading from their Manhattan apartment block. Kerry turned away, fed coins into a newspaper vending machine by the side of the road, and retrieved a copy of *USA Today*. The man and his daughter, with long, dark, curly hair walked past and headed west on East Forty-fifth. His navy blue overcoat, buttoned all the way up, hugged his body while the girl wore an unzipped, thin gray fleece.

Kerry spoke into a microphone hidden under the lapel of her jacket. "We're on." She threw the newspaper into a nearby garbage can and followed them.

"Don't lose them," Mylor said in her ear from the control center. "There'll be no reruns on this."

Kerry made sure there was at least one other person in front of her as cover and kept a distance of thirty to forty feet. At seven-forty-five in the morning, the Midtown rush hour was in full swing, so it took a few moments to fight their way across Third Avenue.

"We're approaching the school now," she said.

"I want you to get real close once he's dropped off the girl," Mylor said.

"Can you say that again?" Kerry pushed the earpiece deeper into her ear. "I'm struggling to hear you over the traffic."

"Don't screw this up. When he's on his own, keep real close and do not let him out of your sight—not even for a moment."

"Got it."

The Montessori school was on the corner of Lexington and East Forty-fifth, above a branch of Chase Bank. Every morning for the past three days, the pattern had been the same: The man had dropped off his daughter at the school at around seven-fifty-five and then continued alone. But this time, both of them walked past the bank.

Kerry looked at the other parents filing into the school with their children. Her throat tightened as she stared at the man, willing him to bring his daughter back. "Something's wrong."

"What is it?"

"He's gone right by the school, and the girl's still with him. This can't—"

"Continue the mission."

"Did you hear what I said? He still has his daughter with him."

"I heard you. Continue the mission."

"Why would he keep the girl? It makes no sense."

"It's the perfect cover." Mylor made a poor job of hiding his irritation.

"Our source has to be wrong."

"The information is solid. Stick with the plan."

"But—"

"This is not a debate. You see this thing through. Do you hear me?"

Kerry stopped walking, but kept her eyes locked onto the target. There had to be a mistake. He was not supposed to have the girl with him. He couldn't be going ahead with it if his daughter was still there. The intelligence had to be wrong. It had to be another day.

"What's happening?" Mylor asked. "Where are you? Keep me in the loop, dammit."

"We're approaching the MetLife Building." Kerry started

walking, closing the distance on the man and the girl. "I'm twenty feet away."

"Whatever happens, you cannot let him enter Grand Central."

"I'm not sure this—"

"Listen to me. You deal with this now. He must not enter the station."

Kerry's heart exploded. She couldn't breathe. The man was almost at the station entrance. If she was wrong, and the intelligence was reliable, she could never live with the fact that she could have prevented the carnage. But his daughter was with him. It had to be wrong.

"Talk to me," Mylor said. "I want to know everything."

"The girl—"

"Do it."

Kerry closed her eyes and tried to swallow. "Okay. I'm on it."

She ran to within five feet of the man and drew her pistol.

"It has to be a clean kill," Mylor said. "He cannot activate the switch."

Kerry aimed at the back of the man's head.

The little girl turned and looked at her. "Daddy," she said, tugging on his arm.

Commuters streaming out of the station scattered for cover. The man swung around and, for a fleeting moment, Kerry saw evil in his eyes. She fired two shots in quick succession, one through his brain, the other through his heart.

The girl screamed as her father fell to the floor.

Kerry ran to the man and fired another round into his head, spraying the girl with blood.

"Daddy, Daddy," screamed the girl, shaking her father. "You've hurt my daddy."

Kerry pulled open the dead man's overcoat and tore at his shirt, exposing his abdomen. His warm blood soaked her fingers.

"He's not wearing the belt." She kept ripping at his clothes. "There's nothing here. Nothing."

The girl looked at Kerry, her little face full of incomprehension.

"What have I done?" Kerry couldn't hold the girl's gaze and lowered her head.

"Is the target neutralized?" Mylor asked in her ear.

"We were—" Kerry fought back the reflux in her throat.

"Is the target neutralized?"

"Yes. We were wrong. He was no threat at all."

"The intelligence was credible. That's all that matters."

"What have I done?"

"You did your job. Now make your way back here as I need you on the SLIDA operation."

CHAPTER 14

Mylor breezed along the wide corridor, a security-encrypted smartphone glued to his right ear.

"Ben," Kerry Ward said, as he passed her open office door. "Something—"

"Not now," he said, waving her away with a flick of his left hand. He carried on his conversation, finishing his call as he entered his office. "Get me coffee and then put me through to Patterson," he said to his PA sitting outside his door.

"Yes, sir," she said. "Kerry has been looking for you. She requested five minutes of your time. She says something important has come up."

Mylor shook his head. "I haven't got time to keep spoon feeding these new people," he said, removing his jacket and loosening his tie.

"She was quite insistent, but I didn't commit you."

"Okay, get her in here when I've finished with Patterson."

When Patterson came on the phone, Mylor closed his office door and slumped back in his chair.

"I gather things are progressing well on Eclipse," Patterson said.

"You've read my report."

"You guys have been busy."

"Sixteen in the bag right now. Are they going to need more?"

"Not that I'm aware of, but I expect Allen will find a few more as he scrapes the barrel. I think he's losing it."

"If there are others, we can handle them."

"Exactly what I told Allen. Have there been any...?"

"Problems?"

"Yeah."

"None, and there won't be any. Least none we can't fix."

"Good. That'll reassure Allen. He needs some good news before he becomes a liability."

"It's all good here. Tell him we're getting on with our job."

"I will, but make sure I'm aware of any potential issues."

"Understood." Mylor terminated the call then opened his door.

"Ready for Kerry?" asked his PA.

"Tell her it'll have to be quick. I'm leaving in a few minutes."

Agent Kerry Ward was in her late twenties. A rising star at the CIA, she'd been the natural choice when Mylor requested the agency find him someone with the brains and drive to fit into his special covert unit. Mylor's own team in Bethesda had been swamped for weeks with all the work Patterson was creating. That meant he had little choice but to look outside when he needed additional resources. He hated having to rely on other agencies for help, particularly that bunch over at Langley. He'd been let down by them too many times before, so there was no way he would rely on the word of the CIA that Kerry was good enough. His standards were much higher than theirs. He needed to see her in action himself before accepting her into his unit, even if it was only on a temporary basis. In fairness, Kerry had handled well the tough task he'd set her. While he had backup on the ground that day, it wasn't required. Kerry did a good job bringing down the suspected terrorist in Manhattan, proving she had the stomach for Mylor's kind of work. Although it was still early days, she appeared to be settling in well.

Kerry wore a tight-fitting suit, emphasizing her perfect figure. She had short black hair and a pretty, angelic face. "Thanks for seeing me," she said, taking a seat in front of

Mylor's desk. She crossed her legs, revealing long, tanned legs when her skirt rose up.

"What is it?" Mylor asked, finishing his coffee. He looked up at the clock on his wall. "I'm out of here in a moment."

"I won't keep you, but I thought you should know something about SLIDA."

"Is there a problem?"

"I don't think so yet, but there may be."

"Go on."

"I've had a couple of people tailing a man named Brodie Tillman. Does his name register with you?"

"Nope. Who is he?"

"He's the former head of technical development at SLIDA. He was included in the cuts that were made just before the sale. I picked up he was pissed about losing his job."

"They all were. That's why they got handsome settlements to keep quiet."

"And all the others took the money and left quietly. Tillman didn't. He took his pay-off, but told the SLIDA board they'd not heard the last of him. It spooked them so they contacted us. I thought he was worth watching. Just in case."

"What have you learned?"

"Not much yet, but one thing is interesting." She uncrossed her legs and leaned forward slightly. "It turns out he's been to see CCP."

Mylor knitted his eyebrows. "What for?"

"I've not been able to find out, but I'm working on it."

"I don't like it."

"It made me uncomfortable too. Of course, it might be innocent. It could be he's after his old job—figures the new owners might need him."

"That's possible, but unlikely. If he still wanted to work there, he wouldn't have alienated the board when he left. Put some more people on it right away."

"It's already in hand."

"Good work. Keep me in the loop on this. I want to know what Tillman is up to. I don't like loose ends." Mylor rose to his feet and grabbed his jacket. "I have to leave."

CHAPTER 15

A cold, biting wind was blowing in from the Upper Bay when Gainham and I climbed out of the yellow cab on Barclay Street. I pulled up the collar of my trench coat and looked up at the DH&W tower while Gainham paid the driver. Hopefully, the meeting about to take place would put our minds at rest once and for all. No doubt, Barrett would roll his eyes at the first mention of Tillman's name, and we'd all have a good laugh about him and his wild claims. Of course, there was nothing wrong with SLIDA. Everyone knew Tillman was a crazy man out to cause trouble.

An attractive, but stern looking, young woman came to collect us from the oversized reception area. "Mr. Barrett is ready for you now," she said. "Please follow me."

We took the elevator to the thirty-second floor and it opened out onto yet another reception desk with giant vases, filled with fresh white lilies, at each end. Three receptionists sat behind it, but they didn't seem to have much to do other than sit there and look important. We walked straight past the desk and followed the woman down a glass corridor. I looked at the meeting rooms as we walked by. Each was named after an American president, but the frosted glass prevented me from seeing who was in each room. From the great views over Manhattan and the thick carpet, it was obvious the bank used this floor for its most important client meetings. This was where DH&W earned its money. Deals completed here moved markets, created corporate empires, and made reputations.

The woman stopped outside a corner meeting room—the

Reagan suite—then tapped on the glass door and led us in. The room was empty, so we took seats at the table while we waited for Barrett.

Gainham tightened the knot in his tie, its bright yellow color clashing with his pink and white, stripy shirt. "How are we going to play this? You know there's a big risk we're going to look like idiots."

"I'm still working on it," I said.

"This could be real embarrassing." Gainham opened one of the bottles of San Pellegrino on the table and gulped some down.

Moments later, Barrett burst through the door.

I stood, held out my hand, and met Barrett's tight grip. "Good of you to see us at short notice, Orlando." I turned to Gainham. "This is Chris Gainham, one of my partners."

"My pleasure," Barrett said, shaking Gainham's hand. "Have you been offered coffee?"

"Yes, thanks. It's on its way," I said, as Barrett joined us at the table.

Barrett rubbed his palms. "Now, what can I do for you? You said on the phone it has something to do with SLIDA."

I looked down at the pad of notes I'd brought with me, then pushed it away. What was the point of dressing it up? Why not just tell Barrett the whole story? So what if we looked stupid? That was a small price to pay to get to the bottom of things. "It may be nothing, but we've hit a problem on the deal."

Barrett frowned. "What sort of problem?"

"As I said, it may be nothing, but we have to be sure."

"I'm listening." Barrett reclined, the chair creaking under his weight. He placed his clasped hands across the front of his shirt.

"We've been approached—"

A catering assistant walked in with two carafes of coffee and placed them in the middle of the table. He looked at Barrett for permission. Barrett nodded and the man left. Then our host leaned forward and poured the coffee. "Please continue, Damon. I'll take care of this."

"We've been approached by the former head of technical development at SLIDA. Apparently, he was let go just before we acquired the company."

Barrett slid the coffee mugs toward us. There was no reaction to indicate he'd heard Tillman's name before. "What did he want? I gather all those they let go received generous termination packages."

"Well," I said, before pausing to take a slow sip of coffee, so I could continue to monitor Barrett for a tell, but there was nothing. "He says SLIDA doesn't work."

Barrett spat out his drink. "I'm sorry." He took out a handkerchief and dabbed coffee from the glass table. "Are you serious?"

Gainham shook his head, looked at me, then bit his lip before studying the top of the table.

In for a penny, I decided to press on with the story. I could hardly stop now. "He says it has never worked and that it's all just a propaganda exercise to convince the Russians and the Chinese to stop building more ballistic weapons."

"Sounds like they were right to let him go. He needs locking up by the sound of it." Barrett snorted. "What did you say to him once you'd picked yourself off the floor?"

"We told him we didn't believe him, of course."

Gainham leaned forward. "We dismissed it," he said. "He'd lost his job so we thought now he's out to cause as much trouble as he can."

"Sounds about right to me," Barrett said.

"He seemed pretty convincing," I said. "Convincing enough for us to come and see you to make sure there's nothing in it."

"I don't know what to say. The man probably needs to go see a shrink. Don't tell me you came all this way to discuss this ridiculous suggestion?"

"I know it sounds crazy, but we have a duty to our investors.

We have to be certain we've spent their money wisely."

Barrett couldn't contain the smirk on his face. "I understand your position, but really. The whole idea is preposterous. Why would the government enter into a supply contract with SLIDA if the bloody thing doesn't work? Think about it."

"That's what Chris said, but we still had to ask."

"I'm afraid you've come a long way for nothing, gentlemen," Barrett said, standing up. "Tell you what I'll do. If it'll make you feel more comfortable, I'll make some discreet inquiries about this chap Tillman. I'll mention him to our client and let you know what I find out. I'm sure they'll have lots to say about him."

"Thanks. We'd appreciate that," I said. "There's just one more question, I'd like to ask."

Barrett sat back down. "I hope this one's a serious point." He smiled again.

"I think it is." I kept a straight face. "When you guys opened up the data room for the first round of bidders to do their diligence, did any of the trade buyers raise any questions about the technical viability of SLIDA?"

The smile slid off Barrett's face. "You know full well I'm not at liberty to discuss what other parties may or may not have said during the sale process."

"Are you saying there *were* questions raised?"

"I'm saying nothing of the sort."

"I'm not asking you to name names. I don't need to know who considered buying the company. I just want to know if the question of SLIDA's viability was raised by anyone else during the due diligence process. That can hardly be a breach of confidentiality."

Barrett's cheeks began to redden. "Look. All I will tell you is that you are the first to raise this."

Gainham, who'd been watching me and Barrett throughout the conversation, leaned forward onto his forearms. "Do you mind if I ask a question?"

"Fire away," Barrett said.

"Were there any trade bidders in the process?"

Barrett looked up at the ceiling, deep in thought. After a long pause, he said, "I don't see any harm in telling you this now." He cleared his throat. "You were the only bidder."

That made no sense. SLIDA was an extremely attractive asset and would have drawn a lot of interest from both trade and financial buyers like us. "You said we were the only bidder. Surely, you mean we were the only *financial* bidder to make an offer?"

"No," Barrett said, staring directly at me. "You were the only bidder." He sat upright in his chair. "Our client insisted we deal only with CCP and that we try to extract the maximum we could from you. In spite of my advice to the contrary, they said there was insufficient time to run a proper auction. They knew all about your recent fund and that you had plenty of cash left to invest. They simply instructed me to create the impression of competition." He leaned back again and in his most pompous voice said, "I like to think we did a jolly good job of it."

CHAPTER 16

When we returned from New York, Gainham and his wife, Carol, asked me to join them for dinner at their Beacon Hill townhouse, two blocks from my own home. Carol was a great cook, and I was pretty sure she and my mom were exchanging notes on my bad eating habits as they both took every opportunity to keep me well fed—not that I ever complained about it.

The topic that dominated our conversation over dinner, as it had throughout the journey back to Boston, was Barrett's startling revelation. I felt guilty about letting work intrude into our evening, especially as Carol had gone to such great efforts to prepare our meal.

"I'm sorry we've been so focused on work tonight, Carol," I said, polishing off the last mouthful of eggplant Parmigiana. "That was delicious. Thanks."

"You're very welcome. It's Chris's favorite. I'm glad you liked it," Carol said, clearing up the dishes.

"What are we going to do about SLIDA?" Gainham asked.

"I really don't know. It still makes no sense that we were the only ones asked to bid."

"Put yourself in the government's shoes. There you are sitting on a massively valuable asset, and you decide to ignore all the obvious trade purchasers and deal with just one private equity buyer. It's economic madness." Gainham threw his hands apart. "Why would they do that?"

"Makes me wonder if there's something in what Tillman said. But I still don't get why the government would commit to a long-term contract if the thing doesn't work?"

"Why don't we sleep on it, Damon? We can discuss it with the rest of the partners tomorrow."

Sleep would have been nice, but I could think about little else in the hours that followed. Next morning, all the partners met to discuss the deal, and none of us could rationalize why the government would talk only to one party. While that was suspicious, most of my colleagues continued to dismiss Tillman as a crank, out to stir things up because he'd lost his job. But I wasn't so sure. There was something about Tillman's manner that made me think he might be telling the truth. After all, if he was making the whole thing up, he'd be leaving himself open to a massive lawsuit. And if the U.S. government decided to go after him, they could make his life hell. What was in it for him to fabricate a story? The man wasn't stupid. He couldn't be; the head of technical development at SLIDA would need to be a damn smart individual. I needed to find out more about Tillman and so decided, in spite of the risk, I'd raise the matter at the next SLIDA board meeting scheduled later that week.

It was only during the drive from San Francisco International to Sausalito that I finally worked out how I was going to deal with the issue. Rather than discuss it openly with the whole board, I planned on raising it with the chairman and CEO first. That way, if the board members were covering something up, I could contain the damage.

The board meeting lasted two hours. The business was still showing numbers ahead of budget, and there were no unusual matters reported. If it hadn't been for Tillman's intervention, I would have been delighted with the performance of this major investment. Rarely had a portfolio company traded so consistently well from the start.

Immediately after the meeting, I asked George Pellerton and Mike Hansen to stay behind. "Something's come up," I said, "and we need to deal with it urgently."

"What is it?" Pellerton asked.

"What do you know about Brodie Tillman?" I studied Hansen's face as I asked the question. No physical reaction except for an almost imperceptible flicker of panic in the CEO's eyes.

"He used to be the head of technical development here," Hansen said, rubbing his goatee. "Why do you ask?"

"Why did he leave?"

"He was part of the cuts we made just before the sale. We told you all about them. Tillman was expensive, and we thought we could cover his work in other ways without harming the business. I think we've proven we were right. You've seen the numbers."

I kept my focus on Hansen. "Did he leave under a cloud? Did he do anything wrong?"

Creases formed across Hansen's forehead. "Not really. I guess you'd say he was okay at his job. He'd been here a long time, so you can imagine he was pissed about being let go." Hansen forced a smile. "Where are we going with this?"

"He came to see me." I waited while Hansen absorbed the news.

The smiled evaporated. "What did he want?"

"He said something alarming." There it was again, a flash of terror in Hansen's eyes. "Something that left me no choice but to raise it with you."

"What did he say?" Pellerton asked, a glaze of confusion across his face.

I lowered my voice. "He said SLIDA doesn't work."

Hansen jolted back in his seat. "The man's gone off the deep end."

"I've never met him," Pellerton said. He looked at Hansen. "Is he stable?"

"Look, I wasn't going to say anything, but we had some concerns about him before he left," Hansen said, looking down at the table. "It's one of the reasons he was on the termination list."

"Why didn't you mention that when I asked you about him a moment ago?" I asked.

"I didn't see any reason to badmouth a former coworker. He's no longer here. I thought—"

"Does it work?" I asked, leaning forward. "Does SLIDA work?"

"Of course, it works. I'm amazed you need to ask the question." Hansen shook his head. "You can't listen to anything Tillman tells you. We would have let him go sooner or later. We had a number of concerns about his stability. Let's just say the cuts ordered by the Treasury Department were a good excuse to remove him."

"Why don't we ask him to come in and meet with us?" Pellerton asked. "That way, we can put him on the spot and find out what he's up to. He sounds like bad news to me."

"That's a good idea," I said. "Let's do that. Let's face up to him and flush out what he wants."

"We'll set it up," Pellerton said before turning to Hansen. "Let's see if we can persuade him to come in after the next board meeting, Mike."

Hansen's face went bright red. "Is that really necessary? I can't see what it will achieve."

"I think we need to get to the bottom of this," I said. "We need to find out exactly what he's up to and put an end to it quickly." I looked at Pellerton. "Let's go ahead and set the meeting up, but I don't want to wait until the next board meeting. I want to do it much sooner than that."

CHAPTER 17

"We've got a huge problem," Hansen said from the other end of the telephone line. "You guys need to tell me how to deal with this. I'm not taking the—"

"Calm down, Mike," Agent Kerry said, sitting behind her desk. "Just tell me what happened."

"Damon Traynor from CCP has just left. He was up here for our board meeting. Afterward, he started asking a whole bunch of questions about the viability of SLIDA." He paused to gulp down some water with two Advil tablets.

"Go on," Kerry said, scribbling a note of the conversation on a pad.

"He said he's been contacted by Brodie Tillman. I knew he'd be bad news. That idiot's been stirring up trouble. You've got to do something."

"Do you know what Tillman said to him?"

"He actually said SLIDA doesn't work."

"Did Traynor believe him?"

"He's not sure. I think he wants to believe the man has a screw loose, but he feels an obligation to get to the bottom of Tillman's claims. There'll be a shit-storm if this is allowed to go too far. You understand that, don't you?"

"We're on top of this, okay?"

"I hear you."

"Did Traynor say what he plans to do?"

"He's already involved George Pellerton."

"Who's he?"

"The new chairman appointed by CCP. He and Traynor go

back a long way. Pellerton wants us to meet with Tillman, and he's asked me to set it up. I tell you, if I see Tillman, I'll wring his freaking neck. Did you see the size of his payoff? And now he does this."

"When is the meeting?"

"I don't know yet, but they want it soon."

Kerry pushed her notepad away. "Okay. Here's what I want you to do."

"I'm listening."

"Just go about your normal duties. If anyone asks you about Tillman, you dismiss him as a hothead. Don't even think about making contact with him. Leave Tillman to us, and if Pellerton presses you, tell him you're arranging the meeting. Act as though you have nothing to hide. You got that?"

"Yeah, yeah. I understand. But what happens if—"

"I told you. We have this under control. Leave it to us."

"I sure hope that's right."

After the call, Kerry raced over to Mylor's office. He had his door open and was on the phone, with his back to the door.

She tapped on the doorframe. Mylor swiveled his chair around and frowned at her. "Got a moment?" she mouthed.

He waved her in, pointing at the seat in front of his desk. He took another five minutes to finish his call, while she thought about how her boss was likely to react to the news about Tillman. Although she didn't know much about him yet, she knew Mylor didn't like surprises.

"What is it?" he asked, replacing the handset.

"You told me to keep you in the loop on Tillman."

"Has he met with CCP again?"

"No, but there's been a development, and it's not good news."

"Spit it out."

"We now know that Tillman met with Damon Traynor, CCP's senior partner. He told Traynor that SLIDA doesn't work."

"He actually said that?"

"That's right. Now Traynor's going around asking a load of questions at the company. And he's arranging for Tillman to meet him, Mike Hansen and their new chairman at Sausalito in the next few days."

"Get Traynor in here as soon as possible. I need to meet him."

"What do I tell him?"

Mylor shook his head. "What do you think? You got into this unit because you're supposed to have a brain. Use it and come up with something."

Kerry thought for a moment. "I could say we're part of the Treasury Department and need to discuss some loose ends arising from the sale of SLIDA."

"That'll do. I'll leave the details for you to sort out. Just get Traynor in here quickly."

"Should we keep watching Tillman?"

"No. We'll pick him up after their meeting. He's not going anywhere before then."

I took a seat in the cavernous reception area at the Department of the Treasury in Washington, D.C. The day before, I'd received a call from a Treasury official inviting me to a meeting to discuss SLIDA. They didn't give me any details on the phone, and I hadn't pressed for any. I simply assumed it had been arranged following our meeting with Barrett in New York. Barrett had promised to inquire about Tillman with his client, so I thought I was there to hear what they could tell me about SLIDA's former technical head. As the department had decided that Tillman should be let go, they must have known quite a lot about the man, and I guessed there had to be a good reason for firing him after many years' service. Hopefully, I was about to learn enough about Tillman to stop worrying about this investment. Depending on how the meeting went, I thought I'd also ask them why there were no trade bidders in the auction process. That still didn't seem right, in spite of what Barrett said about there not being enough time to run a normal process.

I was still deep in thought when I heard, "Mr. Traynor, I'm Kerry Ward." She smiled and held out her hand.

I stood, made eye contact, and reached for her hand. She had lovely straight teeth, deep brown eyes and full lips. I held her hand for a moment too long, and my cheeks suddenly warmed. Was I blushing? I guess it must have been obvious I found her attractive, but she was way above my league. "Sorry, you can have your hand back now. Please, call me Damon."

She pointed across the reception area and began to walk. "Come this way."

I followed her through the security barriers, along a windowless corridor, then up a flight of stairs, her perfume drifting behind her. When we reached meeting room number five, Kerry tapped on the door.

"Come," said the deep voice from inside.

I scanned the room as we entered and wasn't surprised to see another featureless government office—gray painted walls with no pictures or windows. In the center was an oblong wooden table. A man in a dark blue suit stood, walked around the table and shook my hand.

"Ben Mylor," he said. No smile—more an annoyed look on his face. "Take a seat."

Mylor and Kerry sat across the table from me. No drinks were offered. No pleasantries exchanged. They looked at me, but said nothing.

"I gather you want to discuss our investment in SLIDA," I said, filling the uncomfortable silence. *They* requested this meeting. Why did I have to kick off the discussion?

"You could put it that way," Mylor said, tapping the fingers of his steepled hands together in front of his face.

"How would you like to start?" I looked at Mylor then Kerry. She smiled back at me.

95

"We're not really here to talk about SLIDA," Mylor said, slowly.

I tilted my head. "We're not?"

Mylor jabbed his right index finger at me. "I want you to stop doing something."

Some people make you dislike them immediately; Mylor was one of them. Who did he think he was talking to? "I'm sorry. I don't understand."

"You need to stop going around asking questions about SLIDA and whether or not it works." Mylor slammed his right palm on the table. "I won't have it."

"You won't have it?"

"That's what I said."

"Let me be clear. As the owner of SLIDA, I have every right to ask questions about it. Particularly if I'm told it doesn't work."

Mylor made a face. "Who told you it doesn't work?"

"The former head of technical development."

"You mean Tillman?" He laughed. "He wasn't up to the job. He should have been fired years ago. I bet he didn't tell you about his drinking problem, did he?"

"No."

"Didn't think he would. The man was a liability. We couldn't leave him in place during the sale process. He was an embarrassment. He was bound to screw it up."

"But why would he make something like that up?"

"He wants to strike back. With his problems, he knows he'll never work again."

"That still doesn't explain—"

"Tillman needs to keep his mouth shut. We can't have him, or anyone else, going around saying the SLIDA technology doesn't work."

I paused and thought carefully about my next few words. Arguing over Tillman was pointless. What mattered most was our investment, so I dove right in. "Does it work?"

"Of course, it works. I know you've seen the demonstration."

"Sure, but that was just a video. I haven't seen it in the flesh."

"I was on that aircraft carrier and witnessed the whole thing at first hand. Incredible technology. If you ask me, the government should never have sold it."

"So it does work?"

"For the record, yes."

"Then you won't mind joining us for a meeting with Tillman? I've invited him to Sausalito. It would be useful for you to be with us to help clear the air and find out what he really wants."

Mylor leaned onto his elbows. "Listen. This is a matter of national security. We're not about to start discussing the viability of this system with you, Tillman, or anyone else. Can you imagine what our enemies would do if they thought the system didn't work?"

"You won't come to a meeting?"

Mylor looked at Kerry. "I don't think Mr. Traynor here is listening." He turned to me. "I'll spell this out for you. If you, or anyone else at CCP, continue to spread rumors about SLIDA not working, you will regret it. Is that understood?"

"Hey. I'm just doing my job. We've invested a lot of our investors' money into this thing, so I won't sit here and be lectured by you."

"This is no lecture. Consider it more a promise. Just think of the shit you'd have to deal with if I decide to have your firm investigated by the IRS?" Mylor stared at me as if he were looking at something unpleasant stuck to the bottom of his shoe. "Continue asking questions, and we'll grind CCP into the ground. Do we understand each other?"

* * *

After the meeting, Mylor and Kerry shared a car back to Bethesda.

"What do you think Traynor will do?" Kerry asked.

"I don't know, but we can't afford to take any risks with this. I want you to keep an eye on him. I want to know what he does, where he goes, and who he meets. Stick close. The moment you suspect he's stepping out of line, you need to tell me."

"And Tillman?"

"Leave him to me. You just concentrate on Traynor."

CHAPTER 18

"How'd it go yesterday?" Gainham asked, catching up with me in one of the crowded elevators in the lobby of our office building. We were both carrying a paper coffee cup in one hand and a briefcase in the other.

"Not very well would be an understatement," I said, using my elbow to push the button for CCP's main floor.

Gainham looked over the head of the young woman standing between us. "Did you learn anything useful about Mr. T?"

I shook my head. "I'll tell you all about it when we get to the office. It didn't go well at all."

A few minutes later, we were sitting in my office with the door closed.

"He actually threatened you?" Gainham asked. "I can't believe it. Who the hell does this guy Mylor think he is?"

"He talked about national security and how it would be in jeopardy if we or Tillman go around raising questions about SLIDA."

"Incredible! How does a stuffed shirt from Washington think he can get away with acting like that? Our taxes pay his salary." Gainham sipped some coffee. "Did he say anything at all about Tillman?"

"He said he has a drinking problem and that's why they let him go. I do remember him smelling of alcohol when he cornered me in the departure lounge at San Francisco."

"Maybe that's why Mylor was so annoyed. He knows Tillman's a drunk and he sees us giving the loser airtime."

I drained my coffee. "It's possible, but there was something

99

about Mylor's behavior that didn't seem right to me. It was over the top somehow—as if I'd hit a nerve." I reached under my desk and threw the empty cup away. "If Tillman is unstable, then why not calmly explain this to me and agree to face the man down at a meeting? That would put an end to it. Now I'm left asking more questions."

"You don't think you're reading too much into this, Damon?"

I raised my palms. "Hey, I'm not saying I know what's going on here. All I know is that I went to Washington hoping to find a lot more about Tillman and I've come away feeling more uncomfortable about the whole thing. Mylor's reaction wasn't rational."

Gainham placed his paper cup on my desk, stood, and grabbed his briefcase. "If you ask me, I say we drop this now. Let's just put our heads down and keep collecting the money under the contract. SLIDA's trading well and shaping up to be a great investment. Why risk ruining it by rubbing the Treasury up the wrong way?"

"Maybe you're right."

Gainham walked toward the door. "The last thing we need right now is an IRS audit team crawling all over our business. Once those leeches get in…"

"We certainly don't want that."

After Gainham left, I picked up the papers for that day's investment committee meeting and sat on one of my sofas to review them. As I tried to concentrate, my mind kept playing over the meeting with Mylor and Kerry. There was something about his manner that didn't seem right. He'd been too quick to resort to threats. It certainly wasn't the normal reaction of a man with nothing to hide. Strange, too, that Kerry said nothing during the meeting. In fact, the more I thought about it, the more I thought she looked embarrassed by her boss's behavior.

No doubt Mylor could create a bureaucratic nightmare for CCP if he decided to send in the IRS, even though our firm had nothing to hide. I thought about letting it pass, as Gainham suggested, but we still had our investors to think about. What would they expect of me in these circumstances? Surely, they'd want me to put their interests first in spite of any difficulties for CCP. After all, it was their money we'd risked on the SLIDA deal. To ignore Tillman and pretend he didn't exist to shield CCP from the IRS would be a clear conflict of interest. As I thought it through, it was clear I had to continue asking some tough questions about SLIDA. We had to get to the bottom of this investment and find out if it really was okay. While that would be difficult, it was the right thing to do.

I placed the investment papers on the sofa, returned to my desk, and retrieved the business card Kerry gave me as I'd left yesterday's meeting. She seemed more rational, less of a blow-hard, than Mylor. Maybe I could learn something from her. So I picked up the phone and punched in her cell number.

"Kerry Ward," said the voice at the other end.

"Kerry, its Damon Traynor. We met yesterday."

"Yes, I remember." She sounded surprised. There was a brief pause then, "How can I help?"

"I'd appreciate another meeting, if that's possible."

"I'd need to check with Ben to see—"

"Actually, I'd prefer the meeting to be just the two of us. Is that a problem?"

"I see." Another pause. "What would we discuss?"

I thought for a moment. It wasn't wise to mention Tillman again. That would only inflame things. The smart thing to do was to get the meeting arranged first. "Just some more back-ground on SLIDA; things I wanted to ask yesterday, but it didn't seem appropriate given the way the meeting went. Nothing contentious."

"I'm pretty busy right now. Can I come back to you?"

"Maybe I could buy you dinner. I have to be in Washington on business a couple of days next week. When would be good for you?"

"Dinner?"

She didn't sound convinced, but I was making this up as I went along. I had to get her to meet on her own. If she talked to Mylor before agreeing to meet, there was a good chance he'd kill it or, worse still, turn up with her.

"Okay," Kerry said. "Let me check my schedule." I could hear the sound of keystrokes. "How about Wednesday evening?"

"That works for me. I normally stay at the Four Seasons, so I'll book a table there for seven. Is that okay?"

"I'll see you there."

Immediately after the call, I asked my PA to adjust my schedule to free up the middle of the following week. Going to Washington was now my top priority, and everything else could wait.

I'd eaten at the Bourbon Steak restaurant many times before. As well as serving guests at the Four Seasons hotel, it fed many of Washington's power brokers and political elite. I arrived at six-fifty-five and took a seat at the quiet table I'd reserved. It was closest to the window and overlooked Georgetown's Pennsylvania Avenue. The waiter poured me a sparkling Pellegrino as I glanced around the dining room. It was quickly filling up with D.C.'s beautiful people, but I thought there was still enough privacy to discuss what I planned to cover without being overheard. I skimmed the menu, so I could concentrate on the meeting when Kerry arrived. The striped bass sounded good.

"Hi, Damon," Kerry said, when she reached the table. "Sorry I'm a few minutes late." She was wearing a skin-tight business suit with a short skirt. Her make-up looked fresh.

I jumped to my feet and shook her hand. "Thanks for coming, Kerry." I waited for her to sit before taking my seat. "I'm guessing this place must be your local."

She laughed. "I don't think so. Not on a government salary."

After we placed our orders, Kerry looked over my shoulder at the other diners on the nearby tables, before leaning forward. "Listen, I'd like to apologize for Mylor's behavior last week." She smiled. "Let's just say he's not that user friendly. He doesn't get out of the office that much."

It was good to learn I was right—she had been embarrassed by Mylor's outburst. I couldn't take my eyes off her full lips as she talked. "That's okay. I didn't take it personally."

"Good. Now what did you want to discuss?"

An hour later, I'd exhausted all my questions about SLIDA. I already knew the answers to most of them, but they gave me an opportunity to slip in a few about Tillman without making it too obvious what my real agenda was. In truth, I learned very little new information from her. Tillman had been screwing up for years due to his alcohol dependency, and when the sale process started, Kerry's boss had decided it was too risky having him as part of the SLIDA management team, so he was let go— all very consistent with the message I'd received from Mike Hansen after the last board meeting.

"I feel a lot more comfortable about our investment now," I said, finishing the last of my wine. Kerry's glass was also empty. "Would you like another bottle?"

She flashed a naughty smile. "It is very nice."

"That settles it." I waved the empty bottle to the wine waiter, who brought over another of the Napa Valley Hess winery Syrah and poured us both a large glass.

"I'm glad this has been helpful," Kerry said. "You really have nothing to worry about. SLIDA is a good company, and you have the benefit of a watertight government contract."

"I see that now." I took a sip of the fresh glass of wine. "Mmm, it is good. Enough about business. How did you come to work at the Treasury?"

"It's not that interesting a story." Kerry paused to sip her drink. "My father is a CPA, so I guess I have him to blame for my interest in numbers. How about you?"

"Mine's a lawyer. Not something I wanted to follow."

"Did you always want to work in private equity?"

An hour later, the second bottle of wine was gone, and the restaurant was emptying out. I requested the check then signed for it to be charged to my room.

"I've enjoyed this evening, Damon," Kerry said, standing up from the table.

I smiled at her as I stood. "So have I. We should meet up again when I'm next in Washington."

"That would be nice. I'd like that."

"Come on." I tapped her shoulder. "Let's find you a cab outside."

"That's a pity."

"Sorry?"

"I was hoping to see what the rooms are like at the Four Seasons."

CHAPTER 19

After my night with Kerry, I began to feel less worried about our SLIDA investment. While I remained suspicious of Mylor and his bizarre behavior, I believed I could trust Kerry. She'd confirmed Tillman's drinking problem and how it had affected his performance at work. That's why he'd been fired—end of story.

Still hanging in the air, however, was the question why only CCP had been invited to bid. When I'd raised it with Kerry, she'd pleaded ignorance of the sale process and claimed it had been handled by other people at the Treasury. Sellers often do strange things, actions which appear illogical unless you know their private thoughts and priorities. Maybe Gainham was right. SLIDA was hitting or exceeding its revenue and profit numbers, so why rock the boat? After all, our investors wouldn't thank us for causing a storm over nothing. Unless something else happened to support Tillman's claims, I decided to focus my energy on investing the rest of the fund and building our young business. Leaving Tillman behind and planning for the future was a liberating thought.

But you know what they say: "Life is what happens when you're busy making plans." The call came in at three-forty-five on a Thursday afternoon.

"Mr. Traynor, thanks for taking my call," said the voice at the other end of the line.

"My receptionist said you'd only speak to me," I said, sitting at my desk.

"That's right. My name is Adrian Livesey. I'm a partner at

Shipperley Brothers, here in New York."

"We know Shipperley very well. Do you have a deal for us to look at?"

"In a manner of speaking, yes. But it's not a new investment opportunity, if that's what you're thinking."

"Go on."

"One of our clients is a privately held, but substantial, group of companies. They are highly acquisitive. In fact, we've handled many of their previous acquisitions for them. Long story short, they've asked us to approach you in connection with one of your portfolio companies. They'd like to buy it."

I struggled to control the grin on my face. In the course of my career, some of the best investment returns had been achieved by selling portfolio companies in response to unsolicited approaches from motivated buyers. When a determined trade purchaser targets a specific asset, it usually means they've decided it would make a great fit within their group. Because of obvious synergies, that means they're able to pay a high price, particularly if they can have a run at it without competition.

"Well, we only have a few companies in the portfolio at the moment. In principle, all of them are for sale at the right price. Which one is your client interested in?"

"Your largest—SLIDA."

A heady mix of exhilaration and shock ran through me. I stopped breathing. We'd only held the investment a few weeks. Was it possible CCP was about to make the biggest private equity profit in history? Before responding, I tried to compose myself. Whatever happened, I couldn't risk appearing even remotely interested or excited.

"This early on would be an unusual time for us to consider an exit."

"I understand it's early."

"Your client would have to table tomorrow's price today, and even then I'm not certain we'd be ready to sell." I figured there was no harm in managing expectations.

"I thought you might say something like that. My client isn't kicking the tires here. I can assure you they are serious about this."

"I'm sure they're sincere, but whether we're interested will hang entirely on the price."

"They've authorized me to share with you the number they have in mind."

"What is it?"

"Seventy-five billion."

My heart jumped into my mouth, and I held my free hand to my face. Seventy-five billion was three times what CCP had paid for SLIDA, a potential capital gain of fifty billion dollars for the fund—in weeks! And we hadn't even started negotiating yet.

"That's less than we planned to achieve when we put it on the market in a few years' time. I'm not saying it's enough, but I guess it's a basis for an initial dialogue."

"My clients have suggested we all come up to Boston to explore the deal. Would that be possible?"

"Sure. We'd be happy to meet. What's the name of your client?"

"Mendocino Armor."

"I've heard the name before, but know nothing about them. Are they big enough to take on a deal this size?"

"Oh, yeah. We'll give you all the details when we meet. I suggest I email a few alternative dates for us to come up."

After the call, I danced my way to Crawford's office. I had to tell someone right away before I burst with the news. "Diane, you'll never guess what just happened."

Crawford looked up from her PC screen. "Gainham's turned up wearing a matching shirt and tie?" she said, grinning.

"No. This is serious."

"I'm listening."

"We've just had an approach for SLIDA."

"Ugh? How much?"

"The guy from Shipperley Brothers just indicated a starting price of seventy-five billion. They and their client want to meet to explore a potential deal."

"Did you just say seventy-five billion?"

"Yep."

"Dollars?"

"It had better be."

"Fuck me."

I laughed. "Would you settle for working on the deal with me?"

"Sure. I'd love to. Who's the bidder?"

"A group called Mendocino Armor."

"I remember they came up on our sector research when we bought SLIDA. I'll dig the file out and let you know what we have on them."

"That would help. We need to grill them hard when they come here. We need to know they're good for the money."

"A profit of fifty billion in a matter of weeks." Crawford shook her head. "Unbelievable."

"It doesn't get better than this."

When I returned to my office, I started putting together an agenda for the meeting with Mendocino. We'd want to know everything about them: their existing holdings, revenues, profits, net assets, debt level, and borrowing capacity. In spite of Livesey's bullish claims about his client, CCP would have to make sure the buyer really had the ability to consummate a deal of this size. There was no point running up an enormous legal bill if the bidder couldn't afford the acquisition in the first place. And there would be a pile of work to do if the deal went ahead. At least Mendocino was a U.S. company. That would save a lot of hassle as under the original acquisition agreement, CCP needed Treasury Department consent to any subsequent sale of SLIDA. That shouldn't be difficult to obtain when the potential buyer was another U.S. organization—a buyer that in all probability was already approved by the U.S. government as a defense contractor. After all, the clause in the legal documents was only there to prevent a strategic defense asset falling into foreign hands.

A sickening thought suddenly flashed through my mind. *What about Tillman?* The last thing we needed right now was Tillman disturbing sensitive sale negotiations by going around raising doubts about SLIDA. The man was a crank, but he could certainly disrupt the deal—worse still, kill it if he surfaced at the wrong time. I thought it was worth meeting up with him to tell him we'd learned all about the real reason he was fired. If that didn't shut him up, and it turned out Tillman's fear was never working again, we could offer him a job as some sort of technical adviser on defense deals. It wouldn't be a real job, of course, but it would be a small price to pay to guarantee his silence.

I searched for Tillman's telephone number in my Outlook contacts then punched the digits on my phone.

"Yeah," said Tillman when he answered the call. He sounded groggy.

"This is Damon Traynor." There was a delay. Was he struggling to remember who I was? "From CCP in Boston. You came to see me."

"Yeah. I know who you are."

Tillman's tone was miserable. I knew through my work with the homeless shelter how some people can become quite depressed the more they drink. "I know we're meeting again soon, but I'm wondering if we could meet earlier."

"What do you mean we're meeting soon?"

"Hasn't Mike Hansen been in touch?"

"I think I'd remember if he'd called me."

Why hadn't the SLIDA CEO been in contact with Tillman to arrange the follow-up meeting with me and the chairman as I'd requested? I parked my irritation and made a mental note to take this up with Hansen later. For now, that was not my priority.

"Well, I'd like to meet you again to go over some of the issues you raised. I have a couple of ideas I'd like to bounce off you too."

"Sure. I'm happy to meet."

"Would you be able to come to Boston early next week? We'd pay for the flights and everything, of course."

"No problem. I've got plenty of time. I don't have a job. Remember?"

"Actually, that's one of the things I want to discuss with you."

"I realize last time I saw you, you probably thought 'Who is this guy?'"

"Let's just say you certainly gave me a lot to think about."

"I'm real pleased you're taking me seriously now. You don't know how good it feels to have someone actually prepared to listen. I've got lots more to tell you."

"Okay, let's cover it next week. I'll ask my PA to contact you to make all the travel arrangements."

I ended the call. The guy certainly needed help. Offering Tillman a job would be the right thing to do to keep him on side for now—carrot rather stick. There was no way we could risk him jeopardizing the potential sale of SLIDA. The prize was too big.

CHAPTER 20

In the army they called him "the surgeon." When a difficult job needed doing, they'd call on Brad Halley. Always striking at the heart of the enemy with overwhelming force, his passionate, no holds barred, leadership style brought results from the Balkans to Iraq. No matter what the challenge, Halley always found a way to win, whatever the cost.

Three years earlier, the country had voted in General Halley in a landslide. The previous administration had left the country in a financial mess—facing a record debt burden and the highest level of unemployment since the 1930s. Halley was the only candidate who could be trusted to take the decisive action needed. He didn't underestimate the magnitude of the task ahead. During his election campaign he'd held no punches, spelling out the pain barrier the American people were about to encounter. But he promised them he would prevail, and the country would return to its former glory. He'd make America great again. The alternative was unimaginable to him.

But now, for the first time in his life, President Halley was facing the very real prospect of failure. In spite of his monumental efforts, the country he loved—the once great nation he'd seen his brave young men die for—was about to go over a cliff. For weeks Treasury Secretary Allen had been warning him the nation was about to default on its mountain of debt, but Halley had refused to accept it. The Chinese had continued their strategy of refusing to buy U.S. Treasury Bills, and the record pace of U.S. government-owned asset sales had not been fast enough to make up the shortfall. Like it or not, President Halley was about to make history—just not the history he wanted.

"We've sold the low hanging fruit," Secretary Allen said, standing to attention in front of Halley's desk in the Oval Office. "The rest either won't sell or will take too much time and fetch poor prices."

"Don't tell me what we can't do," Halley said, stopping just short of spitting at Allen.

"I'm sorry, sir. I can't—"

"How long have we got? Give me specifics, man."

"At the current rate, I'd say three months, maybe four."

"What about Patterson? Haven't his people been helping?"

"Absolutely. Without him, we'd never have achieved the prices for the assets we've sold so far. His team have bought us at least an extra couple of months."

"That's history. What's he doing on the stuff we're still sitting on?"

"The problem is—"

Halley raised his hand. "I told you I don't want to hear about problems. Give me solutions."

Allen took his time to choose the right words. "The challenge," he said before stepping a few inches back from the desk, "is most of the remaining assets aren't worth anything."

Halley looked like he was chewing a wasp. "That can't be right."

"They're mainly infrastructure related. They just don't make any money."

"What are we talking about? Give me an example."

"Railroads, the postal service, our air traffic control system—"

"Okay, okay. I get it."

"These federal operations consume billions of dollars a year. As they don't make a bean, no one in their right mind is going to buy them."

Halley shook his head in disbelief. "Then get creative."

Allen looked confused. "I'm sorry, sir?"

"Give them to Patterson. He'll know how to make these things look better than they are."

"That won't be easy."

"Look, you gotta tell people what they want to hear. For example, tell potential buyers you've retained the lossmaking parts of the postal service. Tell them. Correction. Show them how the rest makes good money."

"But it doesn't. The Post Office is a money pit."

"You're supposed to be the money man. Do I have to spell it out for you?"

"You want me to inflate the numbers?"

"Do whatever it takes. Lay it on thick then let Patterson work his magic. His people will sort it out. They always do."

"I don't think we have time."

"I don't give a rat's ass what you think. I want you to find more money and fast. We can deal with the consequences once we've stabilized the economy."

"Patterson will need to work miracles."

Halley waved Allen away. "Go do it now."

Allen turned around and walked out of the Oval Office, quickening his pace once inside the corridor and out of Halley's sight. There was only so much pounding he could take. Back in his own office, when his heart rate returned to something close to normal, he picked up the phone and punched in Patterson's number.

"He didn't like it, did he?" Patterson said from the other end of the line.

"Went just like you said it would."

"I told you. Never give him bad news without a solution."

"I tried to reason with him. I even suggested he might consider some sort of conciliatory gesture to encourage the Chinese back to the table. He wouldn't have it."

"You really don't know Halley, do you? He'd never do that."

"He wants us to get as much as we can for the rump of the

assets. I told him that wouldn't be easy—not with the crap we have left."

"Then you'd better figure out a way to give him what he wants."

"I'm out of ideas. I can't see any alternative."

"You need to say the words."

"You know what we discussed. I don't like it, but..."

"Are you and the president instructing me to proceed?"

"I guess we are."

"You better be ready to accept the shit-storm this will create."

"Just do what you have to do. And do it quickly."

"Grab a seat, Ben," Patterson said, pointing to an armchair in his Washington office.

"What have they decided?" Mylor asked, dropping into the chair.

Patterson inspected his fingernails. "Allen's so damn weak."

"Did he actually make a decision?"

"The man has no options left. We're running out of money. It's time to shit or get off the pot."

"How the hell did we get here?"

"Goes back a long way."

"But this kind of mess?"

"Americans have suffered from declining real incomes for the last forty years. How do you mask that reality and keep peddling the American dream? More importantly, how do you do it and still get elected?"

"Debt."

"And lots of it," Patterson said, chewing on a fingernail. "You know the story. As long as the country could borrow at cheap rates, no one cared too much about it."

"Until now. Looks like the music finally stops on Halley's watch."

"I feel for him. He's the only one I've seen with the balls to deal with the deficit and the only one with the guts to address the real problem, but I fear it's too late even for him."

"Did Allen tell him what more we can do?"

"You know Allen. He'll have dressed it up in flowery language."

"But Halley understands the consequences if we go ahead?"

"Allen certainly does. I spelled them out before he met with the president. Allen says they're all ready to proceed. That's good enough for me."

"I'm not convinced Allen has the stomach for it."

"You may be right, but even he wants to keep his job. I'm certain Halley gets it and will do what it takes. He'll be focused on the big picture."

"Then I'm to step it up?"

Patterson nodded yes. "Do what you have to do."

Mylor rose to his feet. "Okay."

"What do you think our chances are, Ben?"

"Fifty-fifty," Mylor said, walking toward the exit.

"That good?"

CHAPTER 21

The law offices of Redman Lyons were located on Second Street, Sausalito, right next door to the Portofino apartment block, in a mixed area of residential and professional office buildings. The small town law firm employed fifteen people, including its two partners, Tom Redman and Gerry Lyons. The practice had focused on real estate and family law ever since its two founders broke away from one of the large San Francisco law firms ten years earlier. Working hours at the firm were steady rather than hectic. Occasionally, there'd be a need for staff to work beyond six in the evening, but no one ever worked on weekends. Most of their real estate deals and family law matters could wait to be completed during the normal working week—a pattern on which Mylor was relying.

Heavy rain meant the Sunday evening traffic on Second Street was even quieter than normal. Once it was dark, no one was around to witness the black SUV drive into the empty private parking lot and pull up behind the low-rise law offices. Two men, both wearing black overalls and ski masks, jumped out of the vehicle and ran to the back door of the building. One of them carried a small tool bag slung over his shoulder. They wiped the rain off and peered through the glass door. No lights on, but the alarm control box, just inside on the left wall, flashed red every five seconds. The man with the tool bag jimmied open the door while the other kept watch. Once inside, they ran to the rapidly beeping alarm panel.

"Thirty seconds," the taller of the two men said, scanning around them.

"Shouldn't be difficult," the other said, using a battery-powered screwdriver to remove the white metal fascia plate. He threw the cover onto the floor then retrieved a pair of wire cutters from his pocket, using them to snip four colored cables in careful succession. The beeping stopped twenty-two seconds after they entered the building.

They used flashlights to search the two floors, before stopping at the document storage room on the ground level and levering open all eighteen of the fireproof cabinets. They emptied the contents—a mixture of legal files and loose papers—onto the floor.

"The fuel," the tall man said.

The other one returned to the vehicle, lifted the tailgate, and hoisted a five-gallon gas tank from the back. A police car sounded its siren. Quickly, the man slammed down the tailgate and hid behind the SUV. Crouching down, he stared through the rain covered windows at the distorted image of the patrol car's flashing red and blue lights on the road in front of the offices. The police car moved on, but he waited until it disappeared and its siren faded into the distance.

"What happened to you?" the tall man asked when the other returned.

"Didn't you hear the siren?" He stood the gas can on top of the documents on the floor.

"Is there a problem?"

"Not anymore."

"Come on." The tall guy pointed to the ground. "Douse this lot, but keep a little back." Then he left the room.

The shorter man opened the can and splashed gas over the papers, soaking the carpet below. Fuel vapor filled the air.

"Put some in here, too," the taller man shouted from Gerry Lyons's office along the corridor. Then he pointed to Tom Redman's office next door. "And in there. Pour any you have left on the stair carpet."

When the fuel can was empty, they ran up to one of the

offices on the second floor. They stood at either side of a large window facing Second Street and cracked open the blinds. The rain pounded hard against the glass, preventing a clear view of the street.

"Do you want me to go outside to see if anyone's around?" the shorter man asked.

"No. We don't have time. Let's do it now." The man in charge reached inside his pocket for a box of matches.

They raced downstairs to the document room where they lit two matches and threw them onto the stack of soaking papers. There was a whooshing sound as the flames ignited and sucked air into the room. They ran to the two partners' offices and set those alight, before grabbing the tool bag and the empty fuel can.

Smoke detector alarms rang out as the men hurried to their vehicle. They flew out of the parking lot and headed north toward the downtown area. In his rearview mirror, the driver could see flames lighting up the top floor of the law offices. He smiled as he removed his ski mask.

The white Marin Cablecom van rolled to a stop outside 355 Humboldt Street. The engineer in the driver's seat reached behind and grabbed a carafe and two plastic cups from the floor. He inspected the cups before wiping them with a grimy rag, then filled them with coffee. Another engineer in the passenger's seat opened a Subway paper bag balanced on his lap and retrieved two breakfast subs. A minute later, the cab was filled with the aroma of coffee and melting cheese.

The engineers sat in the vehicle, chatting and looking out of the front window toward the junction with Nevada Street. Nearly all the homes in this part of San Rafael were the same—mid-century, single-story properties.

A short, redheaded woman came out of the gray shingled property at 229 Nevada Street and glanced across the road at the van. She climbed into a silver Toyota Prius, backed down the driveway, and drove slowly past the two engineers. She looked at them, as if to say "What are you doing here?" The men smiled at her then continued to eat their sandwiches and listen to the radio talk show.

At eight-fifteen, they brushed away the remains of their breakfast then drove into the redhead's driveway. One of them reached toward the dashboard and grabbed a clipboard from the top. He used his pen to check off a few boxes on his form then nodded to his colleague.

They climbed out, walked to the van's large side door and slid it open. One of them picked up a heavy toolbox before locking the vehicle. They sauntered to the front door and rang the bell. A man in his mid-forties opened the door a few moments later. He was still in his bathrobe and looked as though he'd just climbed out of bed.

"Yeah?" the man in the robe asked, rubbing his eyes.

"We're here to fix your cable," the engineer carrying the toolbox said.

"What?"

"Your cable." The engineer with the clipboard rolled his eyes then scanned his form. "Says here you're getting an intermittent connection."

"I've no idea what you're talking about," the man in the gown said, beginning to close the door.

"This is number two-twenty-nine isn't it?"

"Yes." The door opened slightly.

"It says here your wife called last week." The engineer turned the clipboard to face the man and pointed at the form. "Look, she reported an issue on Thursday."

The man in the robe took the clipboard. "Without my reading glasses—"

When the man's attention was distracted, the engineer with the toolbox swung it into the man's chest, knocking him back into the hallway and hard onto the floor. The engineers rushed through the door and one of them sat on top of the dazed man, lying on his back. He struggled to move underneath the weight of his attacker.

"What the—?" the man said, before a white cloth, soaked with halogenated ether, was held tight against his mouth and nostrils.

The man punched out, legs flailing, as he tried not to breathe. Two minutes later, the writhing stopped, and he was unconscious. They dragged him through the hallway, past the kitchen, and to the internal door leading to the garage. Once inside the garage, they dropped him on the concrete floor.

The engineers returned to the entrance hall, taking care to straighten anything that had been disturbed during the struggle. When they were satisfied everything was in its place, they took a few moments to check the rooms of the house. The shower in the bathroom was still running, so they turned it off.

Moments later, they returned to the garage with the toolbox. One of them opened it and retrieved a rope, which he threw over the rafter in the center of the garage. They slid a heavy workbench under the rafter, and one of them climbed on top of it so he could tie one end of the rope. He tugged on it hard to make sure it held tight before forming a noose at the other end of the rope.

It took both engineers to lift the man's limp body from the floor. He made a groaning noise as they placed him onto one end of the bench. They removed his robe, threw it to the floor, then climbed back onto the bench and stood over the man. One of them bent down and held him up, taking his full weight, while the other tightened the noose around the victim's neck.

They nodded to each other. The one holding the man up released his grip, allowing the rope to take the man's full weight as he dropped from the bench. They waited until he suffocated and his breathing had stopped before jumping off the bench. They tipped it over onto its side and slid it beneath the dangling, lifeless body.

CHAPTER 22

"I told you he had a screw loose," Gainham said, taking a large bite out of his turkey mayo sandwich. "I'm not surprised he never showed up." He wiped mayonnaise from the corners of his mouth with his fingers. "We've heard the last of Tillman."

"I'd still like to speak to him," I said, biting into a tuna wrap. "Just to be certain he's not going to screw up our negotiations with Mendocino. We don't want anything to throw the deal."

"I'd rather talk about the profit we're going to make when we sell SLIDA."

"Don't get carried away, Chris. Tomorrow is only the first meeting. It may not go any further. We have to be certain they have the money and they're not just on a fishing expedition."

"I know, but you have to admit it sounds promising. They must be serious if they're paying Shipperley Brothers for advice. They don't come cheap."

Our receptionist, stood at Gainham's office door. "Damon, sorry to disturb your lunch, but I have a Mrs. Tillman on the phone wanting to talk to you about her husband. When I told her you weren't available, she started crying. I told her I'd try my best to find you. Is that okay?"

I looked at Gainham. No words were spoken, but both of us put down our food, rose from our armchairs, and walked to Gainham's desk.

"She's waiting on line two," the receptionist said.

My pulse raced as I hit the speakerphone. "Damon Traynor."

"This is Jean Tillman. I believe you were supposed to be meeting my husband yesterday."

"That's right. He failed to show up."

"I know." She started crying. "He's dead."

My heart fluttered as I slumped into the desk chair. I glanced at Gainham. His face was white, his mouth wide open. "I'm so sorry to hear that. What happened?"

"The police are saying it was suicide, but I don't believe them."

"I'm sorry. I don't know what to say. I can't imagine how dreadful this must be for you."

"I found him hanging in our garage when I returned home from work last night. There was no note. Nothing." More crying.

I turned my palms to the ceiling and mouthed, "What do I say?" to Gainham. He shrugged and bit his lip. "I didn't really know him, but he seemed a little depressed when we met him last time."

"He was depressed over losing his job, sure. Who wouldn't be? But suicide? Never. I was married to him for twenty-five years. I knew my husband. Brodie would never kill himself. Never." Her voice grew angrier with every word.

Gainham made a slashing motion across his neck with his hand. "Finish the call," he whispered. "We can't get involved in this."

"I want to thank you for contacting me, Jean. I know this is a hard time for you. I won't keep you any longer. I'm so very sorry for your loss."

"I haven't finished," she shouted.

Gainham shook his head.

I leaned forward over the phone. "I'm sorry, Jean. Please continue."

"Brodie said he was sure he was being followed. Over the last few days, he became increasingly concerned and began to lose sleep over it. I dismissed it all, of course. I told him he was imagining things."

"Who did he think was following him?"

"He never told me, and I didn't want to encourage him. But he said that if anything ever happened to him then I should call you and give you some contact details. He was very specific about this."

I rested my head in my hands and closed my eyes. *Where's this going*, I thought. "What contact details?"

"He said I should give you the name of his lawyer and do everything I could to persuade you to reach out to him. Will you do that for Brodie?"

"Of course."

Gainham stopped shaking his head.

"His name is Gerry Lyons at a firm called Redman Lyons. It's a small firm in Sausalito, not far from Brodie's old office. He said Gerry would have a file of information for you. I asked Brodie what the file was about, but he never told me. He refused to discuss it. He said it was better I didn't know. I hope it means something to you."

I hesitated before answering. "It might do. I'm not sure, but I promise I'll contact Gerry to get to the bottom of this. It's the least I can do."

"That's all I have to say. Will you let me know what you find out?"

"If I learn anything, I'll let you know. Thank you, Jean."

I terminated the call then looked up at Gainham. "What was all that about?"

"There's more going on here," Gainham said, sitting on the corner of his desk. "I think I may have been wrong. I'm not sure we can dismiss Tillman any longer."

"That's exactly what I'm thinking." I tapped at Gainham's keyboard and powered up Google before reaching across for the speakerphone again.

"What are you doing?"

"Calling Redman Lyons."

"Are you sure we ought to do that? We have no idea what we're dealing with here."

I continued to hit the numbers and after two rings heard a recorded message: "This is the law office of Redman Lyons. We're sorry we're unable to take calls at the present time, following severe fire damage to our offices. If your call is urgent, please leave a message after the tone, and we'll return your call as soon as we can."

After the tone, I said, "This is Damon Traynor from Carada Capital Partners in Boston. I'd like to speak to Gerry Lyons in connection with Brodie Tillman. My cellphone number is 555-263-2323."

"I don't like any of this," Gainham said after I ended the call.

"Me neither." I closed my eyes and rubbed my temples with the palms of my hands. "You realize we can't go ahead with tomorrow's meeting with Mendocino?"

"I know. They're not going to like it."

"No more than I do."

CHAPTER 23

It took a couple of hours to collect my thoughts before picking up the phone and speaking to Adrian Livesey at Shipperley Brothers. It couldn't be a coincidence that Tillman died on the day he was supposed to visit us. While it was possible he'd taken his own life for reasons unknown to me, the timing was suspicious to say the least. And if his wife was right that it could never have been suicide, then what was going on? The fire at Tillman's lawyer's offices had to be related. Something sinister was behind these events, but I couldn't yet connect the dots. No matter how large the potential profit, there was no way CCP could continue with the sale of SLIDA if there was any shred of doubt about it working.

"Mendocino's going to welcome this as much as a turd in a swimming pool," Livesey said at the other end of the line upon hearing our decision. "We're all geared up to see you guys tomorrow, and you're canceling the meeting at this late hour? At the very least, it's unprofessional."

Livesey was always going to take it badly. While I felt I owed him some sort of explanation, I wasn't about to share the real reason behind pulling out of the deal. "I'm sorry, but now we've slept on it, we feel it's too early for us to go for an exit."

"But you knew that last week. Come on, Damon, you're not being straight with me here. This is about price, isn't it?"

"It's just too early for us. It has nothing to do with the price. We'd be happy to speak with you and Mendocino when we're ready in a few years' time."

"Sounds like you're arm-wrestling on price to me."

"I'm sorry if I'm not making myself clear. I don't know what else to say. We have no interest in discussing this further right now."

"I'm not sure your investors would like it much if they learned you'd turned down a good profit."

Was that a threat? Was Livesey suggesting he might approach CCP's investors directly? If he did that, we would never deal with Shipperley Brothers again. "That's none of your business. As fund managers, we're paid to decide when the right time is to sell our investors' assets. Back off."

"I hear you. I guess I'll stand down the team. As I say, Mendocino won't like it. I can't control what they do about this. They may well want to take this further."

"This call has gone as far as it can. Goodbye."

I slammed down the phone. I couldn't blame Livesey for feeling frustrated. I was too. It must have appeared a strange decision to turn down an exploratory meeting with Livesey's client after they'd tabled what everyone knew was a great price. But if we'd gone ahead with the meeting, there was a real risk CCP would have had to withdraw later because of technical concerns over SLIDA. In that situation, the damage would be far worse. SLIDA's and CCP's reputations would be ruined, and the chances of ever selling SLIDA for a decent price would be negligible. Those were risks I couldn't take, at least not right now. First I had to find out much more about Tillman and his claims about SLIDA's technology, and now he was dead, that wasn't going to be easy.

"How'd they take it?" Gainham asked, standing at my door.

"We're no longer on Livesey's Christmas card list."

"That bad, eh?"

"I wish I knew what the hell's going on, Chris."

"I expect we'll learn more when Tillman's lawyer calls back."

"I sure hope so."

"I don't think it'll be good news somehow."

126

"Me neither. None of this feels right to me. It's like we're missing half of the picture." I sighed, my shoulders slumping.

"Hey. How would you like to come round for dinner tomorrow night?"

"That would be great. Thanks. If I sit at home, I'll only dwell on all this."

"See you around eight." Gainham started turning to go when my phone rang.

I picked it up. "Damon Traynor."

"Gerry Lyons from Redman Lyons, returning your call."

I waved Gainham back into my office then hit the iPhone's speaker button. "Gerry, thanks for returning my call."

"You beat me."

"What do you mean?"

"I was going to call you myself, but with our office fire, let's just say we're a little behind."

I frowned at Gainham. "I still don't follow."

"My client, Brodie Tillman, left clear instructions that in the event of his death we were to contact you and send you a file he left with us for safekeeping."

"He didn't mention any of this to me. We hardly knew him. What's in the file?"

"I have no idea. He never discussed it. All Brodie said was that it was related to his work and that you had to have it."

"Can you FedEx it to me so we have it here tomorrow?"

"Ordinarily, that wouldn't be a problem."

"We'll pay the charges, of course."

"It has nothing to do with the cost. I'm sorry to say the file was in our document storage room, and everything in there was destroyed by the fire we had a couple of days ago. Whoever broke into our offices, it appears they were targeting that room in particular."

Gainham stared at me, shaking his head.

"Sounds like a hell of a fire. Is none of it recoverable?" I asked.

"If I tell you our building will have to be pulled down and rebuilt, maybe you'll understand the scale of the damage."

"Wow. I'm sorry to hear that. If anything turns up, anything, please send it to me immediately."

"Of course. I'm not optimistic, though. This has almost put us out of business."

"I'm sorry. Thanks for returning my call in these circumstances. You have my number if you find anything."

I ended the call, stood and walked to my window. I closed my eyes and slowly bumped my forehead on the pane. "You know what I have to do, Chris."

"What's that?"

"It won't be easy."

"Go on."

I turned to face Gainham. "I'm going to go and see Mylor and have this out with him. I don't care how much he threatens us."

"Are you sure that's the right thing to do?"

"Let him threaten us with the IRS. We have nothing to hide."

"I can't help but think that will make things worse."

"It may, but we can't stand back and do nothing. We have to know the truth about this investment and I have an idea Mylor knows a whole lot more than we do."

"If you're going then I'm coming with you."

CHAPTER 24

United Airways flight 282 landed at Washington Dulles International at seven-twenty-eight a.m. The downtown meeting we'd arranged with Mylor and Kerry was scheduled for ten. Gainham and I allowed an hour for the twenty-five-mile cab ride into town, leaving us still with plenty of time to kill.

"I'm starving," Gainham said as we stepped into the arrivals hall. "What do you want to do about breakfast? My vote is we head into town and find somewhere."

"I'm really not that hungry. Let's stay here a while," I said.

"Airport food again?"

"If we leave now, we'll only sit in commuter traffic. I'd rather get a cab when it's died down." I pointed across the hall. "Look, we can grab a table in there."

Before Gainham could put up a fight, I walked toward the Dulles Gourmet Market, where we bought coffee and two muffins, both for Gainham.

"Sure you don't want any of this?" Gainham pointed to the half-eaten second apple and cinnamon muffin on his plate.

"I'm okay." I didn't look up from reading the business section of *The Washington Post.* "This country's in a mess."

Gainham started on the sports section. "I've stopped reading about it. It's all so depressing."

"The federal deficit is way out of control. How did we ever get here?"

Gainham smiled. "Why don't we raise that with Mylor? It might help to break the ice."

"Yeah. Sure. We'll ask him what the Treasury plans to do

about it too." I drained my cup. "I'm going to get another coffee. Want one?"

"I'll have another. See if they have any more of those muffins while you're there."

I shook my head. "I don't know where you put it. You ought to be a lot heavier."

Gainham patted his stomach. "It's all muscle."

I headed to the counter and stood in line. As I looked back at Gainham, he had his head down in the newspaper. *He's a good friend*, I thought. Even though I'd told him he didn't need to come to the meeting with Mylor, he'd insisted on joining me for moral support. He said he didn't like the idea of his friend being bullied by some spineless suit in Washington.

As I turned around to face the counter, something caught my eye. A man in a dark suit was sitting at a table near the entrance door. There was something vaguely familiar about him. He appeared to be staring right at me, but when I made eye contact with him, he turned away and picked up a book. The more I racked my brains, the more certain I was that I'd seen him somewhere before—but where?

I reached the front of the line and placed my order, then turned my head toward the man. He was looking my way again and suddenly appeared embarrassed to have been caught staring. He picked up his book, put it in his briefcase, and quickly left.

"Where's the muffin?" Gainham asked when I returned with two coffees.

"Oh. I'm sorry, I forgot it."

"Don't worry. What's wrong?"

"What?"

"You seem preoccupied."

"I'm okay. It's nothing."

* * *

Just before ten, we arrived at the offices of the Department of Treasury where Kerry met us in reception.

"Thanks for arranging this, Kerry," I said, shaking her hand.

She held my gaze for a few moments and smiled. "I was happy to help."

"This is my partner, Chris Gainham."

"Pleased to meet you, Chris." Kerry shook Gainham's hand then pointed toward the security barriers. "Shall we go through?"

While we followed Kerry along the corridor, Gainham nudged me in the ribs. "She's a looker," he whispered. "You didn't mention that."

I nodded, but said nothing.

When we walked into the meeting room, I looked at Mylor, who was sitting at the head of the table, talking on his cell phone. He made no effort to acknowledge us and continued his conversation while we took our seats.

A few moments later, Mylor finished his call. He looked as though he was sucking on a lemon when he made eye contact with me. No handshakes, no pleasantries, so I made no effort in return. After all, this was not a social meeting.

"You wanted to see me," Mylor said before glancing at his watch.

I leaned forward. "Yes, I wanted—"

"I hope you're not here to stir the shit again."

"Just who do you think you are?" Gainham asked.

"Leave it, Chris," I said, tapping Gainham's forearm. "I'll handle this."

Gainham rolled his head and slid his chair back from the table.

Mylor pointed at Gainham with his chin. "Who's he?"

I ignored the question. "Okay, let's jump right to it." I paused. "Brodie Tillman is dead."

Kerry went pale, looked sideways at her boss and then back at me. "Dead?" she said. "When?"

131

Mylor didn't flinch. "I know all about it."

Kerry's face was a mixture of shock and disgust. She seemed to struggle finding the right words. "How—?"

Mylor raised his right hand. "Hanged himself."

Kerry lowered her head while she absorbed the information.

"He was scheduled to come and see me the day after he died," I said.

"What about?" Mylor asked.

"I wanted to get to the bottom of his claims about SLIDA."

"I told you to stop digging."

"I needed to know if there was any shred of truth in what he was saying."

"I told you he liked the bottle. The man was lying."

"Even so, he could have disrupted a potential sale process."

Mylor narrowed his eyes. "What sale process?"

"We've had an approach for SLIDA. A serious one—at a level we find interesting."

"What is this?" Mylor slammed his palms on the table. "Don't even think about selling."

Gainham snorted. "Is this guy serious?"

"We own the company," I said. "It's up to us whether we sell it or not. We paid you good money for it. You can't take the cash and then tell us what to do with it. It doesn't work that way."

"You need Treasury consent to any sale," Mylor said.

I could see Gainham struggling to restrain himself. "Sure, you can veto a sale to a foreign buyer," I said. "That makes sense. We all accept SLIDA is a strategic defense asset. But you cannot reasonably refuse consent to a sale to a U.S. buyer. That's what the contract says."

"I don't give a shit about the contract. I'm telling you we won't give consent."

"That's outrageous," Gainham said.

"That's how it is," Mylor said, staring at Gainham. "Who are you, anyway?"

"He's one of my partners."

"SLIDA must stay with CCP. There will be no sale."

"What's going on here?" I made no attempt to hide my frustration. "Are we missing something?"

"Just keep collecting the income under the contract and put any ideas about selling it to the back of your mind. In a few years' time, we might entertain a discussion about it, but not now. It's too early."

"We'll be taking legal advice. There was never any discussion about us having to keep the investment for a minimum period."

"There's a bigger national security picture in all this."

"We won't be bound by anything not in the original contract. If we decide it's in the best interest of our investors to sell SLIDA, then we'll sell it. If you continue to refuse consent, then we'll see you in court."

Gainham smiled at Mylor and said, "That'll be an expensive mistake—probably career shortening."

"You really don't want to cross me on this," Mylor said, rising to his feet. "If I hear any mention of a sale or legal action, I'll close you down. This meeting is over."

CHAPTER 25

A silver BMW Five Series pulled up to the sidewalk outside the Department of Treasury, and Mylor and Kerry climbed in the back.

"The office," Mylor said to the driver. He fastened his seatbelt then turned to Kerry. "I'll drop you at the office and go on from there. My daughter has a soccer match this afternoon, and I promised I'd be there."

"Fine," Kerry said, peering out of the window as they passed the White House.

"Why the long face?" Mylor asked after a few minutes of silence.

"I don't know what you mean."

"What's the problem?"

Kerry turned to her boss. "When did you find out about Tillman?"

"Yesterday."

"And you didn't think I should be told?"

"It's not my job to give you a running commentary."

"It was embarrassing in that meeting, learning something important like that from Traynor. How did you find out?"

"I make it my business to know what's going on. So should you."

"But you told me to stop tailing Tillman and focus on Traynor."

"I didn't say close your eyes, did I?"

Kerry sat in silence as they drove onto the I-95 South. "Do

you believe he killed himself?" she asked as they passed the Newington exit.

"Who?"

"Tillman, of course."

"Yeah, sure. You saw his file. I'm surprised it took him so long."

"Why would he kill himself if he'd arranged to meet Traynor? I don't get it."

Mylor shrugged. "I don't know. Ask his shrink."

"Here's a man who tracks down the new owner of SLIDA and tells them it doesn't work. They dismiss him as some kind of wacko. If he killed himself at that point, maybe I could understand it, but not the day before CCP invite him to their offices to discuss his concerns. That doesn't make sense to me."

"You're thinking too much. Take it for what it is. An alcoholic with no job and no prospects decides to hang himself. That's all it is. Period."

Another few minutes of silence.

"I never signed up for this," Kerry said, staring out of the side window.

"For what?"

"Innocent people dying."

"Tillman took his own life."

"What about Frank Marcuri?"

"Who?"

"The chairman of CCP's advisory committee."

"Means nothing to me."

"His helicopter fell out of the sky when Traynor couldn't persuade him to approve the SLIDA deal."

"What are you trying to say?"

"Now Tillman dies the day before an important meeting with CCP."

"And your point is, Columbo?"

"Who?"

"Never mind."

"I don't have a point. I have a question: Are these deaths linked in some way?" She turned to watch Mylor's face for a reaction.

He didn't flinch. "Look, if you can't handle the pressure, I can always have you transferred off the unit to some comfortable office back at Langley, pushing paper around."

"I didn't say I couldn't handle it. You pay me to use my brain. Remember?"

"Well, I suggest you use it on something productive. Stop looking for things in the shadows. Sometimes things are exactly as they seem. No, correction. Most times things are what they seem." Mylor took his phone out of his jacket pocket. "I have some calls to make."

CHAPTER 26

The Barnstable Fire Department was out in full force. A swarm of yellow uniformed firefighters held up traffic at the lights at Main and Millway, as they did every Labor Day weekend. I eased my car forward and lowered the window when I reached the intersection. A young lieutenant shook his charity bucket then leaned into my vehicle. His uniform was immaculate, and in the middle of his helmet he wore a silver plate with a single bugle. I reached over to the back seat and grabbed my briefcase. "Great to see you guys out here again," I said, retrieving two twenty-dollar bills from my wallet and throwing them into the bucket.

The firefighter smiled. "You have a nice day, sir," he said, handing me a sticker for my windshield, showing I'd made a contribution. That way, I wouldn't be stopped each time I crossed that intersection over the weekend.

"And you." I turned left onto Millway and headed toward the harbor. Day trippers were piling onto a whale watching boat moored at the dock. I pulled over for a moment to take in the view. The place was heaving with visitors fighting for parking spaces. My window was still down, and the smell of fried fish filled my nostrils when the sea breeze drifted past the Osterville Fish Cafe. Its small outside dining terrace was packed, as it was on all warm weekends over the summer.

A few moments later, I drove into the driveway of my parents' home. Mom and Dad came running out as I stepped out of the car.

"Great to see you, Son," Dad said, hugging me. "How was the drive?"

"Your sister's here, already," Mom said in between kisses.

"The traffic was bad coming over the Sagamore Bridge, but that was the only hold up," I said, lifting my overnight bag from the back of the BMW. "There's a lot of people up at the harbor."

"It was the same last year. Your mom and I took a walk up there early this morning. It was busy then. We'll stay clear of the area until it quietens down."

"Too many city folks coming down from Boston, I guess," I said, grinning.

The following morning, while Mom and my sister prepared Sunday lunch, Dad and I went out for a walk. We headed east along Commerce Road to avoid the busy beach area.

"I'd like to ask your advice on something, Dad," I said as we took a left toward Indian Trail.

"Always happy, if you think I can help," Dad said.

"I'm struggling to know what to do. I've not been here before."

"Well, let's see if we can come up with an answer together."

Half an hour later, I'd recounted the whole story of the SLIDA deal, from CCP's initial excitement having completed such an important transaction, through the claims Brodie Tillman made, to the recent meeting with Mylor.

"Is this the same deal we discussed when you were last down here?" Dad asked.

"That's right. You'll remember we had some difficulty persuading the chairman of our advisory committee to do the deal. Maybe we should have listened to him."

"He's the one who was killed in that helicopter crash?"

"That's right."

"This Mylor guy sounds like a loose cannon to me. Why is he being so aggressive? I don't get it."

"I really don't understand it either. It feels personal in some way." I stopped walking and turned to my father. "I think there's something sinister going on. Does that sound crazy?"

"Hmm." Dad looked like he was lost in his thoughts.

"Two suspicious deaths, a massive fire at Tillman's lawyer's office, and Mylor acts as though *we've* done something wrong. I don't like it, Dad, but I'm not certain what I can do about it."

"The funny thing is I could put it all down to coincidence if it wasn't for the office fire. You said the papers that were meant for you were completely destroyed?"

"That's what Tillman's lawyer told us."

"Those document rooms are meant to stand some serious heat and that's before we even think about the fireproof cabinets. I'm with you, Son. There's more to this." Dad put his hand on my shoulder. "Come on. We'd better start heading back before the girls begin to worry about us."

We turned around and walked west along The Old King's Highway. The conversation stopped for a couple of minutes while both of us thought.

"You're worried about your investors, aren't you?" Dad asked, raising his voice above the holiday traffic on the main road.

"I feel I've let them down. They've entrusted a lot of money to CCP and they expect us to look after it. If we lose this investment, the whole fund would be under water, not to mention the damage it would do to the firm and our reputation in the market."

"I can understand that."

"Then we have this maniac, Mylor, threatening to wipe out our firm if we continue raising questions. But I can't just sit on my hands and watch this happen."

We turned right down Commerce Road, and the noise of the traffic disappeared behind us.

"Here's what I think you should do."

"I'm listening."

"You're right. You can't ignore Tillman's claims, particularly in light of what happened to him. My advice is to work around Mylor. He may be a blowhard, but there's no point baiting him if you don't need to. Be discrete. Make some inquiries of the other board members at SLIDA. Who knows? You might find that one or two of them are wondering what's going on too. It's possible Tillman may have spoken to them first before coming to you."

"I guess it's possible, although all of them, except the chairman we appointed, were there when Tillman was fired."

"Well, start there and see where it takes you. Involve the new chairman. He may know who's most receptive to a quiet conversation on the board."

I nodded. "I think you're right. Perhaps I've been a little heavy handed up to now. Maybe that's what irritated Mylor so much. Good advice, Dad. I'll start with the board and go from there."

"If that doesn't work, there may be another way I can help."

"How?"

"I know Mylor's ultimate boss."

"You do? How?"

"The Treasury Secretary is Gordon Allen. He and I shared a room in college many years ago. Every now and then, we still catch up at an alumni event. I'm sure he'd take my call if you need me to get the lowdown on Mylor."

That's one of the amazing things about my father. He's the most humble and unassuming person you could meet, and yet the range and depth of his friends and contacts sometimes blows me away. "Don't do anything for now, Dad, but I might take you up on that if we're still struggling in a week or two."

"Well, the offer's there if you need it. Come on. I'm starving."

Tuesday after Labor Day, I called a partners meeting. Gainham and I briefed our colleagues on our previous week's visit with

Mylor. Then I shared my thinking on how we ought to proceed.

"It's a pisser they won't allow us to sell SLIDA," Crawford said, clearing her throat. "That would've solved everything in one go."

"Mylor was clear. The government will not sanction an early exit," I said, looking toward Gainham for support.

"That's right. We even threatened him with legal action, but he didn't seem too concerned," Gainham said.

"In any case, we still have to find out whether we have a problem with SLIDA before we can sell it."

"Are you sure we should continue raising questions about it?" Crawford asked. "If we've got to keep the investment, why not keep our heads down and enjoy the fee income? Do we really want to ruffle any more feathers right now? I can't see what that will do for us."

"That's exactly what—" Gainham said before I put my hand on his shoulder.

"I'll deal with this, Chris." I turned to Crawford. "I think we have to know if there's a problem with SLIDA, even if we plan to keep it. Think what our investors would say if they found out we suspected there was a major flaw in the technology and we just sat on our hands and ignored it."

"Well, when you put it that way…" Crawford said.

"We need to be careful," Gainham said. "I get the impression Mylor's just waiting for an excuse to come down hard on us."

"So, we're agreed? We'll start with the SLIDA board members and take it from there." I looked around the table and collected the reluctant nods from my partners. "I know it's hard, but it's the right thing to do."

CHAPTER 27

Kerry looked up at the clock on the wall outside her office door—six-fifteen. It would be another hour, at least, before she'd have the report ready for Mylor's review. Ordinarily, she'd have finished it hours ago and not be right up against his tight deadline, but these were far from ordinary times.

When she was first handpicked for Mylor's team, Kerry had been delighted and terrified in equal measure. It was flattering that people higher up the chain at the CIA recognized her talents and considered her ready for the challenge, but she wasn't sure she'd measure up to Mylor's exacting standards. Her parents were thrilled and very proud their intelligent daughter was doing so well. Mylor's reputation within the intelligence and security community was legendary, so her move was regarded as a certain route to rapid promotion. Many currently high ranking officers had spent a couple of years with Mylor during their early careers only to see swift advancement soon after. No doubt about it—once Kerry joined Mylor's team, she was on the fast track, just so long as she could handle the pressure.

But the initial euphoria had long since dissipated. She could put up with Mylor's aggressive personality and his unpredictability. She'd been warned about him long before she accepted the position and knew what to expect. And while the nature of the work she was doing had raised ethical concerns, she'd come to terms with them. Her boss had explained how important the activities of the Bethesda unit were to helping the Treasury Department get the most out of sales of government-owned assets. Maximizing those proceeds would help stabilize the economy, so what they were doing was, essentially, a matter of national security. He'd even told her their work was so important it had been sanctioned by the highest levels within the administration.

It was something else causing her to lose sleep and fall behind on her work: A recurring fear that Mylor might be behind the more sinister events surrounding the SLIDA deal. She had no proof, but the suspicion was never far from her mind. There were too many unlikely coincidences—things that just didn't feel right. Maybe Mylor had a point when he'd questioned whether she was up to the job. If success at this level meant becoming more like him, then perhaps she wasn't cut out for all this.

"Mr. Mylor just called," Mylor's gaunt personal assistant said, standing at Kerry's door. She was in her late fifties, with long gray hair, and reminded Kerry of an aging hippy. Apparently, she'd worked with Mylor for almost twenty years. For that alone, she deserved a medal. "He said there's no way he'll be able to get back to the office this evening."

"Oh," Kerry said, feigning disappointment. "That's a shame. What's delayed him?"

"I can't say, but he said he'll see you first thing in the morning to go over the report."

"Okay. Thanks for letting me know."

"I'm heading home now if you don't need anything."

"Don't wait for me. I'm almost done here. I'll print off all the copies we need for the morning."

Over the next hour, Kerry watched as all her coworkers left for home. When she finished her report, she read it through one last time. Mylor had a reputation for throwing documents into the shredder if he found sloppy errors. Then she printed out three copies before sliding one of them into a colored sleeve and walking it over to Mylor's office. His door was shut, as it was most times whether he was in or not. She knocked then, after a moment's delay, walked in and placed the report face down on his desk.

Standing next to the great man's desk, she scanned his office. No personal items, no photos, and no pictures on the wall— nothing to hint at Mylor's personality or show he was human. What was it that made a man so singularly focused on his work? It couldn't be the money. Kerry knew Mylor's pay grade. He'd never become rich on that salary. It couldn't be the lime- light either. All his assignments were low key, under the radar, able to be denied if probed. When Kerry stopped to think about it, she knew nothing about the man. Was he married or di- vorced? He'd mentioned a daughter once, but that was all she knew about any family. Whenever she'd tried small talk with him, he seemed uncomfortable and would move the conversa- tion on to work matters. The man was an enigma.

A sheet of paper lay on the floor between Mylor's office chair and his desk. Kerry bent her knees and leaned down to pick it up, immediately recognizing it as the loose cover sheet from her report. It must have slipped out of the plastic sleeve. As she grabbed it, she rested her weight against the desk. Some- thing moved. The lower drawer of the desk was open. She pushed it back in then stood up.

Later on, when she ran over that evening's events in her mind, she would never know what possessed her to do it—she wasn't that kind of person. Her pulse was racing as she placed her fingers on the top drawer handle. She stopped, breathed deeply and closed her eyes. What harm could looking do? No one would ever know.

Kerry tugged on the handle. That drawer wasn't locked either. She eased it open a little then stopped. If she left now, there would be no harm done, and she would not have pried into Mylor's personal space. Now was the time to stop and leave the room, but something compelled her to go on. Another tug. Inside the drawer was a small stapler resting on top of a messy pile of yellow post-it notes that had a bunch of telephone numbers scrawled on them. At the back of the drawer was an unopened pack of paper napkins and a small bag of half-eaten peanut M&Ms. Kerry smiled. Maybe he was human, after all. No. He'd probably stolen them from a sick child.

Suddenly, Mylor's telephone rang, shattering the silence. Kerry fell backward toward the chair, hitting her left shin hard on the sharp underside of the desk. Her heart pounded her chest. "Shit," she said, lifting herself off the floor. "Idiot."

Wincing, she rubbed her leg to ease the pain. The wooden edge of the desk had broken the skin. She hobbled over to the door. When she reached it, the telephone stopped ringing. She stood still, looked back at the desk, took a few deep breaths, and swallowed. A cocktail of shame and fear filled her brain. The drawer was still open.

She walked back to the desk and slid the top drawer into place, pushing it hard to make sure it was completely closed. Her breathing returned to normal. She'd done nothing wrong. Up to now, she was comfortable she'd not invaded Mylor's privacy. But something compelled her to continue and to see what was in the other drawers. She kneeled behind the desk.

Two thick blue plastic folders filled the second drawer. There were no labels on the outside to indicate their contents. She opened the first one, leaning it on the seat of the chair as she flicked through the papers. It contained what appeared to be a couple of years' worth of personal bills, all marked in Mylor's handwriting with the date he'd paid them. No mention of a Mrs. Mylor on any of the documents. At the back of the folder were a few recent bank statements in his name only. The latest one showed a balance of $4,422 and it seemed to fluctuate around that level for the previous three months, confirming he wasn't doing the job for the money. A pang of guilt consumed her; it wasn't right to be looking at these private things. She stuffed the papers back into the folder and placed it on the top of the desk, promising herself she would just take a quick peek at what was inside the other file. If those papers were personal, she'd stop right there and leave.

The second folder was much heavier, bursting with papers. Kerry stood and rested it on the top of the other folder before opening it. The first half or so contained press clippings from around the world, with no obvious connection between the stories. She stopped at a cutting from the *Financial Times* with the headline "Fund Manager Killed on Tube." The article described a Paul McCann, who was head of investments at the London office of the Gulf States' sovereign wealth fund, and how he was killed on the London Underground after falling onto the rail tracks in front of a speeding tube train. There was speculation about his death. Some suggested it was an accident due to an overcrowded platform, while others thought it might have been suicide. There was a photo of Mr. McCann, a man in his early forties, described as a devoted family man, who left a wife and an eight-year-old daughter.

None of it made sense to Kerry. She flicked on a few pages and stopped at another newspaper photo of a different man standing next to a Porsche. The caption beneath it read "Happier days." The article described how Tom Laudel, a prominent hedge fund manager, had been found dead in his Porsche in woods not far from his Connecticut home. It said he killed himself, but there were no details disclosed.

Kerry straightened her back. What was this file? Why would Mylor be collecting this information? There was no obvious link other than the stories were all from the last few weeks. She started turning the pages again, scanning the headlines, trying to connect them together. All the articles concerned people who had gone missing, had died in accidents or were suspected of committing suicide. How did any of this fit with the work of Mylor's team? Why would he be involved in investigating these deaths?

It was the photo of the helicopter that stopped her in her tracks. The article from the *Boston Globe* described how two people had been killed in a helicopter crash over Boston Harbor—the pilot and a Mr. Frank Marcuri, a prominent insurance executive. Kerry stopped breathing. This was someone she recognized—Marcuri was the chairman of CCP's investor advisory board. Why would Mylor have an article on this helicopter accident? And hadn't Mylor denied knowing Marcuri's name when she'd mentioned it in his car?

Kerry took a few moments to calm her nerves before continuing. The second half of the folder contained typed surveillance reports, listing names, places, and times. She didn't recognize any of the names of those under surveillance. Perhaps they were code names. Toward the back, she discovered a surveillance log on Brodie Tillman, but it wasn't her work. She'd called off her surveillance team when Mylor had said it was no longer necessary. The log in front of her ran well beyond that time. What was Mylor up to? Why call her team off and place another tail on Tillman? And why hide this from her? She checked the dates of the log. Tillman had been followed right up until the day before his death. Kerry held her hand to her mouth to fight the reflux in her throat. Mylor had to be connected to all these deaths.

What am I involved in here?

Her hands trembled as she grabbed both folders from the desk. She had to get out of there. When she opened the drawer to put the files away, they fell out of her hands, the papers scattering over the floor beneath the desk. Panic gripped her.

Crouching, Kerry quickly collected the loose papers together on the carpet, doing her best to sort one folder's contents from the other. When the documents were back in the right files, she raced through the press cuttings pages, stopped at the articles on Laudel and Marcuri and grabbed them. As she folded them, she noticed one of Mylor's bank statements caught up with the Marcuri pages. Then there were footsteps in the corridor outside. No time to put anything back. She had to get out of Mylor's office. Without stopping to think, she stuffed the folded papers into one of her pockets and threw the folders back into the desk. As she was checking that all the drawers were closed, the office door swung open. Gasping, her heart exploded in her chest.

"What the hell are you doing in here?" Mylor asked, standing in the doorway.

Kerry could feel her face reddening. "Leaving my report on your desk."

CHAPTER 28

The Patriots were playing the Pittsburgh Steelers and the Patriots were winning—twenty-seven to twenty-four with less than two minutes left. Keeping my eyes glued to my Sony widescreen, I stuffed the last of a Thai takeout into my mouth.

When my cell phone rang, I ignored it. Whoever it was could wait. As the channel went to another commercial break, the phone rang again. Without looking to see who it was, I answered it. "Can I call you back in a few minutes?" I said, assuming it must be a friend calling that late in the evening.

"Damon, it's Adrian Livesey."

"Look, I can't talk right now. I'll have to call you back."

"Sure. I'll wait for your call. I'm at the office."

What was Livesey calling for that time of night? I had been crystal clear about our position on SLIDA. There was no way we could carry on discussing a potential sale—to anyone.

I continued watching the game, but my mind was now elsewhere. Livesey wouldn't be calling at that hour if it wasn't important, at least to him. I muted the sound on the TV, tapped the recent calls icon on my iPhone, and hit Livesey's number. "You're working late."

"Normal day for me." Livesey sounded surprised to hear from me. "Thanks for calling back. This couldn't wait."

"I'm listening."

"First up, I want to say how sorry I am about my behavior last time we spoke."

What was Livesey up to? The masters of the universe at Shipperley Brothers apologized to no one. Sure, his behavior had been bad, but no worse than many others I'd seen in the investment banking business. Arrogance and big egos were common, particularly on Wall Street.

"There's no need to apologize. I'd already forgotten about it."

"Thanks, but there was no excuse for it." Livesey paused, as though he expected me to say something. I didn't. "Look, there's been a development this evening, and I wanted to run it by you."

"If it's about the SLIDA deal, we've made our position clear."

"It is about SLIDA, but I think you'll want to hear this."

"I doubt it." I braced myself for another argument. What was it about *no* Livesey couldn't understand?

"Since we last talked, we've had a bunch of meetings with Mendocino. They want this asset, Damon. I mean they really want it, and they're willing to do whatever it takes to get it."

"I'm afraid you've been wasting your time. It's not for sale."

"Stop playing hardball for a moment. We both know everything has a price."

"I'm not playing anything. SLIDA's not for sale."

"Hear me out, would you?"

"It's a waste of your time and mine."

"One hundred and twenty-five billion."

"What?"

"Mendocino called me half an hour ago. That's what they authorized me to offer. That's five times your money."

I sat forward on the edge of my sofa. For once, I didn't know what to say. Five times the money in a matter of weeks. That was an incredible offer, but we still had no idea whether SLIDA worked or not. I needed more time to finish my investigation. Even then, Mylor would be no pushover. There'd be months of messy litigation if he continued to refuse consent, although I was confident CCP would win that battle in the end. Contractually, Mylor didn't have a leg to stand on.

"Come on, Damon, you'd be lucky to see a price like this in ten years' time," said Livesey, obviously riled by my lack of response. "Don't tell me it's not for sale now."

"I hear you and I understand your client wants it."

Call me a worrier, but now I was beginning to question why anyone would pay five times as much as we did so soon after our deal. What was I missing?

"Will you now agree to a meeting?"

"Not yet."

"You're unreal. You've got to be shitting me."

"Leave this with me. I will, at least, discuss it again with my partners, but I'm making no promises about selling it. Is that understood?"

"I can't believe we're having this conversation. If you guys turn this down then we'll never do business together again. There must be something in the Boston water. It's affecting your brain."

"You just apologized for your behavior. That didn't last long."

"Talk to your partners and call me back." Livesey terminated the call.

Who did that conceited clown think he was talking to? I looked up at my TV. The Patriots had just lost the game.

CHAPTER 29

"Something's come up on SLIDA," I said, sitting with my back turned toward my closed office door, the iPhone clamped to my left ear. "I need to see you."

"Actually, I've been thinking of calling you over the last couple of days," Kerry said from the other end of the line. "I've learned a few things about Mylor, which I think you ought to know."

"I don't want to involve him at this stage."

"Good. Neither do I."

"Shall I come to Washington, or would somewhere else suit you better?"

"Hold on a moment." Kerry went quiet for a few moments. I assumed she was checking her calendar. "What are you doing Friday?"

"Nothing I can't move."

"Okay. I'll take the day off and come to Boston for the weekend. That way I don't have to explain my absence to Mylor."

"I'll buy your plane ticket."

"That's okay. Just treat me to somewhere nice for dinner. I hear the coastline up toward Rockport is worth seeing."

"I know just the place. I'll pick you up at the airport once I have your flight details."

"Great. See you Friday."

* * *

I sounded the horn of my X5 when I spotted Kerry walking out of the terminal, wheeling her overnight bag behind her. She had such an elegant walk. I still wondered how I'd managed to attract such a beautiful woman. She saw me, smiled, and headed toward the car. I jumped out and kissed her on the lips. "It's good to see you," I said, grabbing her bag. "I've taken the afternoon off, so we can head out of town straightaway and avoid the traffic."

"Sounds good," said Kerry, climbing into the front passenger seat.

I pulled away and drove toward the Sumner Tunnel. "I've booked us a room tonight at this great boutique hotel I know, just south of Rockport. It has a fantastic view along the coast. The food's good too."

"I bet you take all your girlfriends there?"

I felt the blood rushing to my cheeks. "Only the ones I'm trying to impress."

"I feel honored."

"If it's okay with you," I said, taking the ramp onto US-1 at Revere, "I'd like to discuss SLIDA on our way up there. Sort of get it out of the way so it doesn't spoil our weekend."

"Well that is why we're meeting, after all. Although, I have to admit, I have been looking forward to seeing you again."

For a moment, I took my eyes off the road and smiled at her. "So have I."

"You said something happened on SLIDA?"

"It has, and you're not going to like it."

"Why did I know that already?"

"For the record, we don't accept the Treasury can block a sale. The SLIDA acquisition docs were very specific; consent to a sale to another U.S. buyer cannot be unreasonably withheld."

"I know. I've read them."

"I've discussed the whole thing with my partners. They don't like being told what to do any more than I do and that was before I took the phone call this week."

"What call?"

"From the buyer. We turned down their first approach. But it turns out they desperately want SLIDA and won't take no for an answer. They came back this week with a much bigger number. The kind of number that would get me fired if our investors saw me walking away from it."

"I don't think Mylor cares about the numbers. The fact that you've received a better offer won't mean a thing to him."

"It should. It means we have more of an incentive now to challenge him in court, if he persists with his position." I kept the car to the left, taking the 128-N toward Gloucester. "We can't just ignore this offer, Kerry. You see that don't you?"

"Let me guess. You want me to arrange another meeting with him to discuss all this?"

"That's right. But I wanted to gauge your reaction first—see what you thought. You know the man. I thought you'd know how best to approach him."

Kerry looked away. "My advice is to drop it. I know exactly what he'll say. Don't give him an excuse to go after you, Damon. It's not worth it."

"I'm only doing what my investors pay me to do. This is their money, not ours. I can't just drop it because some bureaucrat at the Treasury wants to start throwing his weight around."

Kerry continued staring out of the window. She seemed lost in her thoughts as we drove in silence. Then her face turned serious and she said, "Listen. I'm taking a big risk with what I'm about to share with you."

"Okay."

"And if it ever comes out, I'll deny having said it."

I eased off the gas, wondering what was coming. "Go on."

"I know you've been concerned about Mylor's behavior. I have too—have been for some time, actually."

"You never said anything."

"He's my boss. What could I say?"

154

"I understand, but his attitude is outrageous. How does he hold down his job?"

Kerry ignored the question. "I've been digging around, trying to find out a bit more about him. You know I've only been in his team a short while?"

"You said it's some kind of temporary position."

"That's right. One I wish I'd never taken."

"Why?"

"Because I've learned something I don't like. Something that made me question what I'm doing on his team."

"What is it?"

"I don't want to go into details, so don't push me on this. I can only tell you so much."

"Okay. I won't push you." I reached over and squeezed her hand. "Whatever it is, it's obviously upsetting you. Just tell me what you can, Kerry."

Kerry took a deep breath. "Don't mess with him. I think he's capable of some dangerous stuff."

"He's already threatened us with an IRS audit."

"I'm talking about something much more menacing than that."

"Menacing?" I looked at Kerry. "What are you suggesting?"

"I think he had something to do with Tillman's death. I can't prove anything, but I've seen some of Mylor's files, and what–"

"Are you serious?" What could she possibly know to make her reach that conclusion? "Didn't he commit suicide?"

"That's what Mylor wants us to think."

"Come on, Kerry. The man's a bully, sure, but I don't think a senior Treasury official is going to go around killing people."

Kerry avoided eye contact and chewed on her bottom lip. I could tell she wanted to say more.

"I know it sounds crazy," she said, "but there are some things I can't share with you. You're going to have to trust me when I say I'm not making this up."

"What sort of things?"

"I told you not to push me."

I raised my right palm. "Okay."

Kerry sat in silence for a few moments before continuing. "You remember Frank Marcuri?"

"Of course."

"I think Mylor was involved in the helicopter accident."

I hit the brakes. The driver behind us sounded his horn, so I drove on. "Do you realize what you're saying?"

"Sadly, yes."

"Do you have any proof of this? Because if you do, we need to go to the police."

"No. There is no proof. Let's just say I've seen files that I shouldn't have seen."

"At the Treasury? Is it possible you're mistaken, Kerry? Maybe you misunderstood something?"

"There is a chance, yes. There's no hard evidence to support what I've just told you. But I'm almost certain it's the truth."

While I didn't want to believe what Kerry was telling me, I had to admit some of it sounded credible. After all, Tillman's wife had been adamant her husband didn't kill himself. And both Tillman and Marcuri died immediately before crucial meetings with me. Were these deaths connected? I wondered what else Kerry knew that she couldn't share with me.

"Is there anything else I should know?"

"I've said enough already, but I'm going out on a limb with this for a reason."

"What is that?"

"To protect you. I don't want you to push Mylor any further. Now you know what he can do, my advice is to drop any idea of selling SLIDA. Keep your head down and stop asking questions about it."

"It may not be that simple."

"It looks simple enough to me."

"I don't know that I have a choice."

"I don't want to see you harmed, Damon. Really, I don't."

CHAPTER 30

Denzil Clyne's first arrest was for aggravated assault at the age of seventeen. Now thirty-seven, he'd spent a third of his adult life in prison as a result of a long list of violent attacks. Twice he'd been married, with both partners filing for divorce within two years, citing domestic violence. He'd tried anger management counseling, both in and out of prison. None of it worked. When the pressure was on, Clyne always lost his temper and resorted to his fists. It was ironic that the one crime he was good at, and the way he earned his living, had never led to his incarceration. Breaking and entering was his calling, and he'd yet to come across a security system he couldn't work around. In the New England criminal underworld, Clyne was the go-to person for gaining illicit access to any building.

Clyne parked his Chevy pick-up on Batterymarch Street, fed the meter with enough coins for two hours' parking, and sauntered up Kilby. He wore a blue short-sleeved cleaner's uniform shirt and dark gray pants. The badge on the shirt read Malloney Cleaning, as did the label on the carryall he held in his right hand.

He crossed State Street and walked along the service road behind CCP's office building, glancing over his shoulder without making it obvious. He'd already scanned the area for CCTV cameras earlier in the week and found nothing to worry about. He stopped and looked up at the office tower. While there were a few lights on, the building looked quiet, as it was most Saturday evenings. No lights where he was heading—CCP's twenty-second floor main office suite.

Within minutes, Clyne was inside the building. Two security guards stood chatting at the front reception desk, absorbed by the TV screen next to the waiting area. They had it tuned in to a rerun of *American Idol* and were laughing at the judges' comments. The problem was the elevators faced reception, so any movement would attract attention. Consequently, Clyne slipped into the stairwell and climbed the stairs at the back of the building. This was an occupational hazard for Clyne and one of the reasons he kept himself in good physical shape.

It took only four and a half minutes to reach CCP's main level, where he waited on the stairs until his breathing recovered. The firm's reception area was dark when he left the stairwell. Before reaching for the cutting tool in his bag, Clyne gently pushed the glass door. He smiled as it opened—something he'd learned over the years. Why struggle with locks when one in every ten "locked" doors was left open? Once inside, he stood and let his eyes adjust to the poor light, listening for any sounds. Nothing. The place was empty. The only thing he noticed was a faint odor of cigarette smoke.

Clyne walked past a row of empty offices until he reached Damon's corner room. The briefing note had been clear; he knew exactly where he needed to go. He closed Damon's door behind him then turned on a small flashlight and scanned the labels on the cabinets along one wall. When he found the cabinet he was looking for, Clyne spread its contents on the floor before using his DSLR camera to capture high resolution images of each document. He spent twenty minutes taking photos before placing everything back into the cabinet. He took his time. There was no hurry. What mattered most to him was collecting everything the client wanted. He'd give them no excuse to avoid paying the other half of his fee.

He sat at Damon's desk and examined the few loose sheets of paper lying on top. Nothing of interest. After checking the desk drawers, he shone the flashlight around the edge of the room. There was a laptop case tucked alongside a small bookshelf. He went over and picked it up. It was obvious from the weight of it that the laptop was still inside, so he kneeled on the floor and started putting the case into his carryall.

Suddenly, the office light came on.

"What the hell are you doing?" demanded Diane Crawford, standing in the doorway.

Clyne struggled to focus in the bright light. He grabbed his bag and charged toward the door.

Crawford stood her ground. "I'm calling the police."

"Get out of my way," Clyne shouted.

"I'm not the only one here." Crawford turned her head toward the open-plan area outside Damon's office. "Pam, call the police."

Clyne wasn't falling for that one. "Move out of my way."

"I'm going nowhere."

He punched the side of Crawford's face. She fell backward, hitting her head hard against a desk, knocking her unconscious.

Clyne ignored her and, instead, zipped up his bag before racing out of the office. Fifteen minutes later, he drove away in his pick-up.

"Yeah?" Mylor said, recognizing the incoming call on his cell phone.

"We have some interesting stuff here," the voice at the other end of the line said.

"Go on."

"It turns out Traynor has been ignoring your instructions."

"What's he been up to?"

"From some of their meeting notes, it seems the partners at CCP plan to raise their concerns with the SLIDA board."

"That can't happen. What else?"

"We got his laptop. You won't believe how much money these guys make."

"Tell me something I don't know."

"There is something else, but you won't like it."

"I haven't got all night."

"His calendar shows he met with Kerry Ward."

"I know all about that; I was there. We met with him in Washington."

"I'm not talking about that. She met him in Boston too."

Mylor closed his eyes. "Is there anything else?"

"Yeah." A pause then, "A woman got hurt."

"Who? My instructions were not to go in unless the place was empty."

"We don't know yet. Probably one of Traynor's partners working late."

"Amateurs." Mylor shook his head. "Find out what happened and report back to me. Anything else?"

"No. That's all we have."

"Come back to me as soon as you learn who the woman is."

"Want me to deal with Traynor?"

"No, leave him to me. This requires a little more subtlety."

CHAPTER 31

Lunchtime Sunday, after dropping Kerry back at Logan International Airport, I headed straight for Beacon Hill. Some quiet time at home would help get my head straight. My mind was running overtime trying to process what I'd been told about Mylor. The more I thought about it, the less it seemed plausible. How could a senior Treasury official be responsible for the deaths of Tillman and Marcuri? It made no sense. I didn't want to doubt Kerry, but there had to be another explanation. She had to have been mistaken.

The answering machine's red blinking light in the hallway caught my attention the moment I got home. There were three messages—all from security at our office building—informing me of a break-in and sharing scant details of the attack on Diane Crawford. Why hadn't they called my cell? I jumped back into my car and raced to Brigham and Women's Hospital.

Before visiting Crawford in her private room, I learned that she'd had surgery on Saturday night to stem the bleeding in her brain. The doctors expected her to pull through, but she wouldn't be conscious for a couple of days, and there was no certainty there wouldn't be brain damage. They said they'd know more in a few days. For now, all they could do was let her rest.

"She speaks so highly of you," said Mary Crawford, Diane's mother, who'd spent the night at the hospital. She was sitting next to her daughter's bed with one hand constantly touching the bed cover. "I can't tell you how much she enjoys working at CCP."

"We're lucky to have her in our team," I said.

"She tells me how you go on at her to stop smoking. I tell her the same thing. Maybe now…" She burst into tears.

I walked around the bed and hugged her. "She'll pull through," I said. "I know Diane, she's a fighter—the toughest partner we have."

Mary forced a smile and wiped away the tears. "I'm sorry. She's all I have, since her father died three years ago."

"Have you eaten anything?"

"No. I'm not hungry."

"At least let me bring you a hot drink."

"Coffee would be nice."

Wiping the moisture from my eyes, I walked over to the coffee shop I'd spotted on my way in and ordered two strong lattes. While I was waiting for them to be made, a man in a cheap brown suit walked by the door and headed toward Crawford's room. Only his side profile was visible, but there was something familiar about him. I grabbed the coffees and rushed into the corridor before I lost sight of him. As he turned at the end of the passageway, I thought I recognized him. I was almost certain he was the same man who'd been staring at me at the airport cafe in Washington? What was he doing in Boston?

He slowed down when he approached Crawford's room and looked over his shoulder as though he was checking if anyone was watching. Quickly, I tucked in behind three nurses. Once at Crawford's door, the man held the handle and appeared to hesitate.

"Can I help you?" I asked when I caught up with him. Now we were up close, I could tell he was definitely the same person from Dulles airport. No doubt about it.

The man flinched, but said nothing.

Is this the coward who attacked Crawford? I thought as I threw him a shit-look. "Do I know you?"

The stranger stared at me. "I've no idea who you are," he said, contempt in his eyes. "I must have the wrong room." Then he walked away.

"Who are you looking for?"

He carried on walking and didn't respond.

"I've seen you before and I'd recognize you again," I shouted, watching as he disappeared around the corner.

"Who was that you were talking to outside?" Mary asked when I entered the room and handed her one of the coffees.

I sipped my drink while I chose my words carefully. "Just someone at the wrong room." Another sip. "Did the police say anything about what happened last night at our office? Do they know who attacked Diane?"

"All they'd say was that she was there working alone."

"That sounds like her."

"They think she must have disturbed an intruder, and that was why she was attacked." She pointed to her daughter in the bed. Crawford's face was swollen and bruised, and the top of her head was wrapped in a bandage. "How could anyone do this to her?" She started crying again.

First thing Monday morning, I called a partners' meeting. While I'd phoned them all Sunday night, I wanted to share the latest information I had on Crawford. The good news was she had begun to show signs of recovery overnight. That was something we could hold onto. Rumors about who could be behind the break-in had developed over the weekend, and the partners wanted to explore these. I insisted we stick to the facts, of which there were very few at that stage. That didn't mean I had no theory of my own as to who was responsible. The recent conversations I'd had with Kerry kept playing on my mind. But I couldn't mention any of this to my partners, as Kerry had told me everything in confidence.

163

"What we know now," I said, "is that there was one intruder. The police told me the man was dressed as a cleaner. They have some CCTV footage from a nearby building and in the stairwell, but it's grainy. This was no casual thief, however. They think he was a professional. It appears only my office was entered, and he got away with my laptop. Some of the cabinets in my room were also opened, but nothing seems to be missing. The police think he may well have stolen from the other offices if Diane hadn't disturbed him."

"We ought to split up Diane's workload," Gainham said. "I guess she won't be back for some time."

"I just hope she makes it back," I said. "I don't care how long it takes."

We spent an hour planning how to cover Crawford's work and then how we could increase security. At the end of the meeting, I asked Gainham to join me in my office.

"There's more to this, Chris," I said, closing my door. "This wasn't just a chance break-in."

"What do you mean?" Gainham asked, taking a seat.

"Remember the fire at Tillman's lawyer's office?"

"Of course."

"I think this could be connected."

"You think the same people attacked Diane?"

"I do." I remained standing. "You remember when we flew to Washington and we were killing time at Dulles that morning?"

"Yeah. Why?"

"I swear a man was watching us."

"Huh?"

"I didn't say anything at the time because I thought nothing of it. But I saw him again yesterday."

"Where?"

"Outside Diane's hospital room."

"What? Are you certain it was the same man?"

"There's no doubt in my mind. As soon as I challenged him,

he disappeared. I've no idea what he wanted, but I think he's following us."

"Have you told the police?"

"No. What could I tell them? Officer, I saw a man at the hospital in Boston yesterday and I'm sure I saw him in a coffee shop at the airport in Washington."

"That doesn't sound too good, does it? Do you think he was about to attack Diane again yesterday?"

"It's possible. He may be trying to shut her up. It's likely she saw him before she was injured."

"What should we do?"

"I've arranged for a private guard to sit outside her hospital room."

"I still think you ought to share this with the police."

"Maybe you're—" My phone rang. I walked to my desk and hit the speaker button. "Damon Traynor."

"It's Adrian Livesey. I assume you've got the right answer for me."

Gainham looked confused.

I shook my head. That was just what we didn't need at that moment. More pressure from Livesey. "We're not selling SLIDA. Period."

"Are you completely insane?" Livesey shouted.

"There's nothing for us to discuss."

"Hold on a moment—"

I terminated the call.

"What was that all about?" asked Gainham.

"Mendocino won't give up. I haven't had a chance to talk to you about it yet, but they came back last week with a higher offer. That was me turning it down. We still need to be certain that SLIDA works before we think about selling it. And the picture on that is becoming less clear by the day."

"I guess it makes sense to put them on hold for now."

"Besides, if Mendocino want it now, they'll want it even more in a few years' time."

"I've got to know. How high was their latest offer?"

"Five times our money."

Gainham flinched. "Are you serious?"

CHAPTER 32

"He really is very busy," our receptionist said. "His calendar shows him in back to back meetings. I can give you his PA's contact details if you'd like to call and make an appointment."

"Just tell him the man he met at the hospital is here to see him," said the man in the cheap brown suit, leaning over the reception desk. "That'll get his attention."

"Let me try him for you." She pursed her lips and picked up the phone. "Damon, I'm sorry to interrupt, but I have two gentlemen in reception who say they need to speak to you urgently. I've explained you're in meetings, but they insist on seeing you. One of them says you met at the hospital." She replaced the receiver and smiled at the men. "He'll be here in a few moments." She pointed to the waiting area. "Please take a seat."

I left my meeting and raced over to Gainham's office. "Chris, you'll never believe who's in reception."

Gainham looked up from his PC. "Elvis?"

"I'm serious. The man I told you about from the hospital. He's here and says he wants to see me."

"What's he doing here?"

"I've no idea. Apparently, there are two of them. Can you join me?"

"Try stopping me." Gainham grabbed his suit jacket from the back of his chair.

I picked up Gainham's phone and asked our receptionist to

take the visitors through to the boardroom.

"Did you report the guy to the police?" Gainham asked, putting on his jacket.

"I did. They took his description, but they didn't seem that interested."

"Amazing."

"I can't blame them. All I could say was that I'd seen him before. That's hardly a crime. Besides, the police have now spoken to Diane, and she gave them a description of her attacker. It turns out he looks completely different from my man."

"It's still a bit weird, though."

"Come on. Let's find out what they want."

We hurried to the boardroom. The man I'd seen at the hospital was wearing the same suit, with a cream shirt and no tie. He looked athletic and in his thirties, but it was difficult to tell as much of his face was covered by a close-cropped beard. Sitting next to him was a short man in his fifties. He had on an expensive, blue Armani jacket over a white open-necked shirt and a pair of jeans. He had Asian features, but I couldn't tell exactly where he was from.

No smiles, no handshakes, just a nodding of heads as we took our seats on the opposite side of the table.

"Thanks for seeing us," the younger of the two visitors said.

"You owe us an explanation," I said.

"You'll have it. My name is Tom Chisholm." He turned to his colleague. "This is Ken Wei."

"This is Chris Gainham," I replied, pointing to my partner with the back of my right hand. "You appear to know who I am."

Chisholm smirked. "Yes. We know who you are. In fact, we know most everything about this firm."

I glanced at Gainham. Where the hell was this conversation going? Was Mylor behind these people? Were they some sort of IRS investigations team? Had Kerry been trying to warn me about this on our trip? It was clear she knew more than she could say. But what would the IRS be doing at Crawford's hospital room?

"We're listening."

"We know you received an offer for SLIDA recently," Chisholm said. "A very good offer."

I sat upright in my chair. "We don't discuss portfolio matters with strangers."

"We know you've turned down two offers for the company."

"What does any of this have to do with you?"

"We'd like to understand why you weren't interested."

"Damon just told you politely. Let me spell it out," Gainham said, uncrossing his arms. "Mind your own damn business."

Chisholm held eye contact with Gainham a little too long. Both men looked as though they were about to punch each other.

"Okay, smartass, we won't waste any more time," Chisholm said. "Mendocino is our company. Shipperley Brothers was acting on our behalf."

I jumped to my feet. "We made our position abundantly clear to Adrian Livesey. SLIDA is not for sale." At least they weren't from the IRS or anything to do with Mylor. Thank goodness for that small mercy. They were just a couple of time-wasters, hoping to persuade us to alter our position by forcing a face to face meeting. But that still didn't explain why Chisholm had been following us. "This meeting is over."

Chisholm banged the table with his fist. "Sit down. We haven't finished."

I remained standing. I wasn't going to be dictated to by this hot-head. "Come on, Chris, our visitors are about to leave." Gainham stood.

Wei placed his right hand on Chisholm's left forearm, and leaned forward. "Gentlemen, you should have taken the money when it was on the table," he said in a quiet, but authoritative tone. His accent was more British than American. "Mendocino is not what you think it is. Please, sit down."

Gainham looked confused when he threw me a quick glance.

"You have five minutes before we have you thrown out of here," I said, taking my seat again. Gainham followed.

Wei nodded at Chisholm to continue.

"Mendocino is a private group of U.S. companies with interests in many different defense activities."

I shook my head. "We know all this. We don't need the sales pitch."

Chisholm looked at Wei, who nodded again.

"What you don't know is that Mendocino is a front. Its real owner is the Chinese government."

Gainham threw his hands into the air. "What is this?"

Chisholm ignored him and pressed on. "The U.S. would never allow a strategic defense asset like SLIDA to fall into foreign ownership. Mendocino was set up many years ago to appear as American as Ford or Chrysler."

My brain flooded with a mixture of alarm, shock and confusion. Now, at least, I knew why we'd been followed. "We have nothing further to discuss with you."

Wei leaned forward again. "As I said, Mr. Traynor, you should have accepted our generous offer. That would have been much easier for everyone."

"Our investment is not for sale, least of all to you."

"We are going to obtain SLIDA's technology. If only you had taken the money—"

"That's not going to happen."

"We will contact you soon with the detailed technical information we require—"

"You're not listening."

"I hear you, Mr. Traynor."

"I'd like you to leave. Now!"

"You really do not want to stand in our way."

"Is that a threat?" Gainham asked.

Wei ignored Gainham and fixed his gaze on me. "As my friend here said, we know everything about your firm: its people, their families, and where they all live. We have been watching you for some considerable time. Believe me, we have done our homework. I understand one of your partners is in hospital. Please don't make me spell it out for you."

I rose to my feet. "Go to hell," I said before walking out of the room.

CHAPTER 33

After making sure Wei and Chisholm—probably not their real names—had left, I instructed our receptionist to call the police if they ever showed up again. Gainham and I then returned to my office.

"We have to report this," Gainham said, closing the door behind him.

I sat behind my desk and stared at the window. "We can't do that."

"We don't have a choice, Damon."

"Think about it. If we report it, and word gets out the authorities are crawling all over SLIDA, it could destroy the entire value of our investment." There was also another, more important, reason it would be unwise to take this to the police right now—what I'd learned about Mylor and how dangerous he might be. But I couldn't share that with Gainham. "There's only one way out of this."

Gainham was pacing around the room as if he needed to work off some excess energy. "I'm glad you can see a way out. How did we get into this mess?"

"We're going to see Mylor. If he doesn't want us to sell SLIDA, he'll just have to buy it back from us."

"Do you think he'd do that?"

"This is much bigger than us. This is a problem for the government to fix. It shouldn't be left for us to deal with."

"I doubt Mylor would choose to write us a check. There must be some way we can force his hand."

"I can't see how we can compel him to do anything."

Gainham pulled up a chair at my desk. "What if we went public with this?"

"That would certainly get his attention."

"The government couldn't risk leaving SLIDA with us then. Mylor would have to take it back."

I leaned back in my chair, stretching my clasped hands behind my head. "We can't risk our investment. Besides, Mylor won't like being strong-armed."

"Look, the guys we just met mean business. We need to take control before this thing swallows us up. I know you said the description Diane gave was different, but I think they were behind the burglary and her attack. Maybe they were trying to send us an early message, to show us they're serious."

"I don't disagree. Whatever we do, we don't have much time before those guys come back."

Gainham laughed. "You know, there's some good news in all this."

"If there is, I can't see it."

"If the Chinese have been tracking SLIDA for some time, and are so keen to get hold of the technology, it sort of proves it must work."

"I guess that's right. Tillman was making trouble, after all." I stood, walked to my window, and watched the traffic on the street below.

"Even if we can make Mylor take it back, there's still something pissing me off," Gainham said.

"The price?"

"Exactly. He can't just have it back for what we paid for it. We need some profit on the deal, especially given the pain it's caused us."

"But we know now the Mendocino offer wasn't real."

"We'd need to show some profit for our investors."

"I'd be happy to get our money back right now."

"That doesn't sound like you, Damon."

I turned from the window to face Gainham. "Listen, I've

learned a few things about Mylor and the way he operates. We can't risk making him any more of an enemy than he already is. If he'd take it back for the same price we paid, I'd grab it with both hands."

Gainham tilted his head. "What have you learned?"

"I can't go into details, so don't press me on it. All I can say is that Mylor could be dangerous."

"He doesn't frighten me."

"There's more to this, but I can't say—"

"You can't leave it like that. What have you learned?"

"I'm sorry, but I really can't tell you right now."

Gainham held up his palms. "Okay. I guess."

"I'd like to know what the other partners think before we rush into anything. Let's call a meeting for tomorrow morning."

"We need to move quickly. I'm more worried about the Chinese than Mylor. If they attacked Diane, there's no telling what they'll do next if they don't get their way."

CHAPTER 34

Gainham was careful not to make any noise when he closed the front door of his townhouse behind him. That would only wake up the girls. He slipped the key into his shorts then glanced at his Polar watch—two minutes to six. His regular four-mile morning run took him along Grove Street, right onto Revere, and then onto Charles Street. The traffic was usually light this time of day, which meant he didn't have to stop at most intersections. Breaking his pace for cars was irritating when there was a chill in the air.

Running past The Charles Street Inn, he crossed an already busy Beacon Street at the pedestrian lights outside Starbucks, and continued into Boston Common. A strong smell of fried onions wafted over from the deli behind him. He checked his watch again—six-ten—bang on schedule. Once in the park, Gainham increased his speed, no longer having to worry about cars cutting him up. He sprinted about a hundred yards, slowed down, then sprinted again, a pattern he repeated several times while checking his heart rate on the Polar.

As he ran, he played back in his mind yesterday's meeting. Damon had seemed overly anxious about Mylor, but the real threat was posed by the Chinese. They meant business and weren't going away. Once he got into the office that morning, he'd have another go at persuading Damon to force Mylor's hand. The government had to take SLIDA back and quickly.

Approaching the baseball field, he passed a man walking a black Labrador. Gainham nodded to the man, more to thank him for keeping the dog on its leash than to acknowledge him.

Not all dog owners were that considerate of runners. At the other side of the common, he headed north along a path that ran parallel with Tremont Street for a few minutes, before turning left. The State House's gold dome rose up in front of him. He was now at the halfway point in his routine. Another check of the Polar.

He unzipped his outer running jacket and wiped his brow with the back of his left hand. When he ran past the bank of Persian ironwood trees facing the frog pond, the noise of the traffic building up on Beacon Street grew louder.

In the poor light up ahead was the silhouette of a man. He was sitting on a bench facing the pond and seemed to be drinking from a bottle. Gainham increased his pace a little as he approached the man. He wore a filthy trench coat and had long, gray hair. The smell of alcohol grew stronger the closer Gainham got to the bench.

The man turned his head. "Can you spare any change?" he asked, slurring his words.

"I'm sorry, I don't have any money with me," Gainham shouted, holding up his empty hands.

"Thanks for nothing."

Gainham thought about saying something, but decided to ignore him and turned his head back toward the path.

Suddenly, another man, dressed in a black tracksuit, stepped out from behind one of the trees in front of him.

Gainham darted to the left to avoid him, but the man stepped right into his path. Gainham tried to slow down, but still collided with the man, a sharp pain ripping through Gainham's chest as he fell. He crashed to the ground and rolled onto his back, the taste of iron filling his mouth. He coughed then choked on his own blood.

The man in the tracksuit stood over him and pulled a six-inch knife from Gainham's upper body before using it to slice across his neck. Then he walked over to the drunk on the bench. "There you go," he said, throwing him a fifty-dollar note. "Nice work. Treat yourself to another couple of bottles."

I had almost finished briefing the other partners on the meeting we had with Wei and Chisholm the day before when the call came in on the boardroom speakerphone.

"Sorry to interrupt the meeting, Damon, but I have Chris's wife on the phone," our receptionist said.

"We were wondering where he was," I said, looking around the table.

"She said it's urgent. She sounds really upset."

An icy chill ran down my neck. "Put the call through to my office in thirty seconds."

I ran to my office and grabbed the ringing phone. "Is Chris alright, Carol?"

"Damon, Chris is...He..." She began to cry.

I braced myself for shocking news, tightening my grip on the telephone handset. "Carol. Carol. Take your time."

"Chris was attacked while out on his run this morning."

I closed my eyes. "Is he okay?" There was no answer. "Please tell me he's okay."

"He's dead." More tears.

While I'd expected bad news from Carol's tone, nothing could prepare me for this hammer blow. My breathing stopped, and a crushing cloud descended on me, sucking all energy from my body. My eyes, wide open, focused on the yellow legal pad in front of me. One lone word rose off the page of my hand-written notes: Mylor. Was this his work? Had Kerry been right all along? Had that bastard taken the life of my closest friend?

"I'm so sorry. Chris is like a brother to me. How—?"

"I can't talk now."

"I understand. Can I come over?"

"I'd like that. The police are here, and I don't know what—"

"I'm on my way."

After I finished the call, I dropped my head into my hands.

My best friend had been sitting across my desk just a few hours before, and now he was gone—taken from his wife and young daughters forever. No one would ever enjoy his passion for life, his sense of humor, his loyalty again. My eyes watered. It had to be Mylor's work. Kerry had tried to warn me. Did she fear something like this might happen? Did Mylor know, somehow, that Gainham wanted to force his hand by going public? If he did, that would mean only one thing: Mylor must have bugged CCP's offices. How else could he have known? Where was all this going? The questions kept coming, and the more they came, the more I vowed Mylor would suffer for this. He'd suffer the same loss, the same pain, the same hopelessness.

CHAPTER 35

The days that followed were a blur, filled with breaking the news of Gainham's death to our investors and staff and helping Carol plan the funeral arrangements. Sleep was impossible. In the middle of the night, I'd lie awake, asking myself whether I could have done something, anything, to prevent what happened to my closest friend. Should I have acted more on Kerry's information? Should I have pushed her further for specifics on her boss? What more did she know? What else might I have done to prevent this?

The more I thought about the events of the past few weeks, the greater the urge for revenge consumed me. Who was Mylor? How could a man working for the Treasury Department be involved in the things Kerry had described? It still didn't make sense.

I had to see him—have it out with him face to face.

"Have you any idea what the time is?" asked Kerry, taking my call.

"I'm sorry. I needed to talk to someone," I said, sitting up in bed and holding the bedside telephone in my right hand.

"It's four o'clock in the morning. Couldn't it wait?"

"No, not really."

"What is it? You don't sound very well. Are you okay, Damon?"

"Chris Gainham is dead."

"What? Oh my...I'm so sorry." There was a pause while Kerry absorbed the news. "What happened to him?"

"I'm hoping your boss can tell me."

"I don't understand."

"He was murdered."

"What? And you think Mylor had something to do with it?"

"Who is Mylor, Kerry? I mean, really. Who is he?"

Silence at the other end of the line, then, "I don't know how to answer that."

"It's a simple enough question."

"I told you not to push me when we were in Rockport."

"You also warned me about him. Why would someone from the Treasury be involved in all the things you mentioned? It makes no sense."

"What was Chris doing?"

"What do you mean?"

"Were you guys still raising questions about SLIDA?"

"We'd agreed to explore things further with the SLIDA board."

"And you did that?"

"Not yet. What is it, Kerry? Where are we going with this?"

"I don't think this is Mylor."

"I'm not convinced. I want to meet him. I want to look into his eyes and ask him if he killed Chris. I want to know who the hell he is."

"You don't want to do that. Please don't do that."

"If that animal is responsible for Chris's death—"

"You need to calm down, Damon. Promise me you'll do that. Promise me you won't do anything stupid."

"I am calm. I want you to set up the meeting up for me."

"I can't do that. Not when you're like this."

"Then I'll have to go around you."

"Listen. Here's what I'll do. Promise me you'll do nothing before the end of the week. I'll call you over the weekend, and if you still want to meet him, I'll arrange it. Okay?"

"I'll want to meet him."

"I hear you. Try to get some sleep. I'm really sorry to hear about Chris. I know how close you guys were."

* * *

When I pulled up at my townhouse the next night, I noticed a blue Corolla parked outside. There was no one in it, but the windows were misted up. I was almost up the steps leading to my front door when I heard footsteps behind me. As I closed the door, Chisholm appeared, jamming his right foot in the doorway.

I jumped back. "What the—?"

Chisholm pushed his way into the entrance hall.

"I told you to go to hell," I said.

Chisholm body-slammed me against the wall.

Fury took over and, instinctively, I threw a punch with my right fist, landing him hard on his left cheek.

Chisholm kicked my legs from under me.

I collapsed to the floor, face down.

He kneeled between my shoulder blades and grabbed me around the neck with his right arm, pulling my head back until I began to choke. "I'll snap your neck if you don't stop moving," he said close to my left ear. His breath smelled of tobacco.

I struggled to speak. "Okay."

Chisholm slammed my head onto the tiled floor as he stood. "Get up," he said, retrieving a pistol from his jacket pocket. "I need to talk to you." He pointed to the sitting room with the pistol. "In there."

Coughing, I pushed my body up from the floor and hobbled through to the sitting room, keeping my eye on the gun.

"Close the shutters," he said.

I did what I was told then stood next to one of my leather armchairs. "What do you want?"

Chisholm sat on the sofa. "Sit down where I can see you." He took out a stack of folded papers from his inside coat pocket and threw them onto the glass coffee table between us. "This will take some time."

I sat and pointed to the papers. "What are they?"

"Some of the information we're gonna need on SLIDA. They'll be more. A whole lot more."

"I told you we're not going to help you."

"You'll do what we tell you." Chisholm pointed the handgun toward me.

"And you'll shoot me if I don't? Where will that get you? I'm the only one from CCP who sits on the SLIDA board. I'm the only one with access to what you need."

"I won't shoot you."

"Didn't think so."

"I'll kill one of your partners. The last one choked on his own blood as I plunged my knife into his chest."

A cocktail of shock and contempt barreled through me as I tried to process what I was hearing. This man had killed my best friend and he was in my home bragging about it. I wanted to dive across the table and rip his head off. "You heartless fuck. Chris was no threat to you."

"You needed to know we were serious. We offered you the easy way, but you turned down the money. Twice. Remember?"

"You know he has a wife and two young daughters?"

Chisholm gave a *who-gives-a-shit* shrug. "That should make you think about your other partners all the more. I know they have families too."

"Even if I agreed to help you, your plan won't work."

Chisholm snorted. "And why is that?"

"There's no way I can obtain technical data on SLIDA. I sit on the main board, dealing with strategic matters only. It would raise red flags everywhere if I started asking detailed questions."

"You'll find a way. You're a bright boy." Chisholm slid the papers across the glass table. "Pick them up. I want to make sure you understand exactly what we need."

"This won't work," I said, shaking my head.

"Your next board meeting in Sausalito is coming up. We'll give you one week after that to collect the first batch of information and get it to us." Chisholm threw a card at me.

"Call me on that number when you have it ready for me to collect."

"This will never—"

"You fail to deliver then Crawford will be next."

CHAPTER 36

The moment Chisholm left, I called Kerry. "I have to see Mylor immediately."

"I thought you agreed to wait until the weekend," she said.

"I'll explain everything when we meet. Just set the meeting up."

"Not if you're going to start throwing your weight around."

"I won't. I know now he had nothing to do with Chris's murder."

"You do? What happened to him?"

"Look, just set the meeting up. I'll tell you everything when we meet, but it has to be soon."

"That's going to be tricky."

"Why?"

"Mylor's out of the country next week."

"How about tomorrow? I can meet him anywhere."

"I'm with him in Cleveland tomorrow."

"I can get there."

"Even if he has the time, he won't agree to meet without knowing why you want to see him."

I thought for a moment. What was the harm in Mylor knowing something in advance? "Tell him it's to do with SLIDA and an imminent threat to national security."

"If I do this, Damon, promise me you're not going to use the meeting to ask him to consent to a sale. That would not be wise."

"I understand that."

"Promise me."

"Okay, okay. I promise."

"I'll see what I can do and I'll call you in the morning."

The following morning, my plane landed at Cleveland Hopkins International Airport at eight-forty-seven. I hadn't yet heard from Kerry, but I'd booked the flight in hopes of a meeting with Mylor anyway. Kerry wouldn't let me down; she understood how important this was to me. Once inside the terminal, I checked my voicemail—still no word from her. When my cab dropped me downtown, I found a coffee shop at a hotel on East Ninth Street and Euclid. I figured if the meeting went ahead, it was likely to be somewhere downtown, so I might as well kill time there.

The call finally came in just before eleven. "He's agreed to see you," Kerry said.

"What did you tell him?"

"I said you feared there'd been a breach of national security and that it was urgent."

"Close enough. Where are we meeting?"

"At a place called Beachwood."

"Where?"

"It's a few miles east of Cleveland. Get a cab from the airport. I'll text the address to you."

I decided not to tell her I was already in Cleveland. "What time?"

"Four o'clock. Don't be late. We'll be leaving here at five."

There was no risk of being late. The problem was how I was going to spend the next five hours. "I'll be there. Don't worry about me."

I headed down to the lakefront and took a tour of the Cleveland Browns' football stadium. Dad had always been a big Browns fan. I remember when I was growing up, Dad kept going on about Bernie Kosar, their star quarterback. During the tour, my thoughts turned to Gainham and what a great football

185

player he was at college. We'd had some wonderful times together, and I was only just beginning to realize the massive hole he was going to leave in my life.

By mid-afternoon, I was in a cab leaving the downtown area. As we drove through Shaker Heights, I admired the older established single-family homes with teams of gardeners tending their manicured lawns. Chagrin Boulevard continued east toward Beachwood. I told the driver the address: 67223 Commerce Park Road.

A few minutes later, we pulled up next to a white, low-rise warehouse surrounded by trees. I counted only two windows on the outside. No signs or logos on the building to indicate what went on inside, and only a few cars occupied the large parking lot. I thought it might be some kind of low-profile data center used by the Treasury.

I paid the driver and walked into the featureless reception. White walls, with no pictures, surrounded the small reception counter, behind which sat a dour looking woman in her forties. "I'm here to see Ben Mylor and Kerry Ward," I said.

"Take a seat," she said, without raising her head.

As I sat in the small waiting area pretending to check for emails on my iPhone, a door leading off reception opened. I looked up, and a man in his fifties, dressed in a dark gray suit, walked out. For a moment, he made eye contact with me then continued toward the exit.

Ten minutes later, I looked at my watch for the third time— eight minutes past four. What was Mylor up to? I hadn't come all this way for nothing.

At four-fifteen, Kerry came out to collect me. "Damon, sorry about the delay. Our previous meeting ran over."

I managed a thin smile. "Don't worry about it. Thanks for arranging this for me."

Kerry led me along a brown, windowless corridor, which provided no clues about how the building was used. All the office doors we passed were closed. When we reached the open door of a small corner meeting room, Kerry tapped the doorframe and we walked in. Mylor was sitting on the other side of the table, facing us. As usual, he made no effort to stand up to shake my hand. Kerry took her seat next to Mylor while I sat directly across from him. That way, I could look him straight in the eyes.

"You wanted to see me," he said, pushing to the side a pad with handwritten notes on it. "This had better be good."

There was a small upturn at the corners of Kerry's mouth when she looked at me. Was she trying to say I should, again, forgive the bad-mannered jerk she had for a boss in that half-smile?

"Something's happened," I said.

"You know I don't want to hear about any more offers for the company."

"That's not why I'm here." The relief was obvious on Kerry's face.

Mylor had on his best poker expression. "Good."

"One of my partners has been killed."

"I know."

"You do?"

"Kerry told me. I'm sorry to hear it." His face didn't look that sympathetic.

"Well, that's why I wanted to see you."

"What's it got to do with me?"

"It turns out the people who made the offer to buy SLIDA were not who they said they were."

Mylor tilted his head. "Is this going anywhere?"

I ignored him. "When we turned them down, they paid us a visit. They said they still wanted SLIDA, and seeing as we wouldn't sell it to them, they told us we had to supply them with a list of information on SLIDA's technology."

"And you said?"

"I told them to go to hell, of course."

"You did the right thing. Who were these people?"

"They didn't really say. They told us the Chinese government owned the company that made the offer."

Mylor laughed. "Yeah. I bet they did."

"This isn't funny. They said if we don't agree to supply them with the information they want, something would happen to the people closest to us."

"You've been watching too many spy movies."

I peered into Mylor's eyes and held contact. "The next day Chris Gainham was killed—stabbed to death by these people."

"How do you know it was them?"

"Because last night I had another visit from one of them. He admitted to killing Chris and said if I didn't start supplying the data they need soon, they'd kill more of my partners."

Kerry shook her head and looked down at the table.

"What exactly do you expect me to do about it?" Mylor asked.

"I cannot stand by while these people threaten to kill my partners." I leaned forward. "I want you to buy back SLIDA. You need to take this problem away."

"That's out of the question."

"If you take it back, the Chinese will have no interest in us. We'd have no value to them."

"Lose any thoughts you have about us buying it back. That ain't going to happen." Mylor turned his head to Kerry. "You know, this could be a lucky break."

"I fail to see the luck in any of it," I said.

Mylor got up and poured himself some coffee in the corner of the room. He gulped down some of the warm drink as he thought. "Send me the list of things these people want."

"I don't have to." I reached into my briefcase. "I have it right here." I slid some papers across the table.

Mylor stood next to his side of the table, put down the coffee mug, and picked up the papers. He scanned them, nodded a couple of times, then placed them back down. "Here's what we'll do. We'll share these with our colleagues over at Homeland Security." He smirked. "I bet they'll jump at the opportunity to provide you with something for your new friends. They get to mislead the Chinese, while it takes some of the heat off you."

"That's not what I came here for."

Mylor leaned his weight onto the palms of his hands as he rested on the table. "There's no way we're buying back SLIDA. Get that idea out of your head."

I looked at Kerry. She offered no hint as to whether I ought to push Mylor further. "I don't like it."

"It's the best we can do," Mylor said, lifting his jacket from the back of his seat. "We have to go."

CHAPTER 37

Late afternoon, two days later, I received a bulky set of documents delivered to my office by special courier. The accompanying handwritten note read: "A little something for our Chinese friends. There's likely to be more." It was signed by Mylor. I flicked through some of the papers before placing them back in the large envelope. There was just over a week before Chisholm said he wanted the information or Crawford's life would be in danger. I didn't know what to do. Could I really get away with handing over false data on SLIDA? Wouldn't the Chinese find out it was fake sooner or later? At best, following Mylor's plan would buy a little more time. Then what?

Something else was troubling me too: my complete lack of trust in Kerry's boss. If I started handing over national secrets to another state, Mylor wouldn't think twice about using it against me if it suited his purpose. I'd have no defense. No one would care if the documents weren't authentic. As far as I could see, Mylor's half-baked plan would be too risky and would only sink us even deeper into the mire. I needed to talk this through with someone I trusted, someone whose judgment I respected, and someone who had our interests at heart. That someone was Gainham, of course. I'd always turned to him at difficult times like this.

I was starting to believe my friend had been right all along. Maybe the best way out of this mess was to go to the authorities or go public with what we knew. The only thing stopping me was the information Kerry had shared with me in confidence. She'd seemed terrified of Mylor as she warned me against crossing him during our weekend in Rockport.

Why was Kerry so sure he was dangerous? What exactly did she know? The more I asked these questions, the more I realized what little I knew about the man. I pushed the envelope to one side of my desk then launched Google on my PC. I typed in the search bar "Ben Mylor" and scrolled through the images and web pages in front of me, clicking on the links that might be relevant. None of them matched the man I knew. I even tried searching the website of the U.S. Department of the Treasury. When I found a page headed "Senior Treasury Officials," I expected to see Mylor listed, but I couldn't see him anywhere. Two more hours of searching followed, but still I found nothing. It was as if the man didn't exist; he was a ghost.

I walked to the kitchen and poured myself a large mug of coffee. It was going to be a long night as I decided I wouldn't leave until I'd found something on Mylor. The clock on the wall above the coffee machine showed it was a little after seven. That time on a Friday evening, most of our staff had left, so the office was quiet. As I passed through the open plan area on the way back from the kitchen, a couple of junior analysts tapped away at keyboards and worked on spreadsheets. I stopped and chatted with them briefly. The firm had a full deal pipeline and, by now, some seventy percent of the fund had been invested or committed, so strong had been the flow of opportunities since we'd acquired SLIDA. If we didn't sort out the nightmare that investment had become, there would never be another fund.

Returning to my desk, I began to research U.S. government asset sales over the last couple of months. It was public knowledge the government was strapped for cash and had sold off a record number of federal assets to pay down debt. The news reports I found were filled with commentaries and stories about these desperate deals to raise money. Each time I came across a new transaction, I trawled through the list of advisers and principals, but still I could find no mention of Mylor.

By nine-forty-five, I had identified and researched a list of seventeen federal asset sales, including the sale of SLIDA to CCP. Almost all these transactions had been handled by Orlando Barrett of DH&W, and all of them had been sold to cash-rich financial institutions around the world. None had been sold to a trade buyer, which made no sense to me.

When the last analyst left around eleven o'clock, I checked the glass entrance door in reception was locked. Since Crawford's attack, all of us had been more conscious of office security. I returned to my office and stopped to stretch at the window. The lights of Boston reached out in front of me until they hit the sea. Marcuri had met his death somewhere out there in the cold waters beyond the harbor. I kept playing back what Kerry said—how she thought Mylor was connected with the helicopter accident in some way.

Back at my desk, I looked at my handwritten list of asset sales next to the PC. Starting at the top, I searched for news reports on each company since it had been sold by the government. By the time I'd finished researching the first ten deals, I'd noted six deaths of senior executives at the institutions that now owned the assets. I counted three reported suicides and three accidental deaths, all involving people in their thirties and forties. Now I'm no actuary, but it seemed inconceivable these were chance events. My throat tightened. Was this what Kerry was trying to share with me?

I needed to know more, so I continued my search. The eleventh asset on my list was the sale of the only remaining government-owned oil refinery—a quirk of history since all the others had been sold off decades ago. The business operated from a massive site twenty miles southwest of Galveston on the Gulf of Mexico. It had been sold by Barrett to the Gulf States' sovereign wealth fund one month before we bought SLIDA. The first story I found was from the *London Evening Standard* describing the death of Paul McCann, the London head of new investments at the fund. He'd been responsible for negotiating and completing the acquisition. The article set out McCann's impressive career. He'd been recruited from Europe's leading private equity player, 3i, only two years earlier to step up the investment rate from the rapidly growing cash pile in the fund. He was in his forties and had left behind a wife and an eight-year-old daughter. The coroner had recorded an open verdict on his death. Some witnesses suggested he'd jumped in front of the speeding train at Liverpool Street underground station, while others thought the overcrowding on the platform had led to his untimely accidental death.

Why would a family man in the middle of a successful career jump in front of a train? This was now the seventh death on my list, and I suspected I was about to discover more.

CHAPTER 38

The Virgin Atlantic 747 landed at Heathrow at six-fifty-five a.m. I reached for my overnight bag in the locker above my head and, a few minutes later, joined the heaving masses at passport control. I could have done without the hassle, having managed no sleep on the overnight flight. The British man sitting next to me in business class had kept going on about his debut novel and all the attention it was receiving. I regretted ever asking him, out of courtesy just after takeoff, what he did for a living.

It took an hour to reach the front of the line. The border patrol officer apologized for the delay, blaming the fog. Apparently, all transatlantic flights had come in together once it had lifted. I was in no mood to argue.

"Where to guv'nor?" asked the chirpy driver when I climbed into the back of the black cab outside terminal three.

"Number one Duchess Street," I said, reading the address from my iPhone.

"Hope you're not in a hurry, mate. The M4's backed up. It's a bleedin' disaster. Must've been an accident or something. I reckon we're better off taking the Uxbridge Road."

I shrugged. "Sounds good to me," I said, as though I knew the London road network intimately.

The driver examined me in his rearview mirror. "Where do you work then? The BBC?"

"No. Why do you say that?"

"I drop off a lot of luvvies there."

I frowned. "I'm sorry, but I don't follow."

"Duchess Street is just behind the new BBC building. They've built a palace there—all with taxpayers' money, I might add."

I nodded. All I wanted was quiet so I could take a nap. Was I really going to have to listen to the driver droning on all the way into central London? I leaned my head on the side window and let his words float over me. I must have drifted off as it seemed only minutes later we pulled into Duchess Street.

"Here you go, mate," said the driver, jarring me into consciousness. He pointed across the road to the BBC. "Told you it was a palace, didn't I?"

I yawned. "It certainly is," I said, paying him.

"Thanks. Here's your receipt. Good talking to you."

I glanced at my watch—nine twenty-five. I had about half an hour to kill before my meeting, so I found a Caffè Nero around the corner on Portland Place and bought a double macchiato. I needed the caffeine kick to wake me up.

"I'm here to see Richard Leigh," I said after entering the terrazzo-tiled reception of the Gulf States' sovereign wealth fund headquarters. A few moments later, a slim, graying man in his late fifties came to collect me.

"Richard Leigh," he said, extending his hand.

I smiled and shook his hand. "Damon Traynor. Thank you for seeing me."

"Not at all. Come on through."

We walked into a wood-paneled meeting room just off the reception area. Through the south-facing window, the BBC building filled the view. "It looks impressive," I said, pointing across the street.

"Yes, the BBC extended Broadcasting House a couple of years ago. Not the best of timing in the middle of a recession." Leigh poured tea into two porcelain cups. "You said you would like to discuss our acquisition of the Galveston oil refinery." He placed a cup in front of me before taking a seat across the table. "How can I help?"

I rubbed the bristly shadow around my chin. "I'm not here to buy it."

Leigh's face reflected a strange mixture of disappointment and relief. "Then how can I help you?"

"Look, I'm going to go put my neck on the line here."

Leigh narrowed his eyes. "I'm listening."

"Was there anything wrong with the business when you bought it?"

"I'm sorry?"

"Anything strange about it or the acquisition process?" Leigh looked confused. "You see, we bought an asset from the U.S. government around the same time. Let's just say we've had problems."

"I'm afraid you've lost me."

I paused and sipped some tea while I contemplated a different approach. "I read something about Paul McCann's death."

Leigh straightened his back. "What do you know about Paul? Did you know him?"

"No. I only know what I've read online, but it was enough for me to jump on a plane to come and see you. It looked suspicious to me."

"I think you might have traveled a long way on a wasted journey. Paul died in an unfortunate accident on the underground near our Bishopsgate office. I don't wish to be rude, but I cannot understand what this could possibly have to do with you."

Maybe Leigh didn't know anything and McCann's death was just an accident after all. Maybe I wasting my time there, but having made the journey, I had to find out what, if anything, Leigh knew. It was worth pressing on.

"McCann was not the only person to die in suspicious circumstances." I watched carefully for Leigh's reaction.

He unfolded his arms, but I couldn't tell whether this was news to him. "I don't understand."

"By my count, in recent weeks there have been between five

and ten suspicious deaths of senior execs in investment houses around the world. The one thing they all had in common was they'd recently bought large assets from the U.S. government."

"Mr. Traynor, I'm afraid you have lost me. I cannot help you with any of this. You have come a long way for nothing." Leigh looked at the clock on the wall. "Now, if you'll forgive me, I have another meeting out of the office." He stood and gestured toward the door.

From his reaction, my host must have thought I was an idiot. Now I knew how Tillman must have felt when he'd first tried to make me listen to his far-fetched story. I stood and picked up my bag. "I'm sorry for wasting your time."

"No trouble at all," Leigh said as he led me into the reception area.

I shook his hand. "Thanks for seeing me anyway."

"Goodbye."

Once I was back on Duchess Street, I turned right, and then right again to head north on Portland Place. The traffic flowed against me, making it easier for me to look for a cab. I raised my left arm when I spotted a black cab with its yellow roof light lit up. As it slowed down, I felt a tug on my shoulder.

"Mr. Traynor, please follow me," Leigh said, waving away the taxi. The driver shook his head and mouthed a profanity.

"What's going on?" I asked.

"I'll explain in a moment. Please follow me."

He hurried north along Portland Place without saying a word. Soon after, we entered a 1920s art deco-style building. The sign inside the entrance read: The Royal Institute of British Architects. *What are we doing here?* I thought. *What's Leigh up to?*

"I know just the place." He raced up the stairs. At the top of the wide staircase was a cavernous café with high ceilings and seats spaced well apart. "There, in the corner," he said, pointing to two leather armchairs.

"What is this place?" I asked as I took my seat.

Leigh sat in the other chair. "The RIBA café. I use it all the time. Not many people realize it's open to the public."

A waiter came over and took our order.

"I owe you an explanation," Leigh said when the waiter left. "I didn't want to talk about all this in our office, just in case."

"In case of—"

"It will all become clear."

"So you don't think I'm crazy?"

Leigh smiled. "No, far from it, Damon. May I call you Damon?"

"Of course."

The waiter brought over our drinks—a sparkling San Pellegrino for me and an apple and mango J2O for Leigh.

Leigh slid his chair a little closer to mine and leaned in toward me. "Although I was his boss, Paul was also a good friend. I recruited him from 3i a couple of years ago. He and I both worked there in the early nineties and we'd remained friends ever since." Leigh looked around the room to check if anyone was listening before he continued. "Paul was not the sort of man to kill himself. I know that's what some of the newspapers speculated, but it's just not true." He leaned even closer to me and lowered his voice. "I think he was killed. Someone pushed him in front of that tube train."

A wave of relief washed over me. I closed my eyes. At last, someone else can see what's going on.

"I don't think he was the only one," I said.

"That doesn't surprise me at all."

"Why do you think Paul was killed?"

"He asked too many questions. He'd discovered things about our investment he didn't like and wouldn't let them drop."

"What sort of things?"

"We paid a very full price for the oil refinery. It suited our portfolio well, and we thought it would be one we'd hold for many years. Paul did the deal and he sat on the board. Pretty soon after we acquired it, he discovered the figures we'd been given in the sale memorandum were massively inflated. In reality, the profits were nowhere near as good as we were led to believe."

"Didn't any of that come out in the due diligence?"

"Good question. Like a lot of deals, this one had a vendor due diligence report that came with it. It had been put together by DH&W in New York. We knew them and trusted them."

"Orlando Barrett?"

"Yes. How did you know?"

"He handled our transaction too."

Leigh looked as though he had a bad taste in his mouth and wanted to spit. "I don't trust that man, let me tell you."

"What did Paul do about the numbers?"

"He spoke to me about it and we agreed he should first raise it with Barrett. He put Paul in touch with his client—Ben Mylor at the Treasury Department."

My heart rate increased. "I know him."

"You do?"

"Oh yeah. I've met him. What did Mylor say?"

"He couldn't have cared less. He told Paul to keep his mouth shut or we'd never be allowed to buy another asset in the U.S. Of course, we were stunned by Mylor's reaction. I didn't like it any more than Paul, but we couldn't risk being shut out of the U.S. market, so I suggested we drop it. But Paul wasn't like that. He just couldn't let it go. He started digging further."

As Leigh described McCann, he could have been describing me. "Did he find anything?"

"Oh yes. Plenty. He went back to New York and grilled Barrett. He discovered we were the only bidders for the refinery."

"This is unreal. That's exactly what happened to us."

"I'm not surprised."

"You're not?"

Leigh looked over his shoulder before continuing. "Paul investigated all U.S. government asset sales around the time of our deal. As far as he could tell, all of them went to financial institutions. He spoke to a couple of the other buyers, and it turns out they thought they were the only bidders too."

"Why would the U.S. government do that?"

"Like you, I'm sure, when we bid for assets, we assume we're in competition for them. Indeed, Barrett did a good job of creating an air of competitive tension in our deal—except he was making it all up." Leigh stopped to finish his J2O. "On our deal, we weren't just the highest bidder, we were the only bidder. It turns out the whole auction process was a sham."

"But why would Barrett not run a real auction including trade buyers?"

"That's because they targeted only cash rich buyers. They weren't interested in selling to the trade. They didn't want complicated share or loan deals; they needed straight cash and quickly."

I lowered my head. "Incredible."

"You see, none of us won any auctions at all, we were targeted from the start, and Barrett was told to play his game on the sale process."

"The company we bought had technical problems. Yours had inflated numbers. How did Mylor ever think he'd be able to get away with all this?"

"Because he was clever. Yes, he targeted bidders with plenty of cash, but he also needed one more key ingredient." Leigh paused and stared at me as though he was uncertain whether to continue. "He needed bidders he could exercise some personal leverage over."

"How do you know that?"

"I'm afraid Paul found it out to his cost. I told you he wouldn't stop digging. He went back to see Mylor without my knowledge. He told him he was going to go sue him and publicize the fact that the U.S. government had defrauded us as a buyer, unless Mylor agreed to pay back some of the purchase price to reflect the true numbers. Mylor didn't like it—told him to keep his mouth shut or he'd regret it."

"That's exactly the way he reacted toward us. What did Paul do?"

"He came to see me. The man was in tears. He'd received a set of photos in the post. They showed him with another woman. Paul admitted to me he'd been having an affair with her for years. There was a note with the photos. It was un-signed, of course, but he knew it was from Mylor as it suggested he thought again about speaking out about the deal or contem-plating litigation."

"So why do you think he was killed?"

"The day before his death, Paul rang me. He said he couldn't let his personal life prevent him from doing the right thing and that he was going to tell his wife about the affair, so our fund could still sue the U.S. Treasury. He said he would hate her to learn about it from a complete stranger and that he owed it to her to be honest. I don't know if he ever told her as I never saw him again."

"You think Mylor found out about it somehow?"

"I'm certain of it. If he told his wife about the affair, Mylor's leverage over him disappeared. After that, he couldn't control what Paul would do next."

CHAPTER 39

Next morning, the return flight to Boston was only half-full, so I found two unoccupied seats together in business class and spread out. I needed some quiet space—free of phone calls and other interruptions—to think through what I should do next. I closed my eyes and listened to the hum of the jet engines. I'd spent the night before at the Mandarin Hotel in Knightsbridge, but all I managed was a few minutes of sleep, punctuated by long periods of staring at the ceiling, replaying the conversation with Richard Leigh. For the first time, I was beginning to comprehend the magnitude of the risks we were facing.

The parallels between Leigh's firm and CCP in their experience of dealing with the federal government were overwhelming. Obviously, Mylor wasn't who he said he was. He was a man with immense power, and yet he didn't show up in any Internet searches. Kerry had tried to warn me that he was dangerous, and now Leigh had just confirmed it. McCann had been killed by Mylor's people because he refused to keep quiet.

Exactly who was this man who claimed to work for the Treasury Department? Someone in a position to do these things, and get away with them, had to work for the CIA or some similar federal agency. As much as I dreaded the idea, I had to admit it made more sense than anything else I could think of right then.

"Would you like a drink, sir?" the flight attendant asked, bringing me hurtling back to consciousness.

"Er, yes. Just some water, please," I said, smiling.

The attendant poured some water in a glass half-filled with

ice and placed it on the table next to me. I reached into my briefcase lying on the next seat and took out a legal pad and pen. I started listing out the facts as I saw them, starting with Mylor. That was a very short list. Then I began to write out the questions to which I needed answers, and they kept coming. How did Kerry fit in to all this? Did she know everything Mylor was up to? Could she be trusted? Clearly, she didn't work for the Treasury Department either, even though I'd met her there in Washington. That had to have been a staged meeting. Was she watching me for Mylor? Was that her true role? That thought kept rolling around my head. I didn't want to believe it, but it was the logical conclusion. Kerry had to be on Mylor's side, acting as his eyes and ears. I felt used and betrayed.

The next word I scribbled on my notepad was SLIDA. In all probability, Tillman had been telling the truth all along. The technology didn't work, and yet the government managed to sell it for cash and for a very high price. Clever work by duplicitous Barrett and DH&W. CCP had been shaken down by them, with Mylor behind the scenes pulling the strings. They'd all played us well. And then, when Tillman looked as though he was going to blow the whole thing open, conveniently he dies. His wife said she'd never believe her husband killed himself. She was right—that had to be Mylor's work. That Tillman's secret file was destroyed in the fire at his lawyer's office proved it.

And what about Frank Marcuri? That couldn't have been a helicopter accident, happening when it did. Mylor must have known Marcuri was about to veto the SLIDA deal and had him taken out. But how could he have known something like that? Was Mylor listening in somehow? Had we been followed from the start?

I sipped some more water, and the terrifying questions wouldn't stop coming. How high did this conspiracy go? Was Mylor a renegade out to make a name for himself or was he doing this with the connivance of his superiors? The asset sales

I'd identified so far amounted to hundreds of billions of dollars. With that kind of money involved, this had to go high up. A chilling thought jumped into my head. Did the President know about this? Over the last year, whenever the President made a speech, it was always about the federal deficit and how he was the man who was going to address it once and for all. Nothing was going to stand in his way. Nothing.

I realized then going to the authorities wasn't an option. If this thing really did stretch way beyond Mylor, there was no way I could assess the risk to me and my partners.

Something still confused me, however. How could Mylor ever hope to get away with his scheme, knowingly selling us an asset that didn't work? I gazed out of the window. Down below, stretching as far as I could see, were the ice sheets of Greenland. The answer hit me like a brick to the head: We were never supposed to find out SLIDA didn't work. It made sense now why Barrett hadn't approached trade buyers. There was too much risk they'd discover SLIDA's faults. No wonder, when we'd raised the prospect of selling SLIDA to Mendocino, Mylor had immediately refused consent and insisted CCP had to keep it for the long term. That's why the U.S. government was happy paying annual fees to the company even though the technology didn't work. Mylor, the Treasury Department, and whoever else he was working for, regarded the deal as nothing more than a loan of funds from CCP to the cash-strapped government. The annual fees were like interest payments. Then, one day in the future, when the federal balance sheet was in better shape, the government would buy back the asset, no doubt giving CCP a modest profit for its trouble. No one would have been any the wiser but for Tillman. That's why he had to be killed. It all made some sort of sick sense.

I gulped down more water. The Chinese deadline was fast approaching and yet I still had no idea what I was going to do about it. Whatever I decided, I couldn't risk another partner being killed. The choice was simple yet brutal. Either I would have to start handing over the fake documents Mylor had supplied or I'd need to find a way to force Mylor to take SLIDA back quickly. Both were risky, given what I now knew but facing down Mylor seemed the least bad option. Pretending to cooperate with the Chinese was only a delaying tactic—it wasn't a solution. They'd find out in the end, then what? No, the only permanent solution was to find a way to force Mylor's hand.

Throughout the rest of the flight, I formulated a plan. It was far from perfect, but it was the best I could come up with in the circumstances.

When the 747 began its approach into Boston Logan, a thought froze my brain. On McCann's deal, Mylor had a plan B when his scheme was discovered: blackmail. As Leigh said, Mylor had chosen fund managers with something to hide and who he had leverage over—people like McCann, who were having affairs they needed to hide; people whose silence Mylor could guarantee with the right amount of pressure, should he need it.

What exactly did Mylor have on me?

CHAPTER 40

I'd later learn Dad had just finished eighteen holes at the Cummaquid Golf Club when he turned his phone back on and discovered I'd left three worrying messages for him. I'd stressed in my voicemails that it was essential he called me on my cell—not my office line, which I was now convinced was insecure.

"Is everything okay, Son? You sounded upset," Dad said, from his Subaru in the golf club's parking lot.

"Not really, but I can't go into it right now," I said, sitting at my desk, typing up the notes I'd made on the flight home yesterday. Somehow, setting them out this way helped me make sense of things and focused my mind on what I needed to do.

"You know I'm always here for you if you want to talk."

"I know. Next time I come down, I'll tell you all about it. Right now I need to pick your brain on something urgent."

"You're welcome to pick whatever's left."

"I need a lawyer. Someone you trust. Someone who is completely discreet."

"Well, that sure cuts the numbers down. Is it something I can help with? I know I'm not practicing anymore, but the old gray cells have retained some legal knowledge."

"Thanks for the offer, Dad, but I need someone unconnected with the family."

"Listen, if you're in some kind of trouble, I'm sure—"

"No. It's not like that. I've done nothing wrong."

"What kind of lawyer do you need?"

"The area of law doesn't really matter. I want them to hold some documents for me in safekeeping."

"I see." There was a pause, during which I hoped my father was not going to press me further. Then he said, "There's a guy called Doug Hennigar in Cambridge. He used to work for me many years ago and then went on to set up his own property practice. I hear he's doing well. Would he be okay?"

"Do you trust him?"

"Absolutely. I trained him. He's old school. Client confidentiality is drummed into him. Want me to have a word?"

"That would be great. Would you mind doing it today?"

"Sure. I'll call him right now. What can I tell him?"

"Don't say anything, other than I'm your son and I'll be calling him today or tomorrow."

"Okay. Leave it with me. Once I've spoken to him, I'll text you his number."

"Thanks, Dad. I owe you one."

Fortunately, I managed to meet with Hennigar at his Cambridge office the following morning. I wasn't at all surprised by his reaction to my cryptic request, and I realized he only agreed to keep my sealed envelope in his firm's secure storage room out of loyalty to my father.

After the meeting with my reluctant lawyer, I called Kerry from my car. "I need to see Mylor," I said.

"I'm fine, Damon. Thanks for asking. How are you?"

I was struggling to rationalize exactly what Kerry's role was in Mylor's racket. An intelligent woman like her had to know what was going on. Although the thought turned my stomach, she had to be an integral part of his corrupt scheme. While I still needed her as a means of communication with Mylor, I planned to keep her at a safe distance.

"I'm sorry, Kerry. I've got a lot on my mind right now. Tomorrow is Chris's funeral."

"An apology isn't necessary. I understand. He was a close friend."

"No. He was my best friend."

"Where were you earlier this week? I tried calling you a couple of times."

My guess was she and Mylor already knew I'd been to the UK, so I had to be careful with what I said. "I was away on business. I had to cover a few things off, so I could free up tomorrow. I want to be around all day for Chris's wife."

"Are we getting together again?"

"I'm going to be tied up for the next couple of weeks, but I'll see you when I meet Mylor."

"That's not exactly what I meant. Besides, I'm not sure I'll be there as he doesn't involve me in many of his meetings anymore. He's had me glued to my desk for the last couple of weeks."

"Why's that?"

"I think he's teaching me a lesson."

"For what?"

"He caught me in his office one night, dropping off a report. He accused me of snooping around."

"The man's paranoid."

"Yeah. Don't I know it?" She laughed. "I'll try to make sure I'm there when you meet him. What do you want to speak to him about? He'll want to know."

"He sent me the stuff to give to the Chinese. I've read it, but I need to go through a few things with him first. You can tell him I'm warming to the idea."

"That'll make his day."

"I bet."

"He's not back until the day after tomorrow, so I'll try and get some dates from him then and get back to you."

"Please do it soon. I have to get something to them by the end of next week."

"I'll do what I can."

CHAPTER 41

The following day was the hardest I'd ever faced. Saying goodbye to my best friend was difficult enough, but dealing with Carol's distress was tougher still. I'd known them both for many years, and they'd become family to me. After the funeral, the image of Carol standing by Gainham's grave with their two young daughters kept filling my mind. The guilt consumed me, depriving me of sleep and any capacity to think straight. If only I hadn't been so desperate to complete the SLIDA deal in the first place, none of this would have happened. And if I hadn't brought Gainham into that meeting with Chisholm and Wei, then maybe he'd have been spared.

Exactly one week before I had to deliver the first batch of information to Chisholm, I had another SLIDA board meeting. Thankfully, Mylor agreed to meet me. Kerry said her boss had to be on the West Coast anyway, so they'd suggested we all meet me in Sausalito on the day of the board meeting. I wasn't convinced by that story, but I went along with it. I suspected he wanted to grill the other directors on what we'd been saying about SLIDA and Tillman's claims.

Although the board meeting was scheduled to start at two o'clock, I decided to take a flight which arrived at San Francisco at eleven. There was something I needed to do—something that had been on my mind for some time.

Once on the Redwood Highway, I continued past the exit for Sausalito and headed north for another ten miles. After exiting at junction 452 for San Rafael, a few minutes later, I drove onto Nevada Street. I crawled along the road looking at the house numbers until I found 229. I left the car at the curb, walked up the drive past a Prius, and rang the doorbell.

No one answered. After two more attempts, I gave up and began walking back down the drive. If there was still time before my flight home, I figured I'd try again right after the board meeting. But that would depend on how long my session with Mylor lasted. Given what I wanted to discuss with him, it could either be a long meeting, or a very short one.

"Excuse me. Were you looking for me?"

I turned and saw a petite woman standing in the doorway of number 229. "Are you Jean?"

"Yes. Do I know you?"

"I'm Damon Traynor. We spoke on the phone after..."

"Oh yes, Damon. Please come in." She held the door open.

I followed her into the house. Jean was younger than I'd imagined—around my age, I thought, but that wasn't possible. I remembered her saying she'd been married to Brodie for twenty-five years. She had a warm smile and striking red hair, which was swept back into a ponytail. For a moment, I was reminded of her husband's similar hairstyle.

Jean led me into a small sitting room at the front of the house. "You're lucky to catch me," she said. "I only work half a day on a Thursday. I'm a part-time researcher at USF."

"I'm sorry," I said, taking a seat in the armchair facing the television. "I should have telephoned to say I was coming."

"It's no trouble. I'm just glad you didn't travel all this way for nothing. Would you like a drink?"

"Coffee would be great. Thanks."

When Jean left, I cast my eyes around the room. The furniture was mid-century modern, mainly from the sixties, I thought. That didn't surprise me as Brodie Tillman had always reminded me of a hippy. On the cabinet to my right stood three framed photos, two of which were of the Tillmans beaming at the camera, obviously on vacation somewhere sunny and warm. The third was of Brodie Tillman shaking hands with an older man in a suit in what looked like the SLIDA boardroom.

"That was when Brodie won some technical award at work," Jean said, carrying in a pot of fresh coffee and a plate of cookies. "He was so proud that day."

"Who is that with him in the photo?"

"I don't know his name. One of the directors, I think."

"Do you mind if I take a look?"

"No. Not at all." She placed the coffee and cookies on the table in front of us.

I reached over to the cabinet and picked up the photo. There was something familiar about the older man in the picture. One thing was certain—he was no longer a director. I knew every current board member. "When was this taken?"

"Two or three years ago," Jean said, pouring the coffee.

I studied the face of the man close up. I'd definitely seen him before, but not at SLIDA. The muscles in my neck tightened when I remembered. I'd seen him briefly in the reception of the building in Cleveland when I'd met with Mylor and Kerry. It was definitely the same man.

"Have you come to tell me about the file Brodie left for you?" Jean asked, interrupting my thoughts.

"Er, no." I placed the photo back down on the cabinet. "I'm afraid we never received the file."

"Brodie was adamant he'd left it with his lawyer. I can't imagine why—"

"The file existed, but it was destroyed. When I spoke to his lawyer, he explained how their office building had been devastated by a fire."

Jean's face paled, and she touched her mouth with her right hand. "There has to be a connection," she said. "I told you Brodie would never have taken his own life. Now you say there was a fire that destroyed his file. They have to be connected."

"That's why I wanted to see you." I placed my coffee cup on a coaster on the cabinet. "I owe your husband an apology."

Jean cocked her head. "An apology?"

"He came to see me about SLIDA not long after my firm bought it. He said a lot of things about the company, which I can't go into right now—a lot of things that worried us. The point is I dismissed him. I thought he was trying to make trouble—someone with a grudge because he'd lost his job."

She crossed her arms. "Brodie wasn't like that."

"I know that now. In fact, I think everything he told me was the truth. I was wrong to ignore him. He was trying to help me, and I turned him away. I'm not proud of the way I acted toward him."

"Do you know why he left you a file with his lawyer?"

"I'm only guessing, but I think it contained proof to support what he was saying. I think he must have known he was in some sort of danger and created the file in case anything happened to him."

Jean looked as though she was wondering if she should say something. After a few seconds, she asked, "Did he ever mention a man called Mylor to you?"

I sat upright in the armchair. "What do you know about him?"

"Not much, really, but Brodie mentioned his name several times shortly before he died. Somehow, I suspect he had something to do with his death."

I took a deep breath. "I fear you may be right. I don't have any evidence to support that, but I know enough about that man to share your view."

Jean's eyes welled up. "You don't know how much that helps me."

"It does?"

"I've been telling everyone, including the police, that Brodie would never have killed himself. It feels so good to know you believe me." She started to cry.

I walked across the room and hugged her. "He didn't kill himself, Jean. I'm certain of that. Your husband was one of the good guys."

* * *

I went through the motions at the board meeting that afternoon. The discussion over the financial results was a complete
blur. None of it mattered any longer. Given what Leigh had
told me in London, it was likely SLIDA's numbers were a complete work of fiction anyway.

After the meeting, I stayed in the boardroom, waiting for
Mylor to show up. When he did, Kerry was indeed with him,
but I found it hard to maintain eye contact with her; I couldn't
trust her any longer. The more I'd thought about it, the more
convinced I was that she was Mylor's mole, monitoring my
every move. She'd used me as much as her boss.

"Good to hear you want to work with us," Mylor said,
pouring himself coffee. He slid the carafe to Kerry for her to
pour her own.

"This is not something I *want* to do," I said, sitting at the
head of the table.

"I understand you have some questions for me? Some things
you want to clarify in the data we sent you."

"That's what I told Kerry."

"Shoot."

"But I lied to her."

Kerry put down the carafe. Mylor didn't flinch.

"I knew if I said anything else, you wouldn't agree to meet
me," I continued.

Mylor sipped his drink. "Go on."

"I can't play your game. It would only be a matter of time
before the Chinese discover I'd given them false information.
Then what? They start killing more of my partners, and I'm not
about to risk their lives—not when you can fix this."

Mylor threw me a shit-look. "Fix it how?"

"I told you in Cleveland. The best thing all round is for the
Treasury to buy SLIDA. While I don't like it, we'd even sell it

back to you at the same price we paid. Anything to make it happen."

Mylor shook his head. "I told you that ain't going to—"

"You don't have a choice."

"Think about this, Damon," Kerry said, before Mylor cut her a steely glare.

"I have thought about it. I've thought about little else since we last met."

Mylor jumped to his feet. "This meeting is over." He grabbed his laptop bag. "You're making a big mistake, thinking you can dictate what happens here."

"Sit down. I haven't finished with you yet," I said.

Kerry's jaw hit the floor while Mylor stood still, seemingly unsure what to say. "I said we're done here."

My heart pounded in my chest. I clasped my hands together to hide my trembling fingers, and swallowed the remaining saliva in my mouth. "You will buy SLIDA or I go public with everything I know. And I mean everything."

"You have no idea who you're dealing with."

"Actually, I have a fairly good idea."

"Kerry and I don't work for the Treasury."

"I managed to work that out for myself."

I shifted my gaze to Kerry. She looked down at the table, avoiding me.

"Then you ought to think twice about your threat." Mylor placed his bag back onto the table. "If you knew who we are, you'd stop this right now."

"It's not a threat. I will go public. I've already taken precautions."

"What are you talking about?"

"I've created a file. If anything happens to me, that file will be sent to the press. It contains details of everything, including the two of you."

Kerry's face filled with dread. Mylor's went bright red.

"Then you leave me with no choice," Mylor said, sitting down again.

"Good." My shoulders relaxed slightly. "Here's what I want you—"

Mylor thrust his right index finger at me. "Shut up and listen. I figured you might make a stupid move like this once I heard you went to London."

I stopped breathing. That confirmed everything. If Mylor knew I'd been to London, then he and Kerry had definitely been tracking me. What else did they know? Did they know I'd been to Leigh's offices?

"You won't breathe a word to anyone," Mylor continued.

"I'll do everything in my power to protect the lives of my partners. If that means exposing you and your corrupt scheme, so be it."

Mylor looked at Kerry. "Close the door."

Kerry walked over to the half open door and closed it while Mylor unzipped the bag in front of him and removed his laptop.

"What is this?" I asked.

"You'll see." Mylor powered up the machine, slipped a DVD into the disc drive, and turned the screen so we could all see. "I want you to watch this."

I exhaled loudly through my nose then looked at the laptop.

When the video started, my heart jumped into my mouth, and I froze.

CHAPTER 42

The view from the Oxo Tower restaurant on the south bank of the River Thames took in a wide sweep of the London skyline with St Paul's Cathedral rising up as the centerpiece. Everyone who dined there requested a table close to the window. The privileged few were successful and enjoyed one of the best views in town.

Richard Leigh was a regular, often taking investment bankers and other deal introducers to dinner there. His table for four was in the corner against the window—the most envied spot in the restaurant. His guests that evening were three senior partners from the corporate finance house responsible for bringing his firm its latest investment opportunity. They'd all arrived around seven so they could watch the sun setting over London. They hit the alcohol early and, by ten-fifteen, they'd consumed two bottles of Vilmart champagne, two bottles of Brunello di Montalcino and several large glasses of vintage port. The bill ran into serious four figures, but that was nothing compared to the money Leigh's firm would make on the deal.

When the waiter handed back his company Visa, Leigh gave him a business card. "Could you please call this company and order me a car on our account? Tell them I'm going to Maidenhead. They'll know what to do."

A quarter of an hour later, he said goodbye to his guests and climbed into the back of a Mercedes S Class, giving the driver his home address. The car followed the south bank, past the London Eye and over Waterloo Bridge, packed with late night revelers on their way out. As they headed west, Leigh leaned his head against the leather headrest and closed his eyes. At that time of night, the journey would take a little under an hour, time enough to drift off. It had been a long day and the alcohol was working its magic.

When the car accelerated up the entrance ramp on the M4, he stirred for a moment then closed his eyes again, falling into a deep sleep. Leigh did not hear the vehicle pull off the motorway at junction six for Slough. The driver took the A355 north then left onto Buckingham Avenue, which led into Slough Trading Estate. The industrial area was quiet at that time of night. As the driver turned left into Henley Road, they passed an old silver Volkswagen Golf. The young couple sitting in the back was hardly visible through the steamed-up windows. The driver smiled and shook his head, before glancing in his mirror at Leigh, who was snoring.

The Mercedes drew up outside a two-story, red-brick industrial unit, and the driver blipped the plastic fob attached to his keys. The unit's metal shutter door rolled up, and the car pulled inside. When the shutter door closed, it banged hard against the concrete floor, shocking Leigh into consciousness.

It took a moment for him to realize where he was. "What is this?" he shouted to the driver, pulling at his safety belt. "Where the hell are we?"

A man in a dark boiler suit emerged from the rear of the unit, ran over to the vehicle, and opened the door next to Leigh. At the same time, the driver jumped out and opened the back door on the other side.

Leigh, realizing he was about to be attacked, punched the man in the boiler suit hard on the side of his face, knocking him against the window. "Grab the bastard," he said, staggering to his feet.

Leigh kicked out at the driver when he grabbed both of his legs. Quickly, he pulled Leigh out of the car, dropping him head first onto the concrete floor, before kneeling on his chest.

"Help," shouted Leigh, before the driver rammed his gloved

fingers over his mouth. The other man raced around the vehicle and grabbed Leigh's arms. The driver took his weight off Leigh for a moment while they swung him over onto his front, pulling his arms behind his back.

Leigh wriggled and continued shouting, but he was unable to free himself from the combined weight of the two men. The driver reached inside his coat pocket and retrieved a vial and hypodermic needle. The other man held Leigh still by kneeling on the back of his head, forcing his face into the dusty floor. Leigh struggled to get free as the needle came closer to his head. The driver injected him just into the hairline above the back of his neck then helped to hold him down until he was unconscious. They waited a couple of minutes before standing up.

The driver opened the building's side door and looked outside. It was dark and there was no one around. He nodded to his accomplice, who dragged Leigh, face down, across the floor to the exit. They took one more look outside before lifting him by his arms and legs and carrying him across Henley Road.

Hauling Leigh's limp weight, the men fought their way through the bank of tall conifer trees on the far side of the road and hoisted him over a five-foot-high metal fence, dropping him on the other side. After they climbed over, the driver looked at his watch. Eleven-seventeen. "Twelve minutes," he whispered to the other man.

Ten minutes later, they dragged Leigh clear of the trees and through fifty feet of dense weeds before placing him face down onto the steel rail. They ran back to the cover of the conifers and watched as the high-speed train from London to Bristol approached at ninety miles an hour. When it reached Leigh's body, there was a soft thudding sound, and the train passed by.

CHAPTER 43

The whole sordid act was caught on camera. Nothing was left to the imagination from that night in Katie's Cambridge apartment after we'd been to Arabella's, celebrating our first deal. It was bad enough that the drunken sex itself had been captured, but the video and sound also recorded me the next morning agreeing to pay off Katie to keep her quiet.

What could I say? There was no defense. It wasn't my proudest moment. I'd been scammed by the young woman, and it was clear now that Mylor had set up the entire thing. Leigh had been right—Mylor had chosen the buyer for each asset with great care and cunning.

In spite of the embarrassment I was feeling, I glanced at Kerry, but I couldn't maintain eye contact. Her face was a blend of shock, contempt, and disgust. Even though the video was a setup, it still didn't change the fact I'd slept with the girl. No wonder Kerry was sickened by it.

"Turn it off," I said. "I've seen enough."

Mylor ejected the DVD and waved it in the air. "What would your investors say if they saw this turn up in the mail?" He grinned. "The great Damon Traynor having sexual relations with a minor."

"You know as well as I do there's no way she's as young as she says. She works for you."

"Does that matter? We have her saying she's only fifteen, and then we have you agreeing to pay her off."

"I've done nothing wrong. We all know what's happening here."

"Maybe we ought to let your parents decide. What do you think, Kerry? Shall we send a copy to them as well?"

Kerry gave no answer.

"Somehow I don't think they'll be sharing this little family movie with their friends. Do you?" asked Mylor, sneering at me. "And when your investors see it, well, my guess is you'll be ruined. CCP will fold and you'll never work in private equity again. You'll be lucky to get a job collecting shopping carts at Walmart."

My plan to force Mylor's hand was now in shreds. "What do you want?"

Mylor moved to a seat directly opposite me. "Here's what's going to happen. First, drop any idea you have of us buying SLIDA. One day, we might buy it back but until then, it stays with you. Second, if I even hear a rumor that you've been raising questions about the laser system, the DVD goes to your investors and parents. Is that clear?"

"And the Chinese? What am I supposed to do about them next week?"

"You give them the documents I sent you. Clear enough?"

"I hear you."

"Then we're done here."

"How do I contact you, now I know you don't work for the Treasury?"

"Here." Mylor slid a card across the table. "Use that number. I guess we don't have to pretend anymore."

I picked up the card and read it. All it had was Mylor's name and a cell phone number on it.

"Now get out of here," he said.

I grabbed my briefcase and hurried out, not once looking at Kerry.

* * *

"What's up with you?" Mylor asked.

"Nothing." Kerry said, even though her face indicated otherwise. "I'm surprised. That's all."

"By what?"

"I didn't think Traynor was like that."

"When you've been in this job long enough, nothing will surprise you."

"Do you think he'll keep quiet?"

"Oh yeah." Mylor picked up the DVD. "I know his sort. They're all the same. He won't want to risk this getting out."

Mylor stood and collected his things. "There is one thing I'd like to know."

"What's that?"

"Have you ever met with Traynor when I've not been there?"

Kerry paused, buying time as she put her coat on. "Yes. I have seen him."

"Why would you do that?"

"I've been doing my job, keeping an eye on him. It's what you told me to do."

"You didn't think to tell me?"

"I didn't think you wanted a running commentary on everything. You're always saying you measure outputs not inputs."

"In the future, I want to know if you plan to see him. Understood?"

"No problem. It's never been a secret."

CHAPTER 44

I stared at the flat screen TV on the wall of my den, nursing a cold mug of coffee. At five o'clock on a Sunday morning, there was nothing worth watching, but it sure beat lying in bed trying to sleep. For three sleepless nights, my mind had been dominated by Mylor's video. At least now I knew what I was up against and what leverage the man had on me. That was something.

It was clear, too, that CCP's acquisition of SLIDA was part of a government shakedown of financial institutions around the globe. Mylor had never actually admitted who he was, but I figured he ran some sort of covert operation, and as his corrupt scheme had managed to raise billions for the Treasury in a short space of time, he couldn't be acting alone. He had to have some serious connections within government working with him. This conspiracy had to go right to the top, given the amount of money being raised and Mylor's apparent freedom to do whatever he wanted.

How could I have let myself be used this way? Was making CCP a success so important that I'd been unable to see the clues right in front of me? The crazy thing was I hadn't even done it for the money—I'd always given away most of my wealth. The ugly truth was my pride had blinded me. I had been desperate to see our new firm take off, to show our competitors what we could do. As much as I hated the man, part of me admired Mylor for identifying CCP as a soft target and the way he reeled us in.

I turned off the television and rested my head on the back of the sofa. Allowing Kerry to get close to me had made things even easier for Mylor. They must have been laughing at how effortless I'd made it for them—falling for the attractive woman, believing she was on my side. Sadly, there had been a time when I thought the relationship might go somewhere. I thought she might be the one. Not anymore. Now I knew there never had been a real relationship. I lifted the cold coffee to my lips. *Kerry's as bad as her boss*, I thought. *They both played me well.*

At that moment, I had never felt more alone. I had no one to confide in. Gainham was dead, and I could hardly discuss any of this with my parents. This time I had to work it out for myself. And I had only four days left before I had to start handing over documents to the Chinese. There was little doubt they'd kill Crawford if I refused to cooperate. But if I did cooperate, it wouldn't take them long to discover the papers I'd given them were fake. Then what? They would send me a message, loud and clear. Maybe they'd go after my parents as well. I couldn't take that risk. There had to be another way out.

As I drained my mug, I made the decision. In my heart, I'd known it was what I had to do since the moment I left the meeting with Mylor. I would never risk the lives of those closest to me. I couldn't do that. No, if Mylor was refusing to buy back SLIDA, the only choice I had left—the only choice I could live with—was to go public with everything. Put it all out there—that SLIDA's capability was in question, that we and others had been threatened, and in some cases killed, by Mylor, and that the U.S. government was involved in a corrupt racket on a massive scale.

It was the nuclear option. It would probably bring down the government, and I had no doubt Mylor would follow through with his threat. He'd release the DVD to as many people connected to me as possible, ruining my reputation and destroying the business I'd worked so hard to create. There was also a real risk Mylor would have me assassinated for crossing him.

But as I realized that was a price I was willing to pay to protect those closest to me, an unexpected calmness settled over me.

By seven o'clock, I was running through the streets of Beacon Hill. The cool morning air helped clear my head, and the more I ran, the more certain I became. I was making the right decision. I could and would accept all the consequences, whatever they were. As I sprinted past Gainham's house, I thought of my dear friend and how he would have agreed with the decision. That made it even more right.

The following morning, I was the first to arrive at CCP's offices. I made my way to my corner office and began to scribble out what I would say to Mylor. First I'd stress that CCP did not ask to be placed in this position. Then I'd list out the times I'd offered to sell the asset back to the U.S. Treasury, even for no profit. I'd explain why I could not risk the lives of anyone else by providing false data to the Chinese. Then, finally, I'd deliver my decision: I was going public with everything I knew and I understood the consequences.

As usual, redrafting my note for a couple of hours helped me straighten out my thinking. It was important that Mylor understood how I'd reached my decision. He had to see he'd left me with no real choice. I'd been backed into a corner. Going public was something I was doing reluctantly, and only because it was a last resort.

At eight-thirty, I picked up my telephone and punched in the number from Mylor's card. I cleared my throat when the dial tone started. *This is the right thing to do.*

"Yeah?" said Mylor, answering his phone. He sounded as though he was in his car and using the hands-free.

"It's Damon Traynor."

"What do you want?" Mylor's tone revealed some surprise.

I looked down at my carefully prepared script then pushed it away. On reflection, explaining how I'd arrived at my decision would be wasted on Mylor. I decided I would keep it short and simple as the man wouldn't care. "This all ends today. I'm telling the press everything I know."

I heard the squeal of Mylor's car tires when he must have stood on the brakes. "Are you fucking insane? You know exactly what I'll do. You'll be ruined."

"I've made my decision." I terminated the call.

CHAPTER 45

After the call, I went straight into the boardroom for a meeting with a team of executives, who were visiting CCP in search of funding for a management buyout. It was a welcome distraction, doing something normal, even if it was only for a couple of hours.

I wasn't getting cold feet. In fact, I'd never been more certain of a decision in my life. My plan was to start contacting the press that afternoon. Fortunately, I'd established some great contacts with journalists during the course of my career, so I knew they'd give SLIDA good coverage. But first I had to decide how best to present the story. It had to be right because once the media got hold of it, the thing would have a life of its own. My other reason for delaying was that I needed some time to speak with CCP's investor advisory committee and my parents first. Both would be difficult calls to make, but I owed it to them. They had to hear the news from me rather than second-hand. And immediately after those calls, I'd have to meet with my partners to let them know. That was going to be tough as I knew my action was likely to crater their careers too.

This was going to be the worst day of my life, but it had to be done. There was no other way.

By the time I returned to my office, I had three voicemails from Kerry, each one more frantic than the last, and all of them pleading with me not to do anything until we'd spoken to each other. I deleted them then started working on the press release. Although she'd sounded desperate, Kerry could wait. After all, she worked for Mylor, so there was little she could say or do to change my mind. No doubt, her boss had instructed her to make contact, hoping she could persuade me to think again. As I wrote out the story, Gainham's face flashed into my mind. Somehow it felt I was finally doing something for him as he'd asked me to consider contacting the press the day before he died. If only I had listened, then maybe he'd still be alive today.

It was just before one when I finished preparing the draft release. I printed it out, read it carefully, and pushed it to the side of my desk. I wasn't sure why, but I decided then to call Kerry.

"Thank God you called," she said. "For a while I thought you weren't going to."

"What do you want from me, Kerry?"

"Mylor's gone ballistic. I've never seen him like this. He says you're going to talk to the press."

"That's right. I have the press release right in front of me."

"Don't do it, Damon. Please."

"Mylor told you to speak to me, didn't he?"

"He doesn't even know I'm calling you."

"You can stop the pretense now. We both know what you're up to. I have to admit, you played me well. You both did."

"I know how all this must appear to you, but I had nothing to do with the DVD. That was Mylor's work, not mine. He set you up. I realize that."

I paused. "You can do better than that, surely."

"Mylor's kept me in the dark on much of this too."

"I don't trust you, so save your breath."

"Will you at least hear me out?"

"You have two minutes."

"I want you to be careful. Mylor is capable of some—"

"I'm not worried about him anymore."

"You should be worried. He's dangerous. I don't want you to get hurt."

"If you think this is going to persuade me to stop, you're wasting your time."

"Listen to me, please."

"One minute."

"I told you about Marcuri and Tillman. As well as them, I've counted four other suspicious deaths. I'm pretty sure Mylor is behind them all."

"Then you ought to be ashamed of the work you do."

"I'm not part of this. Yes, I work for Mylor, but I had no idea about any of it when I joined his unit. You've got to believe that."

"You're a smart person. I figure someone like you would know what's going on around her. You're wrong about the other deaths, by the way."

"I'm telling you the truth."

"By my count, there are seven fund managers you people have killed in addition to Tillman and Marcuri."

"Then you know Mylor shouldn't be crossed. I'm begging you, Damon. Don't go public with this."

"Time's up."

There was a long pause at the other end of the line before Kerry spoke. Then she dropped the bombshell. "Richard Leigh is dead."

The air rushed out of my lungs as though I'd been kicked in the stomach. "Leigh is dead?"

"The day after you went to see him in London."

"What happened?"

"They say he took his own life, but we both know that's not true."

"When does this end?"

"Damon, I'm telling you this because I don't want you to be the next victim. Whether you believe me or not, I care about you."

"I have to go."

"Please. Promise me you'll take some time to think it over."

"I can't do that."

"At least give it a few hours."

"Goodbye, Kerry."

I finished the call and let my head fall into my hands. Although I'd only spent a short time with him, Leigh struck me as a decent and grounded man—certainly not someone about to take his own life. The next thought made me want to gag. If I hadn't tracked him down, he'd still be alive today. In Sausalito, Mylor had bragged about knowing the details of my trip to London. This was his work. Kerry just confirmed it.

Mylor had to be stopped.

CHAPTER 46

I reworked the press release several more times before it was right. Then I shredded the printouts of the various drafts before saving the final version in a secure folder on my PC. Maybe it was something Kerry said on the phone. I wasn't sure why, but I decided to sleep on it and send it to the press first thing the next day. There was no reason it had to go out that day. I still had two more clear days before I had to deliver something to the Chinese. Besides, there was an advantage in delaying: I could speak to the chairman of the investor advisory committee and my parents from the privacy of my own home that evening. And even if the worst happened and Mylor's people got to me before I could contact the press, then the file I'd left with Doug Hennigar would do the job for me anyway.

The call came in on my direct line just before six.

"It's me."

I recognized Mylor's voice immediately. "What do you want?"

"Have you spoken to anyone yet?"

"Just about to."

"There's no need any longer."

"Why?"

"The government has agreed to take SLIDA back."

A wave of relief surged through me as I closed my eyes. *Thank God.*

"When?"

"Immediately. That way, once we've documented it, you can

announce you've sold it. That ought to get the Chinese off your back."

"What's the price?"

"You're getting your money back. Don't push it."

Not what I had wanted for my investors, but I was in no position to negotiate. There was simply no time to drag out a deal. The sale had to be announced within forty-eight hours if it was going to eliminate any threat to Crawford's life. The only way to buy more time would be by passing the false information to the Chinese. And no extra money would be worth taking that risk.

"I'll have to live with it," I said with no emotion in my voice.

"We'll prepare the documents. To prevent any delays, we'll need to meet face to face tomorrow to close this. I'll come to you."

"Okay, I'll have a lawyer on standby. What time?"

"I can't make it before seven tomorrow night."

"Seven it is. Just so long as it's done tomorrow."

"I hardly need to tell you to keep a lid on this."

"Understood. Once SLIDA is back in government ownership, there'll be no need for me to talk to anyone."

After the call, I rose from my desk and looked out of my office window. Fading sunlight reflected off the glass towers opposite as commuter traffic lined up on State Street. There was no sense of elation—more one of deep mistrust. What just happened seemed too good to be true. Mylor was an intransigent bully. Was he really prepared to rollover that easily? He had to be up to something. It was strange how he couldn't make a meeting during office hours the next day. After all, the documents could easily be prepared overnight and be ready for the morning. Mylor had to be buying time for some reason.

I reached inside my jacket pocket for my iPhone. I wanted to check Hennigar still had the file safe, in case he had to release it for me. If Mylor was planning something, there was a very good chance I'd no longer be alive twenty-four hours from now.

As I turned away from the window, the flashing green LED light of the smoke detector caught my attention. I wondered whether they were installed in all of CCP's rooms as I hadn't paid any attention to them before. I put my phone back in my pocket and walked over to the boardroom. Looking up at the ceiling, I smiled when I saw two more units directly above the long table.

I'd hatched an insurance plan.

When I returned to my office, I looked in my briefcase for the card Chisholm had thrown at me. Then I walked with it to the elevator lobby to make a cell phone call from there. The last thing I wanted was Mylor listening in on my next telephone conversation.

"Chisholm," said the gruff voice at the other end of the line.

"This is Damon Traynor."

"You're cutting it fine."

"I told you it wouldn't be easy."

"You better have something for me. You know the consequences—"

"I have what you want."

"I'll come and get it."

"Not now. I'm still pulling it together. Can you come to my office tomorrow evening? Say, seven."

"Yeah. That works."

"You know where we are."

Chisholm laughed. "Sure. I remember it well enough."

"So I can clear it with security downstairs, will it be just you, or will both you and Mr. Wei be coming?"

"Both of us. He understands what he's looking at. We don't want you giving us anything misleading, do we?"

"It's all good data."

"See you tomorrow."

After the call, I rubbed my sticky palms on my pants. Then I returned to my office, opened Outlook on the PC, and scrolled down my personal contacts until I found the name I was looking for: Sam Baker.

CHAPTER 47

Three miles northeast of Paderborn, the Sennespringe U.S. military base covered two and a half thousand acres. From the southern tip of the camp, two rapidly expanding housing developments stretched toward the city. To the north were rolling hills covered in dense pine forest. Like the five others in Germany owned by the Department of Defense, the base had been an American asset since the end of the Second World War. Once an important NATO commitment, today they were an anachronism as the Cold War had become a fading memory.

Orlando Barrett climbed aboard the Bell CH-146 helicopter and sat next to Daniel Keller, a slight man in his forties, wearing a dark blue suit and rimless, round spectacles. Keller slid over as far as he could to make room for Barrett's large frame and buckled his safety belt.

"You guys all set?" the military pilot asked, swiveling his head toward the two passengers sitting behind him.

"Ready when you are," Barrett said over the headset he'd just slipped on.

The helicopter lifted into the air and headed in the direction of Bad Lippspringe, one of the suburbs on the edge of the base.

"I'll take a quick circuit first," the pilot said. "Then we'll head over the site as many times as you guys want."

Barrett looked at Keller. "Is that okay with you?"

Keller gave the thumbs up sign. "Absolutely fine."

Moments later, they were hovering over the eastern flank of the camp. "See here," Keller said, pointing to the ground. "That's where the shopping mall development will begin. And over there, the new housing will be constructed."

Barrett nodded. "Very similar to your plans for the Gütersloh site."

Keller smiled for the first time. "Exactly so. Same architect. We've worked with him many times before."

"Will you be bringing in syndicate partners to help fund the project after closing?"

"No. Our fund will finance and retain the whole thing. We have sufficient capital."

"The third-largest fund in Germany, I believe."

Keller frowned. "Actually, the second, and if our expansion plans come to fruition, we will soon be the largest private equity real estate player in this country."

Thirty minutes later, the helicopter landed, and Keller climbed out of the aircraft behind Barrett.

"Okay, let's do this thing," Keller said.

They walked to the waiting Mercedes S Class and were still locked in discussion as the car drove through the base gates. The vehicle headed south then west along the A44, reaching the outskirts of Dortmund just over an hour later. It stopped outside a four-story, brownstone office building on Prinzenstrasse.

The law offices of Eisner Lagerfeld occupied the top two floors. When the two men arrived at the conference room, a sea of suited lawyers was seated around the large oval table, pushing documents back and forth, talking in a mixture of English and German.

The room fell silent when Keller walked to one end of the table and began to speak. "We are ready to close the deal," he said.

One of the lawyers stood. "Please, gentlemen," he said, pulling out two chairs. "Sit here."

Keller and Barrett took their seats at the head of the table before another lawyer slid a pile of papers in front of them. "Please begin by signing these documents," she said.

In a flamboyant gesture, Keller took a Diplomat fountain

pen from his inside jacket pocket and signed the documents before passing them to Barrett for his signature.

When Barrett signed the final page of the sale and purchase agreement, he rose to his feet and stretched out his hand. "Congratulations, Daniel."

Keller shook Barrett's hand to a round of applause from the lawyers. "It has been a pleasure."

While the Champagne was poured, Barrett slipped out of the room, found a quiet office, and hit one of the speed dials on his phone. "I have good news."

"Has it closed?" Kerry asked, sitting in her Bethesda office.

"Let's just say the U.S. no longer owns any of its former military bases in Germany."

"A moment in history."

"I think so."

"Right now the country needs the money more than those properties."

Keller appeared at the open door with two flutes of Champagne. "I hope you can join us."

Barrett nodded. "I'll be there in one moment, Daniel."

Keller smiled and walked away.

"I'm sorry," Barrett said. "I'm being called back in to celebrate the deal."

"You go ahead," said Kerry. "You've earned it. Well done."

"Thanks. Where do you want me to send the sale proceeds? The usual account?"

"Good question. This is my first one overseas. I'll find out and circle back."

"Okay. For now, it will sit in our client account."

Immediately after the call, Kerry started drafting an email to Mylor. He was out of the office, but always liked to hear immediately when new asset sales had been completed. As another twenty-three billion dollars were heading to the U.S. Treasury,

Kerry figured he'd certainly want to learn about this one.

Halfway through typing the email, she stopped, rose from the desk, and closed her office door. She sat back down and swiveled her chair to face the window, wondering how much longer she could stomach working for Mylor. The man was dangerous and out of control. She'd known it was a big mistake joining his team within days of taking up her appointment. If success meant becoming more like her boss and having to accept his moral standards, she didn't want any part of it. But requesting a return to her old job this soon would look bad—it would signify failure—and Mylor was bound to make things difficult. If she really wanted out, Kerry knew she'd have to leave the service altogether and take up a new role in civilian life. The problem was she had no idea where or what that might be. The prospect made her shiver.

It was when she considered Barrett's question about where to send the money from the sale of the German military bases that the crazy idea struck her. As she thought about it, she knew that if she did it, she'd have to move quickly—and there'd be no going back.

Kerry turned to her desk and scrolled through the contacts on her BlackBerry, stopping at Neil Glesinger. A few years earlier, she'd been through the CIA induction training with Glesinger and a handful of other trainee agents at Langley. They'd become a close-knit group and that bond had continued long after they'd each been posted to different departments and stations around the world. Glesinger could be trusted—he was a friend as well as a colleague—and was bound to be discreet and not ask too many awkward questions. If she went ahead with her scheme, at least this part would work without too much trouble. After that, it would become a lot more complicated.

"Hey, Kerry. Great to hear from you," Glesinger said, taking her call.

"How are you? Still on the Asia team?"

"Yeah. I'm enjoying it, though sometimes I feel I'm living out of a suitcase. How about you?"

"I'm on an assignment in Bethesda."

"I heard about that. I'm impressed—means you're moving up in the world."

"I don't know about that, Neil. It's all a bit dull, to tell you the truth. Right now, most of it's working with the Treasury Department."

"I imagine that would be tedious."

"Look, I won't keep you, but I need a favor."

"Name it."

Kerry took a quick glance at her closed door, cleared her throat, and lowered her voice. "Do you have access to any dormant bank accounts out there?"

"I'm sure we do. Why?"

"I can't tell you. I'm sorry, but it's related to my work here. That's all I can say."

"What do you need?"

"Ideally, we're looking for a dormant account in Hong Kong."

"We're bound to have some unused accounts there. Want me to find one?"

"I'd appreciate it. That would save me a lot of work trying to do it from here."

"Has to be dormant, right?"

"Yes. I can't mix this up with other agency business."

"Okay. Leave it with me and I'll come back to you next week."

"Actually, I need it quicker than that. Is there any way you could find one today or tomorrow? I'm under a lot of pressure, and this would really help."

"I'll see what I can do."

"Thanks."

When she finished the call, Kerry took a deep breath and wondered what she'd just started. There was still time to stop, but something inside kept telling her she had to continue.

CHAPTER 48

Boston Logan was buzzing when Mylor stepped off the plane at ten-eighteen a.m. He climbed into the back of a taxi and went directly to the Four Seasons on Boylston Street. By eleven-fifteen, he was sitting in his executive suite overlooking Boston Common, and spread out on the desk in front of him was a Boston street map he'd picked up at the airport. By his calculations, Traynor's Beacon Hill home and CCP's State Street offices were both about a mile from the hotel.

Just before eleven-thirty, someone knocked on his room door. Mylor peered through the spyglass, recognized his visitor, and opened it.

Chuck Alick sauntered in. "Who'd you think it was?" he asked through his thick moustache. A five-foot-ten walking muscle, he was dressed in an ill-fitting suit. His hair dropped down over the back of his collar, making up for a thinning crown. "An intruder." He laughed at his own wit.

Mylor kept a straight face. "We haven't got time to waste. Grab a seat."

Alick shuffled over to the sofa facing the window. "Nice room."

"I needed somewhere close to our target."

"They don't have a Howard Johnson in Boston?"

Mylor ignored the comment and sat in the armchair with his back to the window. He threw a color photo across the coffee table between them. "That's Damon Traynor," he said, as if the name made him want to throw up.

Alick picked up the photo and studied it. "Who's he?"

"He's why you're here."

"Need me to put a team on him?"

"There's no time for that."

"What's the plan?"

"You and I are meeting him at his office this evening." Mylor pointed with his left thumb at the window behind him. "Downtown."

"Then what?"

"After the meeting, I want him taken out."

"Another accident?"

"You got it."

"That doesn't give us long. In that timeframe, it'll be easier to make it a car wreck. I assume he drives?"

"He does—parks his car right under his office building."

"Good."

"You won't have much leeway."

Alick tilted his head.

"He only lives about a mile away," Mylor said.

Alick sucked air in through his teeth. "That's tight in the middle of a city."

"That's not all."

"You're full of good news today."

"He'll have his lawyer with him tonight."

"So?"

"We need to remove him as well."

"Where's his photo?"

"I don't have one—no idea what he looks like."

"That's really gonna help. Can't we leave him until we know more?"

"No. After the meeting, the lawyer will have some documents with him." Mylor reached into his briefcase, pulled out a bunch of papers, and waved them in the air. "These documents. That's what we're signing tonight. I need them back, or they can be destroyed along with him if that's easier. I don't mind. The point is they have to disappear."

"Do we know anything about the lawyer? Does he even drive? Where does he live?"

"Look, that's your job now. I want your best people on this right away. Fly them in from Cleveland. They have to be in place no later than four this afternoon and ready to roll as soon as you and I leave the meeting."

Alick exhaled loudly. "I don't get paid enough for all this."

"Just deal with it. Okay."

"What's the meeting for?"

"You don't need to know the details. Hard as it may seem, you'll be there as my lawyer, so wear a tie."

Alick raised his eyebrows. "You're shittin' me, right?"

"No. Don't worry. You won't have to do any talking. Leave everything to me. I only want you there in case the plan goes tits up."

"I don't know about this. Pretending to be a lawyer? There's got to be a law against that."

Mylor rolled his eyes as he rose to his feet. "Come on. I want to take a walk by their office, so I can show you where we're going tonight."

"I'll need to get my team on the way." Alick took out his phone. "Let me make a couple of calls before we head out."

CHAPTER 49

"Sam, great to see you," I said, collecting my visitor from reception. "Come on through."

Baker followed me into the boardroom. "My brother says hello," he said. "I told him you'd called and I was coming to see you today."

"Send him my best. I still owe him a beer."

"He'll hold you to it."

I smiled, poured us both coffee, then shut the boardroom door. "Look, I know I told you I wanted to set up our conference room for a seminar when we spoke on the phone, but that wasn't exactly true."

Baker put down his coffee mug and wrinkled his nose. "What is it you want then?"

"I need you to do something for me, but I'd appreciate it if you didn't ask me too much about it."

Baker raised his right palm. "Hey, provided I get paid for the work, I'll do whatever you want."

"Thanks. I didn't know who else to trust with this."

"What do you need?"

I pointed at the two smoke detectors above the boardroom table. "You see those things. I need you to wire them up for me."

Baker stared at the ceiling. "I don't understand."

"Is it possible to hide a small camera and microphone in them, if you strip out what's inside?"

Baker threw me another quizzical look then raised his eyes to the ceiling again. "I guess so." He rubbed the bristle on his chin.

"It's not something I've been asked to do before."

"But you can do it, right?"

"You know it's illegal to tamper with them?"

"I understand. You can put them back later on. They'll only be off for a few hours. I know it's a bit of a weird request but, technically, is it possible to do what I want?"

Baker shifted his weight in his seat. "Yeah. I can do it."

"How long would it take?"

"A couple of hours or so. I'd need to buy a few components. They're not something I carry with me."

"Of course."

"I'll order the parts and schedule to fit them next week sometime."

"That's a problem. I need it done today."

Baker swallowed. "There's a supplier here in town. He carries a lot of inventory. I could drive over there now if he has what I need."

"Would you mind calling him to find out?"

"Sure."

When Baker left to collect the parts, I stopped by our reception. "I need to ask a favor?"

"What is it?" our receptionist asked.

"Can you come through to the boardroom so we can discuss it?"

"Now?"

"Yes, please. Leave the phones for a moment. We'll only be a few minutes."

We walked into the boardroom and I closed the door behind us.

"We have two groups of visitors coming here this evening," I said, taking a seat. "I'd like you to stay behind to deal with them for me. They are very important to this business."

She sat across the table from me. "No problem. When are they coming?"

"They're all due to arrive at seven."

"Where shall I put them?"

"In here, but they need to be shown into the room in a certain order."

She frowned. "Okay."

"It's critical that the first people allowed in are a Mr. Mylor and his lawyer. I don't have a name for him or her."

"And if the other group arrives first?"

"That'll be a Mr. Chisholm and a Mr. Wei. If they arrive first, I want you to show them into a meeting room on the other side of reception. They must not be allowed into this room before the others and they cannot meet each other before they're all in this room. I cannot stress that enough."

She narrowed her eyes. "What happens—?"

"Once you've seated Mylor and his lawyer in here, then you can bring Chisholm and Wei into the boardroom. Don't stick around. Just let them get on with it. Okay?"

Our receptionist scribbled a note on her pad. "Who from CCP are they coming to see? Don't I have to let them know before I leave?"

"They'll be here to see me, but I'm likely to be running behind. I have to go out later on and I expect to be back just after seven. If I'm back in time, I'll deal with it, but if I'm not then I'm counting on you to get this right. Just remember how important the order is."

"Don't worry." She pointed to her scribbled notes. "I've got it."

"Once they're all in this room, you can go home. I'll take care of everything else when I get here."

"I don't mind staying until you arrive. It's no trouble."

"No, really, I'd prefer you to leave once they're here. Don't wait for me."

"You're the boss."

* * *

By two o'clock that afternoon, Baker had returned and installed a miniature Bluetooth camera and microphone in each of the two smoke detector casings, so I joined him in the boardroom for a demonstration.

"You're going to like this," Baker said, pressing one of the buttons on the small remote in the palm of his right hand. "This thing sets it to record. Now follow me."

I followed him to the small meeting room next door where he opened the cabinet normally used to hold coffee cups and glasses. "I hope you don't mind, but I've placed the DVD recorder in here, out of sight."

"I like how you've hidden everything," I said. "Can I see the quality of the recording?"

"Of course." Baker retrieved the DVD from the recorder. "Where can we play this?"

"Let's try it on my computer." Then I realized that wouldn't be too clever in case my office was wired. "Actually, there's a machine through here," I said, leading him into a small office off reception.

I placed the disc into the drive, and we both watched as the PC screen came to life.

"Wow. That's very clear. Great work, Sam."

"Thanks. I've tested the sound and that works well too."

"Is it possible to set the recorder on a timer if I'm not here to activate it?"

"Absolutely. Let's go back to the machine and I can show you. It's a straightforward timer."

After Baker left, I collected my briefcase from my office and returned to the boardroom. I closed the door then unpacked a pile of papers from my case. They were the documents Mylor had sent me to pass on to the Chinese. As I spread them out on the table, I checked to make sure they'd be visible from the camera immediately above my head. When everything was in the right place, I locked the boardroom door and walked to reception. Before I handed the key to our receptionist, I told her to keep the door locked.

"I will," she said "Don't worry."

CHAPTER 50

They crossed Congress Street, passing by a branch of Bank of America, and continued along State. A minute later, Mylor stopped and studied his map. "It's just down here on the left," he said, pointing in the direction of Boston Harbor. After another four hundred feet, they took a left on Chatham, which led around the back of CCP's office tower.

"Is this it?" Alick asked when Mylor folded away the map.

Mylor raised his head. "Up there—on the twenty-second floor."

"Are we going in?"

"Not now. I want to take a walk around the building and count the exits."

Alick pointed to the vehicle ramp leading under the building. "That's the only way in and out by car. I'll place one of my guys on foot as close as he can get to the ramp." He looked along the length of Chatham Street. "Coming out of the parking lot, looks like you can go either way here. I'm going to need a team at each end of the street. The guy at the ramp can tell them which way Traynor and his lawyer are headed when they leave tonight."

The metal shutter door at the bottom of the ramp opened. Then a bronze Chevrolet Camaro came out and drove right past them.

"Come on. Quickly." Mylor sprinted down the ramp. Alick chased behind, banging the top of his head on the closing shutter.

"You're getting slow," Mylor said.

"Next time you might consider giving me a little more notice." He rubbed his head then checked his fingers for blood. "I'm getting too old for this."

"You'll live." Inside the garage, Mylor turned right and inspected the parking bays as he walked. "See? They're all marked on the boards at the back. We're looking for Carada or CCP."

When they approached CCP's parking spaces, a white Savana van reversed out of one of them. Mylor and Alick stood to the side, leaned against a car, and pretended to be locked in conversation. Sam Baker glanced out of the van's side window then looked away when Alick made eye contact.

"What's he looking at?" Alick grunted.

"It doesn't matter." Mylor watched as the van drove off. The shutter door opened when it drew close to the exit. "You're right. There's only one way in and out."

"I'd like to take a closer look at the cars," Alick said.

"What for?"

"It would help if I could work out which one is Traynor's."

"I can tell you." Mylor pointed at a silver BMW X5. "That one right there."

Behind them, an elevator door opened. They looked around, and a man stepped out and headed for the BMW.

"Get down," Mylor whispered, crouching behind the nearest car.

Alick followed. "What is it?"

"That's Traynor."

"Looks like he's leaving. Aren't we supposed to be meeting him?"

"He'll be back." They watched as the X5 drove right by, through the open shutter door and up the ramp. Mylor stood. "Let's get out of here."

Once outside again, they completed their circuit of the building, walking up Butter Square—where Alick confirmed it was a dead end—then continuing along Chatham until it rejoined State.

"I've seen enough," Mylor said.

"I'd like to stick around for a while. I want to take another look at the building itself. When my guys get here, we won't have long. The more I can do now the better."

"Okay. I'll see you back at the hotel. Make sure you're no later than six-thirty. We'll get a cab over here this evening."

CHAPTER 51

The Rubbermaid nineteen-quart storage containers were six-fifty each or fifty dollars for ten. In the aisle, Jean Tillman stacked five on top of each other, stood back, and cocked her head. Fifty dollars was a great deal and, while tight, she thought ten would just squeeze into the car. It was worth a try, anyway, so she loaded up her cart and joined the line at the checkout.

It took some maneuvering to steer the wobbly cart across Home Depot's parking lot to her Prius. Although she had to be careful not to catch the back window when closing the hatchback, the containers squeezed in with a little room to spare.

On her drive home, she kept telling herself she was doing the right thing. The memories of her life with Brodie would always be there—nothing could take them away. But it no longer felt right leaving her husband's things out as they had been the day he died. It wasn't healthy.

The plan was to start with the study then, provided she could cope with it, move on to his clothes. For now, Brodie's possessions would be packed carefully into the new containers and stored in the basement. That way, they'd still be nearby. She'd need a few more months, if not years, to summon up the strength to part company with such precious belongings. Eventually, when she felt strong enough, she'd probably take the clothes to the Salvation Army. Brodie would have wanted that—he detested waste.

Organized chaos was the way Jean had always described the study. Files and loose papers strewn everywhere—just the way Brodie had liked it. She'd lived with it, provided he kept the door closed when he wasn't using the room. That way she could pretend it wasn't there. Standing in the doorway, looking at the piles of paper on the floor, Jean smiled. What she wouldn't give to have him back here now making as much mess as he wanted.

She stacked Brodie's technical journals in the containers, rolling each one out the room as she filled it. It didn't take long to realize ten containers weren't even close to being enough for the study, let alone the clothes in the closet. Jean estimated she'd need another twenty at least. And the full containers were so heavy she'd have to ask a neighbor to help carry them down the basement stairs. For now, they could sit in the hallway.

Two hours in, she'd cleared the study floor and rediscovered the color of the carpet. Moving on to the desk, she set to one side those papers that had to be kept then began creating a pile she'd need to take for shredding.

In the top drawer, were Brodie's calendars for the last two years. Jean sat in his chair and flicked through the most recent one, smiling when she reached her birthday. Brodie had circled the date in red exclamation points. She fought back the tears when she reached their anniversary. The entry read: "Dinner with my lovely wife at Casa Romana." Jean remembered the meal they'd enjoyed there and how happy they were. Not long after, Brodie lost his job, and their lives changed forever.

The second drawer contained what looked like a bunch of technical papers from work. She'd never really understood the detailed aspects of her husband's work at SLIDA even though he'd tried to explain it to her many times. At the bottom of the drawer, she found a transparent folder containing some loose papers. She took out a couple of them and began reading.

The first was a copy of a letter from Brodie to Gerry Lyons of Redman Lyons in Sausalito. Her heart missed a beat when she saw what was written.

Dear Gerry,
If you're reading this then I will no longer be alive. In which

251

case, I need you to do something very important for me. I need you to contact Damon Traynor at Carada Capital Partners in Boston and give him the attached file. Damon knows me, so he will not be completely surprised to hear from you when you mention my name.

Please do not open the file. It is best that you do not know what it contains. There is a letter to Damon inside the sealed envelope. That will be all the explanation he needs.

One more thing. I have told Jean that I have left a file with you, but I do not want her to know anything about its subject matter, not even this letter. I would hate to jeopardize in any way the memory she has of me. I cannot stress how important this is.

Thank you for doing this for me.

Yours

Jean stared at the paper in her hands, wiping away the tears running down her cheeks. This letter had to be referring to the file destroyed in the fire. If Brodie had kept a copy of the letter at home, then maybe somewhere there was also a duplicate of the file itself. She pulled open the other drawers, desperate to locate it, but found nothing.

She picked up the transparent folder again, took out the next few pages, and scanned them, looking for anything that might refer to the missing file. A chill ran through her when Jean reached a letter to Damon Traynor. This had to be a copy of what was inside the sealed envelope that Brodie had left with the file. Swallowing, she held it in her trembling fingers and started to read.

Dear Damon,

I know you do not think very much of me. In truth, I cannot blame you. When I first made contact, the story I told you must have seemed incredible. For what it's worth, if I had been in your shoes, I would have dismissed me as an idiot. But, sadly, as you may well have discovered already, what I told you was the truth. I wish it was not so.

My lawyer, Gerry Lyons, will have given you a file with this letter. It contains irrefutable evidence to support my claims. You must decide what to do with this information, but I hope—indeed I pray—you make the matter public and use it to destroy those who have used me and many others like me. While I was content to be part of our government's propaganda exercise, holding out to our adversaries that SLIDA was fully functional, I was not prepared to maintain the charade when the company was offered for sale. I made my position clear to the board. Not long after, they let me go.

If you are reading this letter, you need to know I have been murdered. I am certain of one thing: My death, no matter how it might appear, will have been the work of a man called Ben Mylor. I know very little about him, other than he and his people have done their utmost to keep me quiet and that they have silenced others like me. If you run into him, please be careful. He is very dangerous and will stop at nothing to get his way.

Please do whatever is in your power to use the information I am leaving you to bring Mylor, and whoever is behind him, to justice. They cannot be allowed to get away with this. It isn't right.

I am sorry to leave this burden with you.

Take care

Despair wrestled with boiling rage deep within Jean. Despair because Brodie had mentioned Mylor's name several times before his death. He must have known his life was in danger, but no one would listen to him. Even she had dismissed his fears as irrational. Rage because the man responsible was still out there, probably still doing the same to others and getting away with it.

Whoever this Mylor was, he had to be stopped.

CHAPTER 52

"Thanks, Neil. I owe you one," Kerry said. "The guys here will be pleased. Sure saves us a lot of time."

"Don't mention it," Glesinger said. "Let me know when you need to move the money."

Kerry replaced the telephone handset and stared at what she'd just written on the legal pad in front of her. Seeing the details of the Hong Kong bank account made it much more real somehow. Up to this point, she could still stop the whole thing, and no one would know anything about her scheme. Her stomach went into cramps. If she made the next call, there would be no going back.

According to her watch, it was just after four p.m., which made it a little after ten p.m. in Germany. Too late to call Barrett now. Maybe the right thing to do was sleep on it anyway—take the time to think through all the implications. The risks were massive, and there could well be consequences she'd not yet considered. She breathed deeply and bit on her bottom lip. No, if she didn't do it now, there was a strong probability she'd drop the whole thing. It had to be done now or not at all.

Kerry stood and quickly checked the corridor outside her office before closing her door. When she sat back down, she picked up the phone and hit the numbers for Barrett's cell, half hoping he wouldn't answer.

"Orlando," Barrett said after three rings.

"It's Kerry Ward. I wanted to get back to you on the money."

"The usual account?"

"Most of it, yes. But there are some deal costs we need to settle from this end. I need some of the money to go to a separate account, so we can take care of them."

"I can get the lawyers to settle those for you before I send the money. Just let me have the details."

Kerry's legs were shaking. "It's easier if we do it. It'll take too long that way. Besides, Mylor still has some of the invoices I need."

"Okay. What amounts go where?"

Her heart hammered inside her chest as she picked up the legal pad. "Send all but ten million dollars to the usual Treasury account."

"And the ten million?"

She told him the account number and Swift code.

"Where's that? Looks like Hong Kong to me."

The muscles in Kerry's neck tightened. Barrett was too smart for his own good. "It's complicated. Some of the transaction costs were incurred over there."

"I don't mean to be difficult, but I'm going to need Ben Mylor's written authorization for this. If the money was going to an account we've used before, there'd be no problem."

Kerry's ribcage felt as though it was about to explode. Every fiber in her body screamed at her to abandon the plan and tell him to put all the money in the usual account. Barrett was about to blow open the whole thing. She had to get off the phone and think.

"Okay, I'll get that to you tomorrow."

"Just email it to me as I'll be flying back tomorrow. Once I get the email, I'll instruct the transfers to be made."

"Have a safe trip back."

Her mind went into overdrive the moment she put down the phone. Did Barrett believe her story about deal costs? Had he suspected something was wrong? Is that why he insisted on Mylor's authorization? It was hard to tell.

She waited for her breathing to calm down before deciding

what to do. Maybe she was panicking over nothing. Barrett was just doing his job. After all, he'd seemed quite relaxed about some of the money going elsewhere. Why would he suspect anything? She kept telling herself she could still do this. Nothing had changed.

So why were the stomach cramps back?

After a visit to the bathroom, Kerry returned to her office and closed the door again. She rifled through the hanging folders in her desk, searching for anything with Mylor's signature on it. He loved to issue his edicts by written memo. Surely, she would have saved some of them. A moment later, she came across one. All she had to do now was draft an authorization in Mylor's name and attach his signature. For that she'd have to wait for his PA to go home, so she could use the scanner.

By eight p.m., Kerry had the document ready and scanned. She scrutinized every detail on the screen in front of her. There was nothing to indicate the signature had been taken from another source. It looked like an original authorization from Mylor. After typing an email to Barrett, she attached the document. Her clammy fingers stuck to the mouse when she held the cursor over the send button. This next step would send her to prison if things went wrong—maybe worse. Kerry removed her palm from the mouse, clasped her hands together, and rested her chin on the back of her fingers, staring at the PC screen.

You can do this.

A minute later, she took a deep breath, swallowed, and hit send.

CHAPTER 53

I took a seat in the cramped reception and gazed at the oversized clock on the wall opposite. It was a little after four o'clock—three hours to go before Mylor and the Chinese would turn up at CCP. I reached across to the pile of magazines on the table in front of me and grabbed the nearest thing—a six-month-old copy of the *Harvard Business Review*. As I flicked through the pages, paying no real attention to the content, my eyelids kept closing. It'd been weeks since I'd enjoyed an unbroken night's sleep—there hadn't been a single hour when I hadn't thought about the risks I was running. Closure on the SLIDA affair had to come soon; living this way was intolerable.

"Damon," Doug Hennigar said, extending his fat-fingered right hand. "I'm really sorry, but I didn't have you in my calendar."

I rose and shook his hand. "I didn't have an appointment. I hope you don't mind."

"Not at all. Come on through." He led me into his office. "You hungry?" he asked, offering me a plate of sandwiches that had obviously been sitting there since lunchtime.

Not having eaten since the day before, I took one. "Thanks," I said, glancing at the blue marlin before taking a seat in front of Hennigar's desk.

"You must've come back for the file?"

"No."

Hennigar looked deflated. "I was hoping you'd sorted out everything."

"I'm afraid not." Resting the half-eaten sandwich on my

plate, I leaned forward. "I just wanted to make sure my file is still in a safe place."

"It's locked away in our document room. Can't get safer than that."

"Is it fireproof?"

Hennigar tilted his head. "I sure hope so, but I can't say I've ever put it to a test."

"Would you mind keeping another copy offsite? Somewhere secure."

"We've never had a problem with our safe storage room."

I took a sealed envelope out of my briefcase and slid it across the desk. "I'd like you to take that copy with you when you leave tonight. Keep it away from here at all times."

"Am I missing something here, Damon?"

I made eye contact with him. "I'll be honest with you. If the people I'm dealing with knew you had these documents, they'd stop at nothing to retrieve them."

Hennigar bolted upright and placed his palms flat on the desk. "You don't think they'd try to burn our offices?"

"I'm not saying that, but I want to be sure you have a backup copy. Call it insurance."

"You know, if it wasn't for my relationship with your father, I'd be handing back everything right now. This doesn't feel right."

"Trust me. There's nothing illegal going on here. But my life is in jeopardy and, if anything happens to me, I need people to know about these documents. Once they've been made public, there will be no risk to you."

Hennigar sucked air in through his clenched teeth and looked totally unconvinced. "This whole thing is way above my pay grade."

"Look, no one knows I've given you the files. Hopefully, you'll never have to release them."

Hennigar reclined in his chair and crossed his arms, resting them on his paunch. "Something prompted you to bring this in today," he said, pointing to the envelope I'd just given him. "What was it?"

"Something's happening in the next twenty-four hours. I hope it'll bring an end to the whole thing. If it goes as planned, then there'll never be a need for you to get involved."

"And if it doesn't?"

"I will be killed."

Hennigar flinched. "Can't you go to the police?"

"No. That will certainly get me killed."

Hennigar shook his head. "I don't like this. There must be something you can do."

"There is, and I'm doing it tonight."

The traffic was crawling along, nose to tail, as I fought my way onto I-90. It only thinned out a little when I hit I-93 south-bound. Although my parents didn't know it yet, I planned to spend the night in Barnstable. As long as both sets of visitors turned up at CCP that evening, the plan would fall into place on its own. I didn't need to be there for it to work. In fact, going back to the office anytime soon would be dangerous; Mylor's people were bound to be watching out for me there. I'd even arranged for Baker to call by CCP first thing in the morning, so I could stay out of Boston until everything was ready. He'd extract the DVD and upload it, so I could access it all from Barnstable.

The drive took me two hours, which meant I reached my parents' home at eight minutes to seven—tighter than I would have liked. Around the corner from their home, I pulled up and made a quick call to our receptionist to check she was all set and to confirm I was running late as I'd anticipated. She told me Mr. Mylor and his lawyer had just arrived, and I reminded her to leave once the others were there. I made her promise. After the call, I turned my cell phone off, so Mylor would be unable to trace my location from the signal. Given what was about to play out at CCP, he would have even more reason to track me down and wipe me out.

I drove to my parent's house and parked in the driveway, where I sat in the car for a few moments, imagining what was about to happen and praying it all went smoothly.

"Hello, Son," Dad said, tapping on the driver window.

I bolted upright and quickly opened the car door. "Sorry," I said, climbing out of the X5.

"You look as though you've seen a ghost. Are you okay?"

"I'm fine, Dad. I didn't see you."

"This is a pleasant surprise."

"Do you mind if I leave the car in the garage tonight?"

Dad made a face. "It will be perfectly safe out here."

"I guess you're right. Call me paranoid, living in a city."

Dad laughed as we made our way into the house.

"You're losing too much weight, Damon," Mom said, putting her arms around me. "Have you been eating properly? You look dreadful."

"I'm okay, Mom." I held her tighter than usual and for as long as I could. "It's good to see you." If my plan cratered that night, this could be the last time I'd get to spend with my parents.

"You've timed it well. We're just about to eat dinner."

"That's what I was hoping."

Over dinner, my mind was elsewhere. I knew that Mylor had already arrived, but what about Chisholm and Wei? I was desperate to learn how it had all played out. Making conversation and appearing normal wasn't easy, especially when my parents asked about Gainham's death. They'd met him many times over the years and knew we were very close. Tougher still was coming up with a plausible reason why I'd needed to find a good lawyer. From their reaction, I could tell my parents knew something was wrong. Had Hennigar been in touch with Dad, sharing his concerns? They'd obviously been close at one time, so it was possible he'd said more than he should.

That evening, I knew I wasn't convincing Mom and Dad, but I couldn't tell them the truth. How could I? It would terrify them and that wasn't something I was prepared to do, no matter how desperately I wanted to offload the burden and share it with someone.

CHAPTER 54

The taxi dropped Mylor and Alick outside CCP's building at ten to seven. Mylor looked up and down State Street while Alick paid the driver.

"Where are your people?" Mylor asked, standing outside the revolving glass door.

"They're here," Alick said. "If you could see them, they wouldn't be doing their job very well."

"They'd better be here. There's no room for screw-up this evening."

"We're good. I'm on top of it."

The receptionist smiled at the two visitors when they walked into CCP's offices. "Good evening, gentlemen," she said.

"We're here to see Damon Traynor." Mylor's eyes danced around the offices.

"Can I take your names, please?"

"Mylor and Alick."

"Thank you. Damon is expecting you." She walked around to the front of her counter. "Please follow me," she said, leading them into the boardroom. "Damon should be here in just a few moments."

Mylor scowled. "He's not here?"

"He's on his way back from another meeting. Can I get you something to drink?"

"Coffee." Mylor placed his briefcase on the chair next to him.

"I'll be right back."

"She's cute," Alick said when she left the room.

Mylor started unpacking his briefcase. "Shut up and pay attention."

Alick rubbed the bruise on the top of his head then pointed to the papers on the table in front of them. "What are these?"

Mylor picked up one of the documents then placed it back down. "Nothing for you to worry about. Just a bunch of papers I gave Traynor a while back. I assume he's going to hand them back to me tonight."

Alick scanned the table. "What is this SLIDA thing?"

"Look. You don't need to know any of this. Just leave the talking and the thinking to me."

The receptionist returned with four coffees and placed them on the boardroom table. "The other gentlemen have just arrived," she said, smiling.

"What other men?" asked Alick.

Mylor glared at him. "Probably his lawyers. Relax."

"Damon just called," she said. "He says he'll be here in just a few minutes. He's running a bit behind. I told him you were here already."

When she left the room, Alick leaned toward Mylor. "I thought you said there would only be one lawyer."

"We don't have all the details. Deal with it."

Alick shook his head. "I hope we have enough men."

"Once we've signed the papers, the ones to focus on are Traynor and the lawyer who takes the papers away with him. Anyone else is low priority."

"And I'm supposed to communicate that to my team how?"

"You'll think of something."

The receptionist returned to the reception area to collect Chisholm and Wei, who were sitting on the sofa together. "I can take you through now," she said. "Damon should be here any second."

The two men rose to their feet and followed her. As they approached the boardroom, Chisholm looked through the glass wall. "Who are they?" he asked.

"They're here for your meeting," she said before opening the door.

When they walked in, Mylor and Alick stood and hands were shaken.

"I'm sure Damon won't be long," the receptionist said before pulling the door closed as she left.

Chisholm and Wei walked around to the other side of the table, nearest the window, and sat facing Mylor and Alick.

Chisholm helped himself to one of the coffees and relaxed a little when he saw SLIDA documents on the table. "Why isn't Traynor here?"

"He's on his way," Mylor said, holding the papers he'd brought with him for signing. "But we can get going."

Chisholm sipped his coffee. "Okay. What have you got for us?"

Mylor pushed a bunch of papers across the table in Chisholm's direction. "Take a look at this first."

Chisholm slid them to Wei. "He knows what he's looking at."

"I'm sorry?" Mylor had a confused look on his face. "It's a boilerplate sale and purchase agreement."

Chisholm made a face and looked at Wei, who was already flicking through the document Mylor had just given them.

"What is this?" Wei asked, tilting his head at an angle.

"You guys are supposed to be the lawyers," Mylor said. "That's the SPA."

"What are you talking about?" Chisholm asked.

Alick glanced at Mylor then leaned on the table. "Who exactly are you people?"

"I suggest you let Traynor answer that, but we're not lawyers."

Mylor looked at his watch. Seven-thirteen. "Traynor isn't coming is he?"

Chisholm shrugged. "You tell me."

Mylor threw a shit-look. "What did he tell you we're here for?"

Chisholm pointed to the SLIDA documents on top of the table. "To collect these."

"This is a fucking setup," Mylor said, standing. He grabbed Alick's arm. "We're out of here." He reached across the table, snatched the agreement out of Wei's hands, and threw it back into his briefcase before storming out of the room, followed by Alick. When they raced through reception, the receptionist had already gone, and the main office lights were off. Mylor glanced at Alick. "Do whatever it takes to locate Traynor. Do it now."

"What was that all about?" Wei asked, collecting the SLIDA papers from the boardroom table.

"I have no idea," Chisholm said.

Wei crammed the last of the papers into his bag. "These had better be good."

CHAPTER 55

I woke for the first time at one-fifteen, then again at two-ten and two-fifty-five. After that, I lay awake, staring at the red LED display on the alarm clock in my parents' spare room. I felt exhausted—like a mixture of jet lag and the flu—and yet I couldn't sleep. Every now and then, I'd hear a car slow down outside, and I'd get out of bed to check who was out there. I kept wondering how my plan had worked out and where Mylor and his people were. By now, if everything had gone well, they had to be looking for me, and it wouldn't take them long to work out where I was. I had only a few hours, at best, to make my next move.

By five-thirty, I was sitting in Dad's garden office nursing a strong coffee. I'd kept my cell phone switched off overnight, but I couldn't wait any longer. I turned it on and discovered Mylor had left several rambling voicemails, each one increasingly aggressive and incoherent. All of them commanded me to call back or there'd be consequences. I smiled as I played them back once more before powering off the phone. That Mylor was so angry meant the plan had to have succeeded. So far so good.

I waited another hour then called Baker using the land line. "Did everything get recorded okay?"

"You're going to love the quality," Baker said. "To save time, I went back and picked it up from your offices late last night."

"I can't wait to see it. When do you think you'll have it ready for me?"

"I'm in my workshop now. Give me a few more minutes and

I should have it uploaded. I'll send you an email once it's up."

"Thanks, Sam. You know it has to go to my personal email, not the work one?"

"I remember."

"I owe you for this."

After the call, I booted up Dad's PC, logged onto my personal webmail system, and stared at the screen, willing Baker's email to arrive. Although Baker had seemed pleased, it was only when I'd seen the recording for myself that I'd know how things had actually panned out. The wait was agonizing, and all I could find to do was hit the refresh button every few seconds to force the system to check for new mail.

It finally arrived as I finished my second mug of coffee. With barely suppressed excitement, I clicked on the link to the MOV file, hit the play button, and waited for the video to start buffering. A few moments later, the PC screen was filled with moving images of Mylor and someone I didn't recognize sitting in CCP's boardroom. Everything was crystal clear—even the headings of the documents on the table in front of them were legible. The sound quality was borderline acceptable, but there was nothing I could do about that now. I hardly blinked as the fifteen-minute video played back the night's events in high definition. The scheme had worked better than I could have hoped. Even Chisholm and Wei seemed happy enough with the documents they grabbed from the conference room table just before they left. It would take days, if not weeks, to discover they were fakes, so at least they'd be off my back for now. And by the time they did find out, I wouldn't have to worry about them anyway, provided the rest of my plan fell into place. When the video ended, I dragged the slider and paused it on the best bit—the shock reaction on Mylor's face when he realized he'd been set up. *Priceless.*

Although I had no appetite, I joined my parents for breakfast. I was in no hurry to call Mylor back. No hurry to put him out of his pain. The man could sweat it out a little longer.

After I helped Mom clear away the dishes, I joined Dad on his regular morning walk—down Millway, left onto Main Street, then left onto Indian Trail before joining Commerce Road—forty minutes in all, including the brief stop at the harbor to chat with the tanned men setting up the whale watching boat for the day. When we returned home, I asked if I could use Dad's office for the day. I explained how I needed time to think through some work issues and it would be easier if I stayed out of CCP's offices to avoid all the interruptions. I wasn't convinced Dad bought the story, but it was the best I could do.

I closed the office door and looked across the garden to check my parents were in the house, out of earshot. This wasn't something I wanted them to hear. Then I switched on my phone and punched in Mylor's number.

Mylor answered it after one ring. "Where the fuck are you?" he demanded.

"You don't need to know that."

"We were supposed to be completing the acquisition of SLIDA last night. Do you know what the hell you're doing?"

"I know exactly what I'm doing."

"Who were those people?"

"As if you don't know."

A pause at the other end. Then, "You're playing way out of your league here."

"I'm not playing. I needed insurance."

"For what?"

"I don't trust you. Never have. There's no way you were going to buy back SLIDA last night, unless I had insurance."

"What do you think I went all the way to Boston for?"

"We both know what you're capable of. I wasn't going to leave myself open."

Another pause. "So what happens now?"

"We proceed with the sale but, this time, I know you'll deliver."

"Oh yeah?"

"I'm certain of it. You got a pen?"

"What for?"

"Write down this URL."

"Huh?"

"A website address. Write this down exactly: www.video-linktap.com/2345_rty."

"Now what?"

"Put it into your browser and hit play. I'll call you back in fifteen minutes." I turned off my phone and imagined Mylor's reaction as he watched the recording.

Exactly fifteen minutes later, I made another call. "Seen enough yet?"

"You have no idea what you're doing." Mylor's tone was slow and controlled, but it still sounded as if he was about to explode.

"I've never been clearer."

"If you know anything about me, you'll stop this right now."

"I'm not stopping. You've cost the lives of too many innocent people, including people close to me. The whole thing is corrupt, and I have no intention of letting you get away with it."

"I don't know what you're talking about."

"Save it. We both know what's been going on."

"I don't know what kind of fantasy you have going on in your head."

I paused to avoid reacting to Mylor's provocation. "Here's what happens next. The government is going to announce today that the Treasury has reacquired SLIDA with immediate effect. Is that understood?"

"Or what?"

"If the announcement has not been made by five o'clock today, then this little home video will find its way onto YouTube. While I'm waiting, I'll be thinking of a suitable label for it. Maybe, something like: 'CIA agent filmed passing secrets to the Chinese.' How does that sound?"

"Five o'clock. I may need longer."

"Don't even think about it. You said you were prepared to do the deal last night. Oh, and by the way, if anything happens to me before the announcement, or after for that matter, then I've arranged for a detailed file of evidence to be released to the press. It sets out how SLIDA doesn't work, how it never has, and yet the U.S. government conspired to sell it. The video will be released too. I imagine it will go viral within hours."

"I'll see what I can do. How do I get hold of you?"

"Leave a message on my cell. I'll have it turned off. I don't want you trying to trace me. I'll call in to collect my messages throughout the day."

"I'm making no promises."

"That's up to you."

As I finished the call, my heart was racing. I closed my eyes and exhaled slowly. Was I really close to ending this? Surely, now Mylor had nowhere else to go, he had to comply. And if he tried anything once this was all over, I'd still have the video as leverage. That ought to be enough to keep him in check.

I looked at my watch—ten o'clock. Seven hours of waiting as Mylor was certain to leave an announcement until the very last minute.

CHAPTER 56

"I need you now," Mylor said, marching into Kerry's office, his face red and puffy. He hovered over the edge of her desk and crossed his arms. "Drop whatever you're doing. I want you to come with me."

Kerry quickly closed the open windows on her PC and grabbed her jacket. "Where are we going?" she asked, catching up with him along the corridor.

"I'll explain in a moment." Mylor ran down a flight of stairs, two at a time.

For a moment, a terrifying thought shot into Kerry's head. Had Barrett been in touch with her boss, asking questions about the bank transfer instructions? What would she do if he challenged her on it? There was no credible explanation as to why she would divert ten million dollars of government funds? If Mylor was onto her, she was dead meat.

Following him into a windowless meeting room, she began to relax. It couldn't have anything to do with Barrett as he'd still be on his flight back from Hong Kong. No way would he have had time to contact Mylor.

Eleven senior members of Mylor's team were sitting around the long table. Kerry knew them all, but hadn't worked with any of them. Mylor liked his lieutenants to work alone, in their own silos, assisted only by one or two junior analysts. Only he knew the specifics of each of their assignments and how they knitted together into the bigger picture. That way, he minimized the risk of any leak of confidential information. The one common thread linking all the people in the room was that they were involved in different aspects of Project Eclipse—the top-secret project that had been active for five months now, and the only one Kerry had worked on since being assigned to the team.

When Mylor briefed Kerry the week she joined, he'd explained that Project Eclipse was the most important operation ever handled by his covert unit—a project so critical to national security that, according to him, he reported directly to unnamed members of the Cabinet. In essence, the mission was simple: Use whatever means available to generate funds for the Treasury by orchestrating the sale of the government's least-attractive assets for the largest cash sum possible. So far, Mylor's team had realized in excess of two trillion dollars for assets that were held in the federal balance sheet at a fraction of that amount. By any measure, they had achieved stunning results.

There was only one problem: Mylor recognized no boundaries, no line he wouldn't cross, and no man or woman he would allow to stand in the way of achieving his objectives. For him, the words "whatever means" had no limitations, legal, or otherwise. Achieving the mission was everything. Kerry hated herself for being part of his unlawful scheme and was desperate to end it. But, so far, Mylor had been clever. There was no trail of evidence pointing to criminal activity. What proof she had was all circumstantial, and while the body count had mounted, as far as anyone outside was concerned, Mylor's hands were clean.

Her assumption was that the people sitting around the meeting room table—all of them had been with Mylor for years—knew exactly what he was. In all probability, they were as guilty as him. Whatever happened, she would never allow herself to become like them.

"Sit there," Mylor said, pointing Kerry to the only empty seat. He remained standing. "I've been bringing these guys up to speed on the SLIDA transaction." There was a sea of nodding heads around the table. Mylor stared at Kerry. "I need you to tell us everything you know about Damon Traynor."

Kerry looked at the expectant faces peering back at her. Why exactly had this meeting been arranged, and why had she not been invited to the earlier session? It was clear from the empty coffee cups that this group had been in a private huddle for some time. Did they know she'd been involved with Traynor and had been trying to help him? The panic returned.

"Have I missed something?" Kerry asked.

"This morning, I heard from Traynor. At five o'clock this afternoon, he's going public on SLIDA. He's going to tell the world it doesn't work. Can you imagine the damage that would cause? We simply cannot allow that to happen."

"Why don't we buy it back? We know that would silence him."

Mylor looked as if he wanted to jump across the table and throttle her. "We don't have time for that. Traynor has to be stopped now. This is a matter of national security."

"But—"

Mylor raised his right hand. "This is not a debate. The decision's already made. We need to find him quickly. That's why you're here."

Kerry assumed Damon had gone into hiding somewhere. If Mylor wanted to bring him in alive, he'd have asked the FBI for help in tracking his cell. But that would never happen; Mylor trusted only his own people. Besides, she knew exactly what Mylor would do if he located Damon. He'd become another unexplained fatality. While she couldn't allow that to happen, she had to appear on Mylor's side—at least for now. "What do you need to know from me?"

"Everything. You've been handling much of the SLIDA deal. I want to know who his friends are, where they live, where his family members live, where he goes on vacation, anything that'll help us find him."

Kerry spent the next hour being grilled by Mylor's team. She pleaded ignorance as many times as she could, while still retaining her credibility. When faced with questions to which she simply had to know the answers, she made the facts up, saying anything to throw the wolves off the scent. She had to buy time for Damon, so he could go public with what he knew. Right now, he was the only one who had the capacity to stop Mylor once and for all. The risks he was taking with his life were enormous, and she admired him for it.

The call from Barrett came in at ten past two when Kerry was back at her desk.

"I got back this morning," Barrett said from the other end of the line. "I just heard from the lawyers. The money should be with you now."

"That's great," said Kerry. "I'll let Ben know."

She put down the phone then closed her office door. The morning's events meant she had never been more certain of her next move. She punched a number into her cell phone. "Neil, it's Kerry," she said, swiveling her chair so she was facing away from her door and lowering her voice. "I'm expecting some funds to have hit the Hong Kong account."

"Do you have any idea what time it is here?"

"I'm so sorry. I wasn't thinking straight. I'll call back later."

"Don't worry. I'm awake now. I can log in from here."

"Do you need the account details?"

"No. I have them." There was a pause and tapping on a keyboard. "Yeah, I have them right here." A few more rapid taps. "Yep. Ten million dollars came in yesterday."

"Good, that's what I expected."

"Is the money going to sit there for a while, or do you need it sending on?"

"I'd like to send it to another account as soon as possible."

"Got the details?"

Kerry reached into her purse and found a folded sheet of paper. She read the account details to Glesinger and dictated a payment advice note. "All of it's going there," she said.

"I'll take care of it."

"Thanks, Neil. I'm really sorry I woke you up."

"You're not the first. Forget about it."

"Thanks. Any time you need a favor, just let me know."

"Sure will."

After the call, Kerry reopened her door then sat down and stared at the screen of her PC. The action she'd just taken was permanent and irreversible, but she didn't have a shred of guilt on her conscience. It was a considered and deliberate act in full knowledge of the consequences.

She launched Word and began to type. Minutes later, she'd written a standard resignation letter. In it, she told Mylor, while she was prepared to give notice, she preferred to leave immediately.

She read the letter on the screen then printed it. This wasn't exactly how she'd envisioned the end of her career, but it was still the right decision. She'd known this moment was coming for some time—ever since, under Mylor's orders, she'd shot the suspected terrorist in Manhattan. That day, outside Grand Central Station, she'd killed what turned out to be an innocent man in front of his daughter. And for what? To prove she had the stomach for it, to show Mylor she was fit to join his elite unit, and to further her own career. All of it was meaningless. Ever since the shooting, she'd been plagued by flashbacks of the little girl's face. How was she coping without her father? Would witnessing his assassination haunt the child for the rest of her life? Kerry wished she could unwind it all.

Kerry picked up a pen, signed the letter, and placed it into a sealed envelope. Then she walked to Mylor's office where his personal assistant was sitting outside his closed door. "Can I ask you to give this to Ben?" Kerry held out the envelope.

The PA looked up from her screen. "You can take it to him yourself, if you like. He's not in a meeting."

"That's okay. As long as he gets it today, it's fine. I have a meeting to go to."

The PA pointed to her inbox. "Leave it there. I'll see he gets it."

Kerry smiled, dropped the envelope into the tray, and returned to her office to collect her purse. She had no regrets as she looked around her office for what was probably the last time.

She pulled the door closed behind her and left the building.

CHAPTER 57

The websites of CNN, Bloomberg, and MSNBC were open on Dad's PC, but there was no announcement about the deal. Nothing. This had to be the longest wait of my life, with each passing hour seeming more like a day. At exactly one minute past five, I placed the battery back into my phone and turned it back on for the first time in two hours. Nothing from Mylor either. *What's he up to?* I thought. *Does he think I'm bluffing?*

On my voicemail, however, were three messages from Kerry. She said she needed to speak with me urgently. Sure she did. If I called her, she'd only drone on about how dangerous her boss could be. That threat didn't work on me anymore. She'd say anything to persuade me not to publish the video and my file of information. Kerry worked for Mylor. As much as it was a bitter disappointment for me, I'd long accepted she was not on my side; she never had been.

My options were becoming fewer by the minute. If I released the video immediately, what leverage would I have left against Mylor? It was the nuclear option. Yes, it would certainly destroy him but, in retaliation, he'd send his DVD to my investors and parents. But if I didn't act soon, his people were bound to locate me, and the consequences of that happening were unthinkable.

I decided to give him one last chance, so I punched in his number.

"Yep," Mylor said after four rings.

"Where are you on the announcement?"

"What announcement?"

"I warned you what would happen. It's now after five."

"Then you'd better get on with it."

"You want me to release the video?"

"What does it show? All the documents on the table were fake. I should know; I gave them to you. So you caught me giving false information to the Chinese. Seems to me, I deserve a pat on the back for that."

I couldn't believe what I was hearing. Mylor was playing hardball and calling my bluff. Did he really think he could ride this one out?

"No one will care about the authenticity of the documents." I was desperate to land a punch but knew my words sounded weak. "All they will see is a senior U.S. agent working hand in hand with the Chinese. You try bouncing back from that."

"Is that all you have?"

Panic consumed me. What else did I have? Nothing. Mylor had outplayed me again.

"I'll give you until six. I won't contact you again. At six o'clock the video goes live."

I couldn't get off the phone fast enough, so I terminated the call.

Why would Mylor take the risk if he could buy SLIDA back from us at cost? That would quietly bring this to an end for everyone. It didn't make sense.

CHAPTER 58

Mylor was slowly tapping his fingertips in front of his face when the phone rang.

"We've picked up Traynor's cell phone signal," Alick said from the other end of the line.

"Good work," Mylor said. "Where is he?"

"Shows him somewhere down on the Cape."

Mylor waded through the papers underneath Kerry's resignation letter until he found the notes she'd prepared that morning, setting out what she knew about Traynor. "We've got him. His parents live in Barnstable. He has to be there."

"Where is that?"

Mylor searched on Google Maps. "On the north shore—a few miles along the Cape. Where are you now?"

"I-93, heading south out of Boston. The traffic's a nightmare."

"I'll text you the address. My guess is you'll be there in just over an hour if you put your foot down."

"I'm on it."

"Traynor is an imminent threat to national security."

"Understood."

"I want no loose ends."

"I've got this."

When I reached for my phone, I realized I'd left it switched on. It had been active since my last call with Mylor almost half an hour earlier. He was bound to make use of the cellular network to track down my location. My first thought was the safety of my parents. Somehow, I'd have to get them out of the house quickly. I was about to hold down the power off button when the phone rang. The screen displayed Kerry's name. What could she want? Mylor had already made his position clear. I knew I should turn off the phone, but something made me take her call.

"What is it, Kerry?"

"I've been trying to get hold of you all day," she said, her voice full of panic.

"I know. I got your messages."

"Why didn't you call me back?"

"Because you work for Mylor."

A pause, then, "I think he's going to kill you."

There was no news in what I'd just heard, but hearing the words spoken out loud chilled my spine. "Why are you telling me this?"

"Because I care about you."

I said nothing. Was it possible I'd misjudged Kerry? Had I been wrong to assume she would always side with Mylor? She sounded sincere enough.

"Mylor has a whole team working on finding you," Kerry said. "I know what he's capable of. He'll stop at nothing to silence you."

"Did he mention the video?"

"What video?"

"You remember the documents he sent me to pass on?"

"Of course."

"Well, I recorded a video last night. It shows Mylor handing them over to the Chinese agents who were threatening us."

"No wonder he was running around like a chicken with its head cut off this morning. I'm amazed he let himself be set up that way. How did you do it?"

"Doesn't matter. I told him the video was going live on YouTube if he didn't acquire SLIDA."

"That explains a lot. What was his response?"

"He called my bluff. Says he doesn't care if I release it. He thinks no one will care about him passing false intelligence to the other side."

"That sounds like him."

"I gave him until five, but he ignored that deadline. Now, I've given him until six."

"That's less than half an hour from now."

"I think he'll ignore this one too."

A long pause at Kerry's end, then, "I may be able to help."

"I sure could use some."

"What if we could make it look as though he was doing more than passing information to an adversary?"

What exactly did Kerry have in mind? Did she have more incriminating evidence against her boss?

"I don't understand."

"I can give you something that'll make it seem he's been taking payments in exchange for information."

"If I had evidence like that—"

"Write this down. You haven't got long."

"I'm listening."

"34-23-22-79-2."

"What is that?"

"It's Mylor's personal account at Citizens Bank."

"How did you—?"

"Don't ask."

"What am I supposed to do with it?"

"Nothing. It's already been done. Earlier today, ten million dollars was transferred into that account from a bank account in Hong Kong."

"What? How did you get—?"

"It's best you don't know. I can assure you Mylor's account details are right, and the money is very real. You don't need to know any more than that."

"I don't know what to say, Kerry. This will stop him in his tracks."

"Now maybe you'll believe I'm on your side."

"I'm so sorry I misjudged you."

"I decided I couldn't work for Mylor a long time ago. The more I learned about him, the more I found things I couldn't live with. He has to be stopped one way or another."

"What will you do?"

"I resigned today. I'll take some time off to think it through. Anyway, that's a conversation for another day. You need to get hold of Mylor as soon as you can."

"Can I call you later tonight?"

"I'd like that, Damon. Good luck."

CHAPTER 59

I waited until six o'clock in case Mylor decided to roll over on his own—not that I expected him to change his mind, but there was no point putting Kerry at risk if I didn't need to.

No call came.

At two minutes past six, I called him.

"You weren't going to contact me again," Mylor said.

"I assume your position hasn't changed?"

"What do you think?"

"Then you leave me with no option but to release the video."

"Do your worst, son."

"It goes live right after this call."

"Listen, I haven't got all night to sit here talking to you."

"There's one thing I forgot to mention last time."

"Oh yeah?"

"I've added a bit more description to the video."

"Have fun. It'll be the last bit of excitement you get."

"Is that a threat?"

"Not really," Mylor said. "More of a promise."

"That's exactly why you have to be stopped."

"This conversation is over."

"Don't you want to hear what I've added?"

Mylor exhaled loudly. "You have thirty seconds."

I stood to deliver the punch. "Have you checked your bank account recently?"

"What?"

"You should. I think you'll find it interesting."

"What do you—?"

"Let's just say the note mentions your bank account and helps explain what the video shows. I'd like to tell you more, but my thirty seconds are up."

I terminated the call and quickly turned my phone off. I leaned against the wall behind my father's desk and closed my eyes. *Thank you, Kerry.*

Mylor opened a web browser, went to his bank's secure website, and entered his login details and password. He clicked on his account and scanned the statement of recent transactions. A heart-stopping cocktail of horror, shock, and rage ran through him as he read the details of the massive deposit made earlier in the day.

Transfer from Hong Kong—$10,000,000.00

"What the fuck?" he said out loud. His PA came rushing to his door. "Shut the fucking door," he said. She disappeared, closing the door behind her. Mylor looked back at the screen and clicked on the deposit, but no more information was available. He looked at his watch. The bank would be closed. He couldn't find out anything about it until the morning.

When he called Traynor's phone, it went straight to voice-mail. "Call me back immediately," he said. "We need to talk."

Staring at his PC screen, he tried to make sense of what was happening. How the hell did Traynor get access to his personal bank account and where did the money come from? The consequences began to sink in. Traynor had video evidence of him betraying his country for money. If this got out, he'd be facing a long prison sentence, if not worse. He called Damon's phone again and left another voicemail, this time barely disguising the alarm in his voice.

Then Mylor remembered Alick was still on his way to Barnstable. Not knowing what Traynor had done with this incriminating evidence or who he'd shared it with, he needed Traynor alive, if he was ever going to contain the threat.

He hit the speed dial for Alick. "Where are you?"

"About fifteen minutes away. The traffic's been—"

"Call it off."

"Are you sure? I'm almost there."

"For fuck's sake, just call it off and get back over here."

I waited until seven-forty-five before returning Mylor's calls. In the hour and a half since we'd last spoken, he'd left six messages, each one sounding more desperate than the last. By now, I figured I had his attention.

"You wanted to speak to me?" I said, keeping all emotion out of my voice.

"Has the video gone out?" Mylor asked.

"Let me see." I sat there, quietly enjoying the moment, letting him wriggle on the end of the rope for a good minute. "Just finishing the upload now. The exact description that went with it reads: 'CIA agent, Ben Mylor, passing confidential defense information to the Chinese in exchange for money.' I hope you don't mind, but I've taken the liberty of disclosing your bank account details to make it easier for the story to be verified."

"What do you want to stop this?"

"I'm not sure I could if I wanted to."

"Look, you've won. Stop the damn upload and tell me what you want."

I waited a few more seconds. The upload hadn't even started, but it felt good hearing the panic in Mylor's voice as he took some of his own medicine.

"I want the government to buy back SLIDA. That's all I've ever wanted."

"And that will be the end of it?"

"You give me what I want, and I'll keep quiet about you collaborating with an enemy."

"Your deal will be announced first thing in the morning."
I finished the call then punched the air.

CHAPTER 60

I parked my X5 in a public parking lot near CCP and walked down State Street to the Marriott Long Wharf Hotel. Until I'd seen the deal announcement for myself, I wasn't going anywhere near the office. Even though I had Mylor over a barrel, he still couldn't be trusted. No telling what a desperate man like him might do.

After my final call with Mylor, I'd spent most of the night on the phone, updating each of my partners from the pay phone outside Mattakeese Wharf, a restaurant at Barnstable Harbor. I owed each of them an apology and an explanation for my recent absence from the office and I needed to tell them what had been agreed on SLIDA. I told them everything and why we were lucky to be getting our money back on the ill-fated deal.

I scheduled a partners' meeting for eight a.m. in one of the Marriott's meeting rooms overlooking the Boston waterfront. When I walked in at ten to eight, I expected to be the first to arrive. Instead, I entered the room to a round of applause and a sea of smiling faces.

"You're late," Crawford shouted from across the room. She was standing with one foot inside and one foot on the balcony, smoking a cigarette. Her right arm was supported in a sling.

My eyes welled up. "It's great to see you back, Diane. I didn't miss the smoke, though."

Crawford threw the stub on the balcony and hobbled back into the room. "I hear the place fell apart without me."

I nodded. "Something like that."

"Why didn't you tell us what was going on?"

"Once you'd been attacked, and we lost Chris, I had to deal with this alone. I just couldn't put more lives at risk."

Crawford shook her head. "I still can't believe Chris isn't here with us."

"Me too. I miss him so much." I looked at my watch. "It's coming up for eight." I turned on the wide screen TV at one end of the room, picked up the remote, and scrolled through the channels until I found Bloomberg. As eight o'clock approached, everyone sat, the room grew quiet, and I turned up the volume.

"Some breaking news at this hour," said the Bloomberg presenter. "The U.S. Department of the Treasury has just announced it's buying back the strategic laser infrastructure for the defense of America. The business, known as SLIDA, was acquired by Boston private equity firm, Carada Capital Partners, earlier this year for twenty-five billion dollars, setting the record for PE deals at the time. The detailed terms of the buyback deal have not been released."

Spontaneous applause broke out in the room. I looked around and soaked up the beaming smiles from my partners. *Chris should have been here to share this moment,* I thought.

"Pity we only got our money back," Crawford said.

"It could have been a whole lot worse," I said.

An assistant manager from the hotel tapped on the open door and entered the room. He looked at me. "Mr. Traynor, your visitor has arrived."

"I'll come out," I said, ignoring the quizzical faces of my partners. A minute later, I walked into the meeting room followed by a woman dressed in a smart business suit.

"Everyone, I'd like to introduce you to our latest senior hire. This is Kerry Ward, who's going to be heading up our due diligence activities from now on."

"Welcome, Kerry," Crawford said. "Damon told us what you did for us. We're all so grateful."

I pointed to an empty seat next to me. "Take a seat, Kerry. I'd like you to get to know the team."

After the meeting, we returned to CCP where I showed Kerry her new office, complete with its view over downtown.

"I don't know what to say," she said.

I put my arms around her. "Say nothing." I held her close to me and kissed her on the lips.

CHAPTER 61

In the days that followed, I settled into a normal working routine, sinking my teeth into new transactions, meeting management teams, and negotiating deal terms. It felt good to be back and focused on investments rather than looking over my shoulder in fear for my life. I was confident Mylor wouldn't come seeking retribution as the evidence we still had against him would make sure of that. As for the Chinese, we'd heard nothing more from them since the government had reacquired SLIDA.

In the financial press, the firm received acres of positive coverage on the SLIDA deal, although some commentators had begun asking why the government had bought back an asset they'd sold only a few weeks earlier. It made no sense, particularly when the federal deficit was still crippling the country. I did my best to dodge those awkward questions when journalists called to interview me. I told them I was paid to worry about my investors' interests, not run the country.

Kerry enjoyed diving into the fine detail of our new deals, learning the ropes and understanding what made the difference between a good investment and a bad one. She was a quick learner, and I had no doubt she'd fast become an asset to the firm. Her critical skills and enthusiasm meant she was bound to succeed in her new role. The one surprise she'd shared with me early on was the hectic work schedule and long hours in private equity compared to working for the government. That made me smile. I told her she'd soon get used to it. Besides, since she'd moved into my townhouse, I'd know if she was struggling with the work and would be there to help.

Two weeks after the sale of SLIDA, I took a call on my cell phone.

"I'm wondering whether you found the information for me?" Jean Tillman asked.

"Not yet," I said. "I'm sorry. Things have been hectic here. I was going to call you this weekend to explain."

"I really don't want to wait any longer. Could you make it a priority?"

"I'll see what I can do, Jean. Please leave it with me and I'll be in touch soon."

Guilt played on my conscience after the call. I didn't like lying to Jean, but what else could I do? I took a folded piece of paper out of my top desk drawer and held it. Everything Jean needed was in the palm of my hand, but I couldn't give it to her. I stared at the handwritten note: *230 Gordon Square Lane, Richmond, Virginia*. The writing was Kerry's. Both of us knew why Jean wanted the information, but we also understood what she was likely to do with it. By holding back Mylor's weekend home address, we were trying to protect Jean from doing something stupid.

Our partners' meeting had gone on longer than anticipated that evening, so I was late getting back. I'd tried calling Kerry before I left the office and again on my drive home, but she'd not picked up the land line at the townhouse or her cell. When I pulled into the garage and saw her car, I assumed she must have gone for an evening run without me.

The house was dark, and when I turned on some lights, I noticed Kerry's briefcase was in its usual place in the hallway. Then I spotted her Nike running shoes in the downstairs closet, so she couldn't be out running.

It was only when I walked into the kitchen that I became concerned. On the counter were chopped onions, peppers, and an open can of plum tomatoes. Why would the house be dark if Kerry had started preparing dinner?

"Kerry," I shouted. "Kerry."

No answer.

Every nerve in my body screamed at me that something was wrong. I ran upstairs to the master bedroom and turned on the light. Lying on the bed in front of me was Kerry, on her back, motionless, her eyes wide open. An empty bottle of pills was on the floor next to the bed. Covering my mouth to suppress the urge to gag, I stood frozen, staring at the woman I'd come to love. When my brain finally reengaged, fear consumed me as I edged closer to the bed and felt for a pulse. I already knew she was dead.

Mylor!

CHAPTER 62

Part of a private, gated enclave, Gordon Square Lane was occupied by enormous, multi-million dollar properties, sitting in five-acre wooded lots. Number 230 was a seven-thousand-square-foot, two-story, red-brick McMansion backing onto hiker trails near the prestigious Country Club of Virginia golf course.

In the far corner of the golf club parking lot, I managed to park my X5 in the same spot I'd used on the previous three Sundays. It was ten past six in the morning when I stepped out of the car—enough daylight to find my way through the trees, but dark enough to hide in the shadows. I wore a black tracksuit and running shoes, with a gray backpack strapped to my body. If the golf club's private security, or any of the owners of the nearby houses, stopped me on what was private land, I'd say I was looking for the hiking trails at the edge of the forest.

But I'd not been challenged on any of my prior reconnaissance visits when I'd sat, hidden in the undergrowth, watching the rear of number 230 through my binoculars. Every Sunday morning, the pattern appeared to be the same. The kitchen light would go on around six-thirty, then Mylor made drinks for him and his wife before carrying them up to the master bedroom. About an hour and a half later, the kitchen became a hive of activity with the couple having breakfast with their daughter, who looked to be around seven or eight.

By now, I could recognize the signals when the mother and daughter were preparing to leave the house. At nine-fifteen, the young girl would run upstairs and come back down a few moments later dressed in soccer gear. For the past three weeks in a row, they'd left the house in a blue Mercedes E Class no later than nine-thirty, returning just over two hours later.

That morning, everything appeared to be following its usual pattern. When the daughter came downstairs dressed in her sports outfit, I cut a hole in the black chain link fence behind the property using metal cutters I'd brought in my backpack. While Mylor was distracted saying goodbye to his wife and daughter, I sprinted across the back lawn and crouched behind the building. My breathing was labored as I sat on the rear terrace, listening for the Mercedes to drive away.

When I heard the familiar crunching sound on the gravel drive, I took several deep breaths to control my nerves. Inside my backpack was a Smith & Wesson double-action, semi-automatic pistol. The magazine was already loaded with a round in the chamber. My heart felt as though it was about to burst when I disengaged the safety. That was the only moment I had second thoughts about what I was doing there.

I closed my eyes and thought of Kerry. Somehow, thinking of her helped calm me down. My breathing now steady, I stood, kicked the backpack against the wall of the house, and edged my way around to the front of the building. At the end of the drive, the metal gates banged as they closed behind the exiting Mercedes. The car accelerated down the lane, but I waited until I could no longer hear it.

With the pistol gripped in my right hand, I rang the doorbell then squeezed against the side of the brick porch so I couldn't be seen.

"What have you forgotten?" Mylor asked, unlocking and opening the door.

Immediately, I kicked it open with my right leg. The edge of the door hit Mylor hard in the center of his forehead, gashing the skin and knocking him to the floor.

"Stay where you are," I shouted, pointing the gun at him while slamming the door shut.

Mylor looked at the gun. "What the fuck?"

"Shut up, you piece of shit." I held the pistol steady.

He sat up and leaned against the wall, raising the palms of both hands. "Okay, okay," he said, blood dripping from his head wound.

"You have no idea how many times I've thought about this moment." My voice was surprisingly calm and deliberate.

"You haven't got the balls to shoot me. We both know that, so put the gun down."

I squeezed the trigger and a bullet ripped into his right knee. "I told you to shut up."

Mylor screamed and writhed around on the floor, clasping his knee. "You can have anything you want. Please, just let me live."

I stood over Mylor's contorted body, so I could look into his eyes. "I don't want anything from you." With the pistol held eighteen inches above his head, I smiled. "It's enough to watch you suffer."

Mylor's face took on a glaze of horror and fear as he absorbed my words. "You must want something."

"You don't seem at all surprised to see me. That tells me everything I need."

"Why are you here? You got your money back."

I put another round in his right ankle, and blood spattered on the beige wall. "That one was for Kerry."

Curled on the floor in a fetal position, trying to hold his knee and ankle at the same time, Mylor squealed in agony.

"You couldn't let it go, could you?" I said.

"I haven't seen her since she left." Mylor struggled to get his words out.

Standing hard on the side of Mylor's bleeding ankle, I twisted it into the carpet. "She outplayed you and you just couldn't accept it," I said, although Mylor was unlikely to hear me above his wailing.

I waited for the weeping to subside before continuing. "How

does someone like you afford a place like this? Don't tell me you did it all for the money."

"Can I please sit up?"

"If it helps you talk. Sure." I stepped back, keeping the weapon trained on him.

"I'm going to need some help."

"If you want to sit up, you're going to have to do it on your own."

Mylor rolled his weight onto his right side, inch by painful inch. The floor beneath him was drenched in blood.

So he could use his good leg to push himself up against the wall, I moved back a little further.

The telephone rang, distracting me for a split second.

Mylor thrust out his left leg and swung it as hard as he could against my shins.

As I lost my balance, instinctively, I gripped the gun and let off another shot. My head crashed against the top of a wooden console table during my fall. For a fleeting moment, I lost concentration and dropped the pistol. It landed between the two of us.

Mylor drove through his pain and charged at the weapon.

I grabbed at the pistol, reaching it just before him.

Mylor picked up the console table's broken leg and plunged the sharp end deep into my thigh, turning it when he hit bone.

The surge of pain delayed long enough for me to sink another round into Mylor's chest. I watched him roll against the wall as I struggled to my feet.

Mylor was lying on his left side, facing away from me, when I limped over to him.

"Please, call an ambulance. I don't want to die." Mylor's words were strained as he struggled to get air into his lungs.

"I'll get you some help, but first you need to tell me something."

"Anything. Just call for help, please."

I held my left hand over the blood weeping from my thigh,

my need for information more pressing than the pain. "I know you were just the bag carrier. How far did your conspiracy go?"

At this point, Mylor was drifting in and out of consciousness, his breathing becoming more erratic.

I stood over Mylor's body and watched his face. When he opened his eyes, I said, "Tell me who you worked for and I'll let you live."

"Allen, Patterson..." Blood and saliva bubbled from his lips as he spoke, "...and Halley."

A few seconds later, the life drained out of Mylor's body.

CHAPTER 63

Dad's first reaction was shock, then outrage, soon followed by a deep desire for justice. I told him everything—how I'd been targeted by Mylor's team in the first place; how stupid I'd been allowing myself to be set up by the young woman in Cambridge; the murders of innocent people around the world, including my friends, Gainham and Kerry; and even my retribution against Mylor. I held nothing back, and it felt liberating sharing the burden with someone I love.

Both of us knew what had to be done. The world needed to learn about the criminal conspiracy being directed from the White House before others were killed. While I wanted to release the file held by Doug Hennigar, it was Dad's idea to go see Treasury Secretary Allen first. Dad remembered his former college roommate as a decent man and was still struggling to accept he was part of the administration's illegal scheme. Because of his lawyer training, he kept saying the evidence I had was largely circumstantial and that it would be compelling if we could get Allen to turn. I figured there was nothing to lose in trying my father's way first. If Allen denied everything then I'd release what I had anyway.

It was a week before I was fit enough to travel. The wound to my leg had required surgery, but I was able to get around with the use of crutches upon my discharge from hospital. Dad contacted Allen to say he and his son were visiting Washington and suggested we meet for a drink one evening. Allen took the bait and invited us to his Georgetown townhouse.

We arrived at eight. Pleasantries were exchanged and, after a quick tour around their Victorian home, Allen's wife politely left him alone in the den with his two visitors.

Dad put down his glass of wine on the mahogany side table next to his armchair, glanced at me, then turned to our host. "This is not entirely a social visit."

Allen looked confused. "I see. Why didn't you say when you called?"

"It won't take long. My son has something to ask you."

"I hope I can help."

I retrieved an envelope from my inside jacket pocket, opened it, and extracted most of the contents. "Do any of these faces look familiar to you?" I asked as I spread color printouts on the coffee table in front of Allen. Each print contained a portrait.

Allen cocked his head. "What am I looking at?"

"You don't recognize them? Maybe their names will jog your memory." I grimaced as I leaned forward toward the table, pulling on my wounded leg. "This one is Frank Marcuri," I said pointing to the first picture. "The others are Tom Laudel, Paul McCann, Richard Leigh, and Brodie Tillman."

Allen flinched at the mention of Tillman's name. "I'm sorry; I don't know any of them. Should I?"

I took the remaining two pictures out of the envelope. "How about these?" I placed photos of Mylor and Kerry in front of him. "Surely, you know these people?"

Allen went pale and covered his mouth with his left palm. "Oh my—"

"It seems you recognize them," Dad said.

"He should," I said. "These are just some of the people he and Mylor killed."

Allen cradled his head in his hands. "I should have known. You're Damon Traynor from CCP."

"That's right. The firm you shook down on the SLIDA deal. Was it worth spilling all this blood for?" My voice became louder as I struggled to contain the fury inside me.

"Please, my wife is next door. I never wanted any of this.

You have to understand the pressure I've been under."

"Tell that to their families." I said.

Allen raised his head, but avoided eye contact. "What do you want?"

Dad looked at me. "Tell him, Damon."

"In twenty-four hours, a file of information will be released to the press." I pointed to the pictures on the table. "Believe me when I tell you we have a lot more than this."

"That means you have a few hours to do the right thing," Dad said.

Allen remained seated, stunned and silent, as we stood and walked out.

After his visitors left, Allen retreated to his study and typed on his laptop. Two hours later, and long after his wife had gone to bed, he printed out eight pages of detailed notes and placed them in an envelope. Then he looked up the home number for one of his contacts in Outlook and called them.

"It's Gordon Allen. Sorry to call you so late. I have something for you."

Half an hour later a courier came to Allen's home to collect the envelope. Allen returned to his study, poured himself a large single-malt, and knocked it back in one slug.

Then he opened up his desk drawer and took out a pistol. He put a single round in the chamber, placed the barrel up against his palate and blew his brains out.

It was just before three a.m. when the president was woken by his unexpected visitor. He was still wearing a bathrobe when he left his private quarters and joined George Patterson in the Oval Office.

"This had better be good, George."

"Mr. President, I have bad news." Patterson handed him two

sheets of printed paper. "Twenty minutes ago, this story appeared on the *Washington Post* website."

President Halley read only as far as the opening paragraph before dropping the papers on the floor. "How?"

"Allen. Who else?"

"We're fucked!"

At eight a.m., President Halley and George Patterson, Director of National Intelligence, resigned from office. Three months later, they were both indicted on charges of racketeering and conspiracy to commit murder.

Not long after Halley's administration collapsed, the Chinese recommenced buying U.S. Treasury bills.

As for me, I wasn't surprised the police never came knocking on my door. After all, if you kill a ghost, it's hard to be charged with his murder. But I knew I'd spend the rest of my life looking over my shoulder. Wanting to make the most of what life I had left, I handed over the reins at CCP to Crawford, bought a home on the Cape near my parents, and devoted myself to working with homeless people.

The strange thing is, I never did find out whether SLIDA works.

ACKNOWLEDGMENTS

I'd like to thank my wife, Jules, for her support and encouragement. Writing can be a selfish pursuit, and so I remain ever grateful for her tolerance and understanding.

Martin Bodenham was born in the UK. He is the author of the financial thrillers *The Geneva Connection, Once a Killer,* and *Shakedown.*

After a thirty-year career in private equity and corporate finance, Martin moved to the west coast of Canada, where he writes full-time. He held corporate finance partner positions at both KPMG and Ernst & Young as well as senior roles at a number of private equity firms before founding his own private equity company in 2001. Much of the tension in his thrillers is based on the greed and fear he witnessed first-hand while working in international finance.

http://www.martinbodenham.com/

OTHER TITLES FROM DOWN AND OUT BOOKS

See www.DownAndOutBooks.com for complete list

By J.L. Abramo
Chasing Charlie Chan
Circling the Runway
Brooklyn Justice
Coney Island Avenue

By Trey R. Barker
Exit Blood
Death is Not Forever
No Harder Prison

By Eric Beetner
Unloaded (editor)
Criminal Elements
Rumrunners
Leadfoot

By Eric Beetner
and Frank Zafiro
The Backlist
The Shortlist

By G.J. Brown
Falling

By Angel Luis Colón
No Happy Endings
Meat City on Fire (*)

By Shawn Corridan
and Gary Waid
Gitmo

By Frank De Blase
Pine Box for a Pin-Up
Busted Valentines
A Cougar's Kiss

By Les Edgerton
The Genuine, Imitation,
Plastic Kidnapping
Lagniappe
Just Like That (*)

By Danny Gardner
A Negro and an Ofay

By Jack Getze
Big Mojo
Big Shoes
The Black Kachina

By Richard Godwin
Wrong Crowd
Buffalo and Sour Mash
Crystal on Electric Acetate

By Jeffery Hess
Beachhead
Cold War Canoe Club

By Matt Hilton
Rules of Honor
The Lawless Kind
The Devil's Anvil
No Safe Place

By Lawrence Kelter
and Frank Zafiro
The Last Collar

By Lawrence Kelter
Back to Brooklyn
My Cousin Vinny (*)

(*)—Coming Soon

OTHER TITLES FROM DOWN AND OUT BOOKS

See www.DownAndOutBooks.com for complete list

By Jerry Kennealy
Screen Test
Polo's Long Shot

By Dana King
Worst Enemies
Grind Joint
Resurrection Mall

By Ross Klavan, Tim O'Mara
and Charles Salzberg
Triple Shot

By S.W. Lauden
Crosswise
Crossed Bones

By Paul D. Marks and
Andrew McAleer (editor)
Coast to Coast vol. 1
Coast to Coast vol. 2

By Gerald O'Connor
The Origins of Benjamin Hackett

By Gary Phillips
The Perpetrators
Scoundrels (Editor)
Treacherous
3 the Hard Way

By Thomas Pluck
Bad Boy Boogie

By Tom Pitts
Hustle
American Static

By Robert J. Randisi
Upon My Soul
Souls of the Dead
Envy the Dead

By Charles Salzberg
Devil in the Hole
Swann's Last Song
Swann Dives In
Swann's Way Out

By Scott Loring Sanders
Shooting Creek and Other Stories

By Ryan Sayles
The Subtle Art of Brutality
Warpath
Let Me Put My Stories In You

By John Shepphird
The Shill
Kill the Shill
Beware the Shill

By James R. Tuck (editor)
Mama Tried vol. 1
Mama Tried vol. 2 (*)

By Lono Waiwaiole
Wiley's Lament
Wiley's Shuffle
Wiley's Refrain
Dark Paradise
Leon's Legacy

By Nathan Walpow
The Logan Triad

(*)—Coming Soon

CPSIA information can be obtained
at www.ICGtesting.com
Printed in the USA
LVOW11s1615301017
554295LV00003B/656/P